"I HAVE A PL.... ....O."

Thomas sat up, planting his shiny black boots in the soft grass. "My plan was to live among the people in India and learn their ways. In that way, I could better discover the sources for the riches I sought."

"And you were obviously successful."

A rustle of wind caught his coal black hair as he nodded. "By the time I'd been there two years I had made enough money to buy my own ship. Once I had reduced my shipping costs, the wealth followed."

"So I presume you now own a fleet of ships." Felicity kept her tone light enough to mask the direction of her thoughts. She could think of nothing save what Lady Catherine had told her about him.

"And mills both here and in India."

He was close enough for her to touch. She could smell his sandalwood scent. She found herself wondering if the Indian woman had loved him. Had she, too, been drawn to his undeniable masculinity? Then Felicity wondered what it was like sharing a bed with him, the bronze hardness of his body stretched beside her. Her hand flew to the locket and she caressed it. *I'm sorry, Michael.* She could not be disloyal to her husband's memory. Why was she thinking about lying with another man? It was unforgivable.

Thomas's eyes followed her movement, lit on her black gown, and a somber look replaced his mirth. "I picture you in a blue dress," he said . . .

Dear Romance Reader,

In July of 1999, we launched the Ballad line with four new series, and each month we present both new and continuing stories set everywhere from medieval England to the American West—the kind of passionate, romantic stories you love best, written by the most gifted authors. At the back of each book, we'll tell you when you can find subsequent books in the series that have captured your heart.

Getting this month off to a dazzling start, is **The Bride Wore Blue,** the debut story in our charmingly romantic series *The Brides of Bath,* from award-winning newcomer Cheryl Bolen. In the most picturesque of cities, the *ton* lives by its own rules—until, that is, love breaks them all! Following her much acclaimed *Bogus Brides* series, beloved author Linda Lea Castle sweeps us back to the spectacular atmosphere of medieval England in her newest keeper, **Promise the Moon.** This is the first story in her compelling series *The Vaudrys,* in which three long-lost siblings rediscover each other against a backdrop of passion and intrigue.

Also this month, Lori Handeland returns with **Nate,** the highly anticipated fifth book in her sexy, compelling *Rock Creek Six* series, in which a pastor's daughter and a gun-for-hire discover how love can overcome even the most difficult obstacles. Another one you won't want to put down! Finally Kathryn Fox begins *Men of Honor,* a stunning new series on the danger-filled lives of the Royal Canadian Mounties. In this first book, **Reunion,** she takes us deep into the snowy wilderness—where tenderness and passion are challenged by the hardships of life on the northern frontier. Enjoy this extraordinary selection!

Kate Duffy
Editorial Director

The Brides of Bath

THE BRIDE WORE BLUE

CHERYL BOLEN

ZEBRA BOOKS
Kensington Publishing Corp.
http://www.zebrabooks.com

ZEBRA BOOKS are published by

Kensington Publishing Corp.
850 Third Avenue
New York, NY 10022

All kensington titles, imprints, and distributed lines are available at special quantity discounts for bulk purchases for sales
promotions, premiums, fund raising, educational, or institu-
tional use.

Special book excerpts or customized printings can also be
created to fit specific needs. For details, write or phone the
office of the Kensington Special Sales Manager: Kensington
Publishing Corp., 850 Third Avenue, New York, NY 10022.
Attn. Special Sales Department. Phone: 1-800-221-2647.

Zebra and the Z logo Reg. U.S. Pat. & TM Off.

First Printing: January 2002
10 9 8 7 6 5 4 3 2 1

Printed in the United States of America

Prologue

He was going to die. Lying on the dark roadside, his long hand splayed over the oozing hole in his side, Thomas Moreland felt the life draining from his young body. He lamented the loss of his future more than he dwelled on the searing in his side or the nearly unbearable pain that spiked through him at any futile attempt to move his legs. He would never cross the seas to make his fortune. His youth had been misspent on his obsessive pursuit of saving money for the passage to India. It sickened him to remember all the years he had shoveled horse dung and denied himself visits to the alehouse and the courting of ladies. All for naught. For his every farthing now lined the pockets of a pair of knife-wielding highwaymen.

Only a green fool such as himself would have ventured this road at night. Tomorrow, horses would once more carry travelers along its dusty path. A verdant landscape would replace tonight's eerie clumps of silvery trees.

And he would be dead.

The unexpected rattle of a carriage on the lonely country road stunned him. If only he could get the

driver's attention. It was no easy task for a man whose
legs were now incapable of movement. Lying on his
belly, he began to move forward, propelled by his powerful arms. His pain was so great, he hoped he did
not lose consciousness.

The carriage slowed, and Felicity Pembroke peered
out of her window to see what the problem was. In
the moon's glow she saw a young man crawling into
the lane, a trail of dark liquid on the dirt showing his
progress.

"The man's been hurt!" she cried, demanding that
the coachman stop.

"Oh, my lady, you mustn't!" her abigail shrieked.
"It's all a ploy to get yer jewels."

"Look for yourself, Lettie," Felicity said. "The man
is seriously injured."

The maid peeped out of the window. "It's a trap."

"Papa saw to it that we are well guarded," Felicity
said.

The equipage came to a stop, and the coachman,
armed with a rifle, stepped down and opened the carriage door.

"Go aid that poor man," Felicity snapped at the
coachman.

Aiming his rifle at the injured man, the coachman
gingerly walked up to him. "What ails ye?"

"I've been robbed and stabbed," Thomas croaked,
nodding toward the lower part of his body, "and I think
my legs broke when I was pushed from my horse."

Still gripping his weapon, the coachman lowered it.
"Got yer horse, too?"

"Yes, and it'll fetch a hundred guineas for the
damned blackguards."

John dropped his aim and called back to the coach. "Come give me a hand, Jeremiah."

The two men carried the wounded man to the carriage where Felicity instructed them to put him inside.

"But he's bleeding like a sieve," Lettie objected.

"And caked with dirt," the coachman added.

Felicity's voice was impatient. "We'll put him on the rug."

The servants lifted the large man. Even in a painfully seated position, his legs were too long to stretch across the seat Lettie had vacated, and he was unable to bend them. "I think the kneecap's shattered," he muttered.

All Felicity could see was the blood gushing from his side. The poor man was going to bleed to death while they worried about where to put his useless legs. "Have we something to bind the man with?" she asked frantically.

The two servants shrugged.

She sighed. "If you gentlemen will turn your heads, I will remove my petticoat to use for a bandage."

"Oh, my lady!" Lettie shrieked. "Ye can't go and do that."

Felicity whirled on her. "And why can't I?"

"It just ain't ladylike."

"My dear Lettie, this man may bleed to death if we don't help him."

The abigail's remorseful gaze dropped to her lap.

The next sound was the tearing of Felicity's petticoat into strips to bind the wounded man.

The pain from bending his knees to fit into the carriage seat must have caused Thomas to black out. When he awoke, he experienced a numbing sense of comfort, of sweet feminine smells and warmth like his mother's bed when she'd nursed him through the croup. He opened his lids and beheld the most beautiful face he had ever seen bending over him. She needed only a halo atop her golden ringlets to look like an angel. She smiled when his eyes opened, causing deep dimples to crease her squared cheeks. Her creamy skin was flawless, as were her perfect white teeth. Her great blue eyes sparkled when he spoke.

"May I know your name?" he asked her in a hoarse whisper.

"I am Felicity Pembroke."

"Soon to be Mrs. Harrison," Lettie interjected. "She's to wed Captain Michael Harrison next week."

A most fortunate man, Thomas thought.

"Can you hold on for the hour it will take to get to London and my very excellent physician there?" Felicity asked in a soothing, melodious voice.

He nodded and fell back into the hard side of the carriage.

He was going to live after all.

One

"I daresay I could become foxed from breathing the air in your chamber, George," Felicity scolded her sleeping brother.

The young man being addressed—George Pembroke, the viscount Sedgewick—rolled over in his bed and pried open a single green eye to gaze at his elder sister. He squinted against the bright sunlight filling the room through the tall casements. "What ungodly hour is it?" he croaked.

"It's well past noon and time you got up. We must talk."

"But I didn't get to bed—"

"I know very well what time you got to bed for it was precisely at the same time I was rising." Felicity held out a cup of strong coffee. "Drink this."

He sighed heavily as he rose to a sitting position, ran a hand through his tousled golden hair, took the delicate porcelain cup and saucer, and proceeded to drink the steaming brew, wincing. "You could at least have sweetened it."

She drew up a chair and sat down to face him. She hated having to berate her brother, for he was only indulging in the same pursuits enjoyed by the other young bucks of his acquaintance. But the other bucks did not have a father who had departed this world leaving his offspring with more debts than his estate could rectify.

George's gaze fixed on a packet of papers she held. They looked like tradesmen's bills.

"It was all I could do not to embarrass you last night when you were deep in play at the Assembly Rooms," she chided. "You promised no more gaming, and I have it on good authority you played all through the night."

"Demmed spies," he muttered.

"How much did you lose?"

He gave her a cocky look. "What makes you think I lost?"

"Are you telling me you won for once?"

His face fell. "No."

"Just as I thought. You're exactly like Papa. Because of his losses at the gaming table, another family now inhabits Hornsby Manor, which should be yours."

"I'll get it back, just you wait and see. My luck will turn."

He was far too optimistic for his own good, Felicity thought. "How many times do I have to tell you, economy, not Lady Luck, will get Hornsby Manor back? I thought when I got you out of London and we came to Bath, you would quit your lavish ways, but you've run up enormous bills with tailors and livery stables." She flung the bills at him. "An advantage to making your home in Bath is that you don't have to keep your expensive mounts. We can walk everywhere we need to go."

He looked remorseful. "I'll sell my bay tomorrow."

"Today!" she snapped. Though she was only a year

older than George's twenty-three years, she had always treated him as a child.

He took another sip of coffee. "Very well."

She could never suggest the one thing he needed to steady his ways—a wife—for he had yet to become enamored of decent young ladies. She frowned at the distasteful thought of the doxies George and his chums associated with. "We'll never find a suitable match for Glee as long as her brother is unable to dower her. If you don't mind that you've dragged the family name through mud, can't you at least care about your younger sister's future?"

He frowned. "I do care. Was trying to make things right last night when my luck failed me. And I don't see why I alone have the responsibility for Glee's future happiness. If you'd only marry the colonel, we'd have enough—"

"I could never marry the colonel," she protested, "no matter how good he's been to me—to us." Her eyes ran over the black gown she wore. Michael had been dead four years now and still she wore widow's black. "I can never marry again. No man can ever take Michael's place."

George sat up straight and spoke softly. "It grieves me that you still mourn Harrison so keenly. You've got to allow yourself to live again, Felicity."

A wistful smile crossed her face. "I don't have to be married to live, you goose. Do I have to remind you I have become quite the grand dame of Bath society? And I mean to see you and Glee properly married."

He winced at the mention of his own unwelcome nuptials.

A knock sounded on the door, and the butler announced that Mrs. Carlotta Ennis was belowstairs, calling on Mrs. Harrison.

"I'll be right down," Felicity said.

Though the two women were quite different, Felicity and Carlotta had become friends while both were married to Guards officers in the Peninsula. They were of the same age, both of privileged backgrounds, both beautiful, and both had been widowed at a very young age. While Felicity grieved that she and her captain had not been able to conceive, Carlotta regretted the son she had borne and did her best to avoid.

The raven-haired Carlotta, wearing a lavender morning dress, rose and took her friend's hand when Felicity glided into the room, greeting her with dimpled smiles and cordial words. The two sat next to each other on a damask sofa.

"I came straightaway to tell you the newest *on dit,*" Carlotta said smugly. "My maid's sister has just been employed at Winston Hall. It seems a fabulously wealthy nabob has purchased the estate and takes possession this very day."

"I hardly see why this is of great interest to me," Felicity said.

Carlotta's large lavender-gray eyes shone with mirth. "The nabob is a bachelor."

"I am sure he would be much too old for Glee. Remember, she is but seventeen."

"It wasn't your sister I was thinking of," Carlotta quipped. "What about you or me?"

Felicity glanced at her own black dress. "You know I intend to stay Mrs. Harrison until I die."

Carlotta rolled her eyes. "Oh, yes, Michael's martyr.

I, for one, mean to remarry. And I certainly would not object to marrying a man of wealth."

"But what of rank? What if the nabob's from a family of low birth?"

"With his money, he'll be accepted."

Felicity frowned. "Edward, though he had no title and no money, was of good birth. Surely you owe it to his memory and to your son to avoid a misalliance."

"Pooh!" Carlotta said. "I allowed my first marriage for love. My second will be for fortune. It grows tedious getting by on Edward's meager pension."

Felicity frowned. "I cannot help but feel pity for poor Lady Catherine. 'Twas bad enough losing her home—"

"But losing Winston Hall to a man who's not of noble birth will surely destroy her," Carlotta interjected with a mischievous smile. "She's such an utter snob."

Stanton knocked on the drawing-room door and announced that Colonel Gordon was calling.

On Felicity's instruction, the butler showed the man into the room.

Though his hair was graying, Colonel Gordon's lean frame of well-toned muscles gave little evidence of his thirty-nine years. Because of his family's wealth, he had become a colonel by the time he was thirty. His face was handsome, and his tailoring impeccable. Leaning on a silver-headed walking stick, he limped into the room, the bad leg a testament to his shortened duty in the Peninsula.

"How good it is to behold the two most beautiful ladies in Bath," he greeted, bowing to them before stiffly lowering himself into a chair facing them.

"I've just been telling Felicity about the nabob who's bought Winston Hall."

"So I've heard," he said drolly. "It's all over Bath. Perhaps we will see him at the Pump Room today. That is, if you ladies will do me the goodness of accompanying me."

"You and Carlotta go on," Felicity said. "George and I have matters that demand our attention today. And I scarcely need drink the odious water for I enjoy excellent health."

Carlotta cast a furtive glance at Felicity. "Don't be too hard on the boy."

Felicity pursed her lips and glared mischievously at Carlotta. "And don't always take up for George. One would think *you* were his sister."

Carlotta and the colonel rose, Carlotta taking his proffered arm. "But, my dear," Carlotta said to Felicity, "nary a drop of blue blood runs in my veins."

Felicity watched as they left the room. A pity the colonel fancied himself in love with her, for he and Carlotta would have suited each other. Many a time Carlotta had lamented that the handsome colonel was wasting the best years of his life on Felicity.

Thomas Moreland settled his large frame against the soft leather chair and ran his eyes over the tall wooden cases filled with leather-bound books. It was all his. All of Winston Hall was now his.

A year shy of his thirtieth birthday, and he had amassed more riches than he'd ever dreamed of back in the days when he cleaned horse stalls for two shillings a week.

From his pocket he withdrew the torn white linen he had carried from one end of India to the other. He had washed his blood from it and dried it in the sun six long years ago. It was a piece of his rescuing angel's petticoat. Felicity Harrison's.

Next, he read the runner's report and the letter from the solicitor he had paid an exorbitant sum to glean other information.

Now, it was his turn to rescue Felicity Harrison.

Two

Glee Pembroke flipped an errant lock of curly, rich, red hair from her fair oval face and addressed her sister. "Does not Mr. Salvado have the most wonderful brown eyes you have ever beheld?"

"I cannot own that I have ever noticed the color of the dancing master's eyes," Felicity said, stooping to pick up discarded slippers that littered the floor of her sister's chamber.

"Have you not been struck by his handsomeness?" Glee asked.

Felicity scowled at her sister. "I declare, there is not a man in breeches who does not appeal to you. It is hoped your taste will become more discerning once you enter society."

Glee looked up hopefully. "Then you will permit me to attend the assemblies?"

"Very soon," Felicity said, sitting down on Glee's full tester bed. "But you must present yourself with more deportment than I have been able to detect in you heretofore. Remember always, you are the daughter of the viscount Sedgewick. You must not babble on incessantly about the merits of every man who pays you court, and you must quit your outrageous flirting."

Glee's large green eyes narrowed. "I know. 'A lady is to remain quiet and never offer her opinion unless

solicited,' " she mimicked. "You have told me millions
of times."

"Then I fail to see why my advice goes unheeded
when you admit to hearing it *millions* of times."

The girl ignored her sister and walked to her
clothespress. "Think you I should wear my ivory
gown to my first assembly?"

"I think the ivory an excellent choice—that is, if
you do not cheapen it with golden sashes and hordes
of ostrich plumes."

Glee spun around to face Felicity. "You're a fine
one to instruct me on how to dress when you wear
nothing but those hideous black garbs. Your year of
mourning for Michael was up three years ago, and I
came out of Papa's mourning nearly a year ago. Everyone says you'd be the most beautiful woman in Bath
if only you'd wear color."

Felicity checked her rising temper. "But you see,"
she said calmly, "it matters not to me if I am considered beautiful. I have loved and been loved. Now, it
is your turn, my sweet."

The chamber door creaked open, and Lettie poked
her head in. "Oh, here ye are, Mrs. Harrison. Stanton's
been looking for you. A gentleman has requested to
see you privately." She crossed the carpet and handed
Felicity a card. A gentleman's card.

Felicity read it: Thomas Moreland of Winston Hall.

The nabob! "But I do not know the gentleman,"
Felicity told her abigail, then directed herself to her
sister. "It's the new owner of Winston Hall."

"It would be most unseemly to refuse to meet him,"
Glee said.

Felicity removed herself from the edge of Glee's
bed, cast a glance into the looking glass on the opposite wall, and strolled toward the door. "Very well."

* * *

His back was to her when she entered the drawing room. He was a large man. Not fat but very tall. She noticed his broad shoulders funneling down to a trim waist. She noticed, too, the excellent quality of his superfine coat and the breeches that molded to his muscled legs. His hair was black, and when he turned to face her, she saw that his skin was bronzed by the sun, no doubt from the warm climate of India. And he was handsome. Not at all the picture she held of corpulent, bejeweled nabobs.Were he ugly or old or young she would have greeted him with kindness. But this man's handsomeness froze Felicity, leaving her self-conscious and stiff. Must he glare at her with those somber black eyes? Despite that a hint of sadness swept across his face, she could not feel sorry for him. His very stance bespoke power and pride.

She resolved to give tit for tat.

"I am Felicity Harrison," she said. "We have not been introduced to each other before, have we, Mr. Moreland?" Her voice was wrapped in haughtiness. There was something vaguely familiar about him, but she was sure she had never before met a Mr. Thomas Moreland.

He walked toward her and bowed. "No, I've not been introduced to you, but I know much about you. I have come today to make a business proposal to you."

She moved toward the door. "All business matters are handled by my solicitor. His name is—"

"Malcolm Fortesque."

She stiffened and her blue eyes rounded. "You have talked with Mr. Fortesque?"

"The matter I wish to discuss, while a business

proposition, is of a private nature. Between you and me."

She still had not asked him to sit. "I cannot enter into business with a person I don't know."

"I propose to rectify that situation, Mrs. Harrison."

She stepped backward. "Perhaps you are ready, sir, but I assure you, I am not!"

He pulled from his coat a stack of small papers and moved toward her. "I have settled these vouchers of your brother's in the amount of four thousand pounds. May we talk?" His dark gaze, solemn and intent, caught hers, and quite oddly she was unable to look away. Her heart drummed madly. She was thankful when his gaze shifted to the sofa.

"Have a seat, Mr. Moreland," a stunned Felicity said in a shaky voice.

He sat on one side of the sofa, clearly intending her to sit on the other side.

Felicity settled in a chair facing him. Why had the impertinent man taken the liberty of settling *her* brother's debts? "What do you want for the vouchers?"

He handed them to her. "They are yours."

She reached across the distance separating them and took the papers with a trembling hand, her eyes never leaving his. "How may I repay your generosity?" All manner of sordid thoughts popped into her head.

"You have something I want, and I have something you want."

Her heart pounded in her chest. "Pray, enlighten me, Mr. Moreland."

"I am a very wealthy man, Mrs. Harrison. I can settle all your brother's debts and your father's debts, and settle an annuity on you, your brother, and your sister."

It was the answer to her prayers. But like a foul head after a night of indulging spirits or an unwanted babe following a romp in the hay, such pleasures could come at great cost. Did the man want Hornsby Manor? It was not hers to give. "What could I possibly offer that would be worth such an enormous sum?"

He stretched out his long legs on the Oriental carpet. "As you must be aware, I am not of noble birth. I'm not ashamed of what I am. In fact, I'm rather proud that I've risen to where I am by virtue of my own cunning and hard work. I don't care if I'm accepted into your world, Mrs. Harrison. But I do desire that my sister enter into an alliance more fortunate than her birth recommends. Dianna—being ten years younger than I—has been raised with the privilege my money can purchase. She has gone to the best schools. Her clothes are the finest London mantua makers have to offer. She has had the best drawing masters and dancing masters and music teachers. She is nineteen now, and none of the men in our own class are her equal."

Felicity's back bristled. "I hardly see what I can do about that."

"You, Mrs. Harrison, are one of the most respected matrons in Bath. I don't purport to launch Dianna in London, but I think—with your help—we can assure her success here in Bath."

"Then you want me to introduce her into society here?"

He nodded gravely, his black eyes searching hers. "Unfortunately, I am part of the package, for I would have to accompany my sister."

"Do I understand you correctly, Mr. Moreland? You want me to bring you and your sister into my circle.

Eat at each other's houses, accompany each other at assemblies and musicales and strolls through town?"

"You understand correctly, Mrs. Harrison."

She bit at her lip and avoided his pensive eyes. It sounded too easy.

"I won't make you give me your answer until you've met Dianna. You must see for yourself that she will not be an embarrassment. I propose that you and your family dine at Winston Hall tonight. Then you can see for yourself if you think my sister and I will be able to manage in the *ton*." He got to his feet. "My carriage will call for you at seven." Hat in hand, he strolled to the door and left the room.

The odious man had not even waited for her answer. What audacity! He even knew they did not own a carriage. He had underhandedly spied on her, and she disliked him excessively.

He rode his phaeton the three miles back to Winston Hall, surprised he had not seized her in his arms when he beheld her. For her blond beauty shone as brightly as it had in the dim carriage six years ago. He had thought if he could just see her once again—hear her sweet voice—his thirst for her might slake. Perhaps she wasn't as beautiful as he remembered. But, if anything, she was even lovelier in the glare of sunlight with her smooth golden skin and flawless face. Her voice was the same yet different. But, then, one did not speak to an arrogant mogul as one would to a dying youth. She had been kind beyond belief that night; today she was proud and—something else—bitter? defeated?

She was smaller than he had thought. The tip of her golden head barely came to his shoulders. He wondered what it would feel like to have her smoothly curved body molded into his own, what it would feel like to enclose her slimness in his arms. The thought evoked an immediate physical response that surged through him to settle in his groin.

Underlying his powerful reaction to her was the disappointing observation that she still wore black for her long-dead husband.How could he ever compete with the dashing Captain Michael Harrison? He had met the man just once. The time he had taken Thomas from the surgeon's to procure him passage on a clipper to India. At *her* request, the captain had arranged for Thomas to work for his passage, preparing food from a seat in the galley, for Thomas had not been able to put weight on his legs for another month.Captain Harrison had been all that was gentlemanly. Not only was he the second son of an earl, but he was also as fine looking a man as Thomas had ever seen. With bittersweet regret, he pictured the manly officer with cultured voice and ready smile. And impossibly broad shoulders and a tall, powerful frame. *Damn him.*

Since becoming wealthy, Thomas had learned everything he could about Felicity Harrison right down to the name of the tenants of Hornsby Manor.

He had not precisely lied when Felicity asked if she'd ever been introduced before. For he had not told her his name that night on the dark country road. And it was obvious now she had forgotten the wretched man whose life she had saved on a winter night six years previously.

With bitter realization he knew that capturing Felicity Harrison's long-buried heart was going to be the most difficult challenge he had ever faced. Learning the customs and language of a faraway nation had been much easier. He had studied the Hindi language from the age of fifteen and had mastered it while he lived among the dark-skinned people. He had learned their ways and got far better prices for their sought-after goods than the rich nabobs who cooled themselves in the lavish palaces they had erected in India.

But chiseling through Felicity's icy heart might prove impossible. For she had changed greatly. Six years ago, she did not care about rank. She wanted only to save a man. It had not mattered that he was not a gentleman. But now . . .

He looked off into the gently sloping hills. Now, she was different.

For the second time that day, Felicity entered her brother's chamber.

His valet had just removed his coat. "You will be most happy to learn that I got a hundred guineas for my mount."

"That is very good, I am sure," Felicity said distractedly. "But I must talk to you in private. Let us go to the library."

"What have I done now?" he questioned, following his sister from the room.

"This time, nothing."

She closed the library door and instructed her brother to take a seat. She sat on a settee beside him.

"Why all the secrecy?" he asked.

"There is something of a very private nature I wish to discuss with you."

"You're not marrying Gordon! Upon my word, I didn't mean for you to sacrifice——"

"I'm not marrying Colonel Gordon."

He eyed her suspiciously. "You ain't planning to shackle me, are you?"

She smiled, and her dimples seemed to light up the darkened room. "I'm not planning to shackle you, either."

"Then what in God's name?"

"I received a most unusual proposal today."

His ears perked. "A proposal?"

"Yes. You've heard of the nabob who bought Winston Hall?"

He nodded slowly, his eyes narrow.

"Well, he came here today. The man knows everything there is to know about us. It wouldn't surprise me if he knew what you ate for breakfast. Anyway, he settled four thousand pounds' worth of your gaming vouchers."

The young man's eyes widened. "My vouchers?"

"Yes. And he knows all about your debts and Papa's. He told me he would settle all of them for what seems to me a very inconsequential payment."

George squared his shoulders and faced her, his brows drawn together. "What payment?"

"He . . . he wants me—and I suppose that means you, too—to sponsor him and his sister into the upper echelons of Bath society. His sister is nineteen, and he says she's too polished to settle for a man of her own class."

"Polished, my arse!"

"George!"

"I'm sorry, pet. But it ain't right to saddle you with righting my wrongs."

"I wouldn't be righting them. Mr. Moreland would."

"So Moreland's the name?"

"Yes. It seems he's enormously wealthy."

"Well, I don't like his proposal." He stuck out his lower lip.

"I think it's a small price to pay for the generous settlement he proposes."

"There's more to his proposed settlement?"

"Yes. He would pay off all your and Papa's creditors. Don't you see, you could get Hornsby Manor back? And in addition to that, he will make settlements on the three of us."

"His sister must be a real dragon," George muttered.

"You can see for yourself tonight. He has invited us to Winston Hall for dinner. After that, I can give him my answer."

He stood up and met her gaze. "Well, I don't like it one bit. What kind of a fellow is he? Coarse?"

She thought a moment before answering. "While he did not at all strike me as being coarse, he's not exactly amiable. He's quite an ogre, going about spying on our affairs."

George frowned. "I won't set foot in the man's house."

"I'm not saying we will go along with his proposal, but what would it hurt to see them at Winston Hall? No one need know we were there. And his sister might not be nearly so obnoxious as her brother."

His hands fisted. "If you really want me to go, I will. But I'll not permit you to go along with the fiend's scheme."

Three

Felicity dressed her finest for dinner at Winston Hall. She wore her black silk. When the carriage from the hall called for them, she eyed it appreciatively—even enviously—but refused to acknowledge its grandeur. Such pride escaped her sister and brother. While praises gushed from Glee's mouth, George commented that a better set of matched grays he had never seen.

Inside the carriage for the brief ride to Winston Hall, Glee could not contain her delight. "I daresay I've never sat upon anything this soft before."

"I expect your bed is," George contradicted.

Glee screwed up her face and swiped her fan at him, then turned to Felicity. "Explain, please, how we have the good fortune to be the first in Bath to dine with the nabob."

Felicity cast a warning glance at George. "Our brother is considering entering into a business arrangement with Mr. Moreland. And, please, do not refer to him as a nabob. It is most unseemly."

"Is Mr. Moreland married?" Glee inquired.

"I don't believe so," Felicity answered.

Glee's brow lifted. "He doesn't live alone in that huge palace?"

"I believe he has a sister," George said.

Felicity was desirous of changing the subject, for

she distinctly did not want Glee to know of Mr. Moreland's unusual proposal. The girl had never been able to keep a secret in all her life, and Felicity found the prospect of all Bath knowing about Mr. Moreland's arrangement most unwelcome. "Does not Glee look uncommonly good tonight?" Felicity asked her brother.

He glanced at the girl's soft, cream-colored muslin dress that was covered with elaborately embroidered flowers of snow white.

"A most becoming dress," he said. "If I didn't know you, I'd take you for eighteen."

That comment seemed to raise Glee's spirits. "I suppose the Moreland girl will be wearing the latest fashions from London."

"Probably have to make 'em out of stage curtains," George muttered.

Felicity scowled at him.

"Is Miss Moreland fat?" Glee inquired.

"We do not know what the young lady looks like," Felicity said. "George is being obtuse."

Soon Felicity saw that they neared Winston Hall. Many windows of the palace-like building were bright yellow with candleglow, and huge lanterns lighted the massive front entrance. The man was spending a fortune on candles, Felicity reflected.

The coach pulled up a U-shaped gravel road and stopped in front of the door. The crimson-liveried coachman let down the steps for them while a footman—also dressed in crimson livery—opened the huge door to the house. Within seconds Mr. Moreland and his sister greeted them in the great marbled foyer.

Gazing at the elegant Dianna Moreland, Felicity was immediately relieved that George's predictions of the young lady's appearance were grossly incorrect. Miss

Moreland was rather taller than average and somewhat slim, with the same black hair as her brother and brown eyes, not the black of her brother's. Despite the darkness of her hair and eyes, Miss Moreland's complexion was extremely fair and free of flaws. Her hair at once recalled the careless simplicity of Roman goddesses.

And Glee had been correct about the young woman's dress. The sheerest, finest silks in the palest pink layered seamlessly to create her stunning gown. A duchess could not have dressed any finer.

Upon first examination of Miss Moreland, Felicity was willing to give Mr. Moreland credit for speaking honestly of his sister. The girl would certainly not cause embarrassment. But Felicity still was not willing to accept Mr. Moreland's proposal. While withholding a pleasant greeting from the odious nabob, Felicity greeted his sister with cordiality and was rewarded with a soft, genteelly spoken reply. The girl would do well in society, Felicity thought. In fact, Glee could learn deportment from her. Goodness knows, she had not learned from Felicity.

"Have you been to Winston Hall before?" Thomas asked.

"Yes," Felicity said. "We are acquainted with the daughter of the previous owner."

"Would that be Lady Catherine?" he asked.

Of course, a man like him would always know the ladies, Felicity mused, nodding. "It's a lovely home you have *purchased.*" In her circle, lovely homes were inherited. She was not willing to lower the barrier between herself and the nabob. At least not yet.

The corners of his mouth lifted ever so slightly. "Then I won't bore you with a tour." He led them into the brightly lit dining room. No fewer than three crystal chandeliers were suspended from a richly gilded ceiling above the huge dining table, which was covered with a white cloth and set for five.

To Felicity's chagrin, she was seated next to the owner. She had known he would spare no expense in offering a highly commendable meal, and he did not. Even the wines he offered with each course were of the finest French vintages. How he procured them, she did not want to know. She had also expected that he would boast on his offerings, but he did not. He displayed the careless disregard of the four footmen and the exquisite porcelain and the out-of-season delicacies as would a peer who had been born to such wealth.

Miss Moreland was shy, but Glee, who sat next to her, was not. By the time they were on the third course, the two young women were speaking with great animation. Glee imparted to the girl tidbits of information on the goings-on in the Upper Assembly Rooms as if she had in fact been there dozens of times.

By the time the fourth course was uncovered, Glee admitted she awaited her first visit to the assemblies. "We must accompany each other our first time there," Glee ventured.

Dianna threw a frightened glance at her brother, who almost imperceptibly inclined his head, then she acknowledged how very agreeable the plan was.

As the ladies conversed, Thomas turned his attention to George. "Do you enjoy hunting, Lord Sedgewick?"

"I'm actually quite keen on shooting but have had little opportunity to do so in the two years we've resided in Bath. The last time I went was a year ago when I joined friends at Blanks's lodge in Scotland."

Felicity was always amazed at how well George

spoke in company. In her presence he conversed as he did with bosom companions. She had held her breath expecting his response to be something like *Bloody well miss it since we had to let Hornsby Manor.* Then, she recalled that he alluded to *Blanks's* hunting lodge. "My brother is referring to his best friend's hunting lodge. His friend's name is not Blanks. It's Mr. Blankenship."

George looked at her with mock indignation. "I've always called him Blanks. Ever since Eton."

"I attended neither Eton nor Harrow," Thomas said.

"You *can* read?" George asked.

Thomas gave a hardy laugh. "Yes, I most certainly can. I could read almost before I could talk. My father, who had taught himself to read, insisted I learn at a young age. You see, he was a bookseller."

"Thomas has always been a prolific reader," Dianna added. "He taught himself how to speak four languages."

Felicity could almost hear herself sigh with relief. *At least he was learned.*

"He must be very much like Felicity," Glee said. "Papa said she's had her head in a book since she could sit up."

Thomas smiled at her. "May I inquire who your favorite writers are? Perhaps we share at least one interest, Mrs. Harrison."

Felicity knew he spoke of more than books. "I should blather endlessly about the genius of Lord Byron or Mr. Scott, but to be quite honest, I admit to reading and rereading everything ever written by William Shakespeare."

Thomas's eyes sparkled. "We may be better strangers."

Felicity smiled at him. It was the first time her lips

had betrayed her. She found herself matching wits with him. *"As You Like It,* sir."

He nodded, a satisfied smile on his face.

"I declare," Glee said, looking from Thomas to Felicity. "I cannot conceive of what you're talking of."

"I believe my brother quoted Shakespeare," Dianne humbly offered.

"Oh, I comprehend!" George said. " 'Twas a line from *As You Like It.*"

Like a prim governess, Felicity nodded stiffly at her brother. Peering into her glass of wine, she said, "It quite surprises me, Mr. Moreland, that you have had time to read Shakespeare, for I cannot think it terribly profitable."

"One cannot make money four-and-twenty hours a day, Mrs. Harrison."

When the sweetmeats were laid, Thomas invited George to shoot with him. "There is a small lake within a thicket behind the hall where grouse are to be had."

"Upon my word, don't mind if I do take you up on your generous offer," George replied.

They agreed to shoot on Wednesday; then the men removed themselves to drink port while the ladies retired to the saloon.

Though she had been disinclined to like Miss Moreland because of her dislike of Mr. Moreland, Felicity found nothing objectionable in the demure young lady. In fact, Miss Moreland in every way embodied quality. Her voice was cultured, her demeanor graceful and unaffected. She was evidently well educated and by nature sweet.

In short, she would be a good influence on Glee, who borrowed tastes and opinions as others might change bonnets.

After the men joined them, Felicity offered to play the pianoforte if Dianna favored them by singing. Felicity had lifted her brows when Dianna announced her selection, for it was one that required a high degree of musical talent.

And Dianna surpassed expectations once again. Felicity would gladly have played all night just to hear Miss Moreland's sweet voice.

Even George stood watching the young singer in a daze of admiration, which greatly surprised Felicity. She could not remember George ever suffering through such a performance with anything but bored courtesy.

When the number was finished, Felicity encouraged Dianna to favor them with another, and George enthusiastically doubled the request.

When Dianna finished, Glee said, "I could not possibly follow such a performance, for my family will agree that my musical talent is most inferior to Miss Moreland's."

"Although your talent is not as great," Felicity soothed, "your style very well matches your selections. You have nothing to be ashamed of, my sweet."

"Please, Miss Pembroke," Thomas said, "we would be honored to hear you sing."

Casting off her shyness, a sparkling Glee came to stand before the instrument her sister was playing. There was no need for the two to exchange information for Felicity immediately began playing the tune she knew Glee performed best.

Glee's performance met with enthusiastic approval.

Afterward, the five played loo until it was time to return to Bath. Thomas and Dianna walked Felicity's family to the waiting carriage. George was all that was cordial to Dianna while Thomas handed Felicity into the carriage. "May I call on you tomorrow, Mrs. Harrison?" he asked.

She threw a quick glance at George, whose countenance was inscrutable; then she met Mr. Moreland's gaze and answered him simply. "Yes."

On the way home George and Glee sang the praises of Miss Dianna Moreland.

"I think she's quite the prettiest girl I've ever seen," Glee said, looking at Felicity, "expect perhaps for you before you stopped wearing colors."

"Must say, she'll do us credit," George added.

Felicity was pleased. Though she would never admit it, even Mr. Moreland was not nearly as crass as she had imagined him to be. To think, he even read Shakespeare! She thought about the evening spent at Winston Hall and had to admit that, except for his using the asparagus fork on the scallops, he gave no sign that he had not been born to wealth and privilege.

Once they were at their house back in Bath, Felicity begged a private word with George. He followed her to the library and closed the door behind him.

"So you're going shooting with the nabob!" Felicity quipped with mock indignation. "What about your resolution not to consider the man's proposal?"

Her brother shrugged. "Fact is, I liked him. Nothing of the shop about him. Appears a perfect gentleman, and there can be no doubt his sister is every inch the lady."

"Does that mean you will go along with the man's proposal?"

"As it happens, I think it might prove to be an excellent arrangement. The pair of them are not likely to cause embarrassment."

She clutched her black shawl closer around her. "Then I will give him my answer tomorrow."

Four

Felicity was determined to leave earlier than usual to avoid being home when Mr. Moreland called. She abhorred the idea of accepting his charity almost as much as she rankled at the thought of *selling* her family's long-standing prestige. Of course, George's utter capitulation to the nabob assured they would have no other choice but to agree to the man's unusual proposal. She just did not want to seem too eager. After all, she had her pride.

Lettie draped a black spencer about Felicity's shoulders. Felicity took a last glance at her looking glass, swept from her chamber, and descended the stairs—just as Stanton was showing Mr. Moreland in.

Thomas looked up at Felicity. "Going out, Mrs. Harrison?"

Felicity colored. Hadn't the man told her he would call this morning? It was one thing being rude when one did not have to face the recipient of the rudeness, but to have to face him was altogether embarrassing. "I . . . I was going to dash over to the lending library."

"Perhaps you will allow me to convey you there. I have come in my curricle."

Already he was planning to flaunt the connection in public. Her lips thinned with displeasure. "That won't be necessary, Mr. Moreland. The short walk will do me good. But I can do that later—after your visit."

She brushed past him and into the drawing room, with him following. "Please close the door, Stanton," she instructed the butler.

Felicity walked to the window and drew open the draperies, allowing more light into the yellow and gold room; then she sat on the sofa.

Thomas lowered his large frame into a nearby settee. She wondered if he would fit in one of the Louis XIV chairs. She doubted it.

"Allow me to thank you for an enjoyable evening last night," Felicity began. "My family was most impressed."

He cocked a brow. "And you?"

"I found nothing offensive, Mr. Moreland. In fact, I must agree with you about your sister. She is all that you implied and more. I believe she would be a good influence on Glee, who is at present a bit flighty. Miss Moreland is genteel, intelligent, and quite lovely."

His wide smile revealed even white teeth and extended to his flashing black eyes. "I'm gratified that you find I did not exaggerate."

"Not in the least! I would be honored to be seen with Miss Moreland."

His face grew serious. "What of her brother?"

Felicity was at a loss for words. She could not meet his gaze. "I find nothing offensive in your manner, Mr. Moreland." She fumbled with her gloves, beginning to remove them, then putting them back on.

He got to his feet. "I will endeavor not to be *offensive* when we pick up you and Miss Pembroke tonight for a visit to the Upper Assembly Rooms." He turned and walked toward the door before turning back. "By the way, your brother's debts have all been settled."

She could feel her anger rising. "How did you know I would accept your proposal?"

"I am accustomed to getting what I want, Mrs. Harrison." He tipped his head to her, then departed.

Hands on her hips, she fumed. "Arrogant creature!"

Her trumped-up plan of going to the lending library quickly forgotten, she scurried upstairs, throwing off her spencer and barking orders for Lettie to awaken Glee. "We've got to get her a dress ready for tonight."

Within moments, an excited Glee, still wearing her night shift, threw open the door to Felicity's sitting room. "I shall be allowed to go to the Assembly Rooms tonight? Please say it's so!"

Felicity stopped searching through her worktable and glanced at her sister. The smile Glee could not possibly repress lighted her face, and her green eyes twinkled with mirth. She reminded Felicity of a wondrous child skating on winter's first frozen pond.

But Felicity realized with bittersweet finality that Glee was no longer a child. Indeed, she stood as tall as Felicity, and her lithe body smoothly curved like a woman's. She hovered at the precipice of womanhood, ready to become the mate of some man Felicity prayed would cherish her. As Michael had cherished Felicity. Felicity touched the locket that hung always from her neck. Because it held Michael's miniature and a lock of his hair, she felt close to him whenever she fingered it. "To be sure. What do you think about the pink gown?"

Glee frowned. "Pink is dreadful on redheads."

"How can you say that! It brings out the pink in your cheeks and lips and goes well with your milky complexion, my sweet."

"I refuse to make my first impression wearing the

dreadful color. I would prefer the aqua, but I know it would not do for my first dance."

"There is the white one you wore last night," Felicity offered.

"And have Miss Moreland think I only own one dress?"

"What matters is how you will look tonight, not what Miss Moreland thinks."

Glee began to dance around the room. "I wonder what Miss Moreland will wear tonight? No doubt it will be something very elegant."

"And appropriate."

"What of the length of ivory sarcenet we purchased last month? Could we not fashion it into a simple gown?" Glee threw a hopeful gaze at Felicity.

"By tonight?"

"You're a fast seamstress, and you won't have to spend any time getting ready yourself," Glee said. "One black dress is much the same as another."

"Very well. It's *your* appearance that counts. Look through Akerman's and see if there's something we can modify."

As he rode back to Winston Hall, Thomas was grave. Having so recently been in the same room with Felicity should have made him happy. During those years he was in India, he would have given a king's ransom just to see her lovely face once again. Now he was assured of seeing her on a regular basis. And the thought brought gloom.

Not that his feelings toward her had changed. He still worshipped her. He had shamefully rejoiced when he had learned she was a widow, but he never imagined she would still be wearing black after four long years.

He also lamented that Felicity's innocent trust and warm compassion of six years ago was as long buried as her Captain Harrison.

Thomas wondered if he would ever be able to chisel through the ice that enclosed her heart.

By the time their escort arrived that night, Felicity was exhausted. She had sewn for so long her fingers ached, as did her back from bending over her needlework throughout the morning and afternoon. She had barely finished Glee's dress in time to throw off one of her own black dresses for another, the silk gown she had worn the night before. Her only jewelry was Michael's locket.

Lettie swept Felicity's blonde ringlets back and pinned them, then stood back to admire her mistress. "Miss Glee will look lovely indeed, but none will ever compare to you. A pity you won't wear colors."

"Pooh! Count me well satisfied if Glee makes a fortunate match," Felicity countered, not even bothering to cast a glance at her own reflection in the looking glass as she hurried from the room.

She had already assured herself of Glee's extremely agreeable appearance and now desired to have a brief conversation with Mr. Moreland before Glee came downstairs. She had asked Stanton to request Mr. Moreland await her privately in the library.

As she entered the dark room where a lone candle burned, he quickly stood up and bowed. And her mind went blank. It suddenly struck her that she had never seen a more handsome man. He was so very large. And powerfully built. Pride and arrogance and an un-

expected flicker of amusement marked his angular
face and his black, all-knowing eyes.

A duke could not have been more formidable nor
better dressed. For despite Mr. Moreland's casual simplicity of dress, his tailoring was impeccable. His
black silk cutaway coat nearly matched the dark sheen
of his casually styled hair, and the white of his linen
was the same shade as his teeth.

Felicity's eyes traveled the length of Mr. Moreland's
classically formed body. She was reminded of
Michelangelo's *David*. And she swallowed. How could
a man of his size maintain so flat a stomach and so
narrow a waist? she wondered. His gray breeches
seemed molded to his muscled thighs. She could tell
no false supports were needed beneath his white silken
stockings where his manly calves formed an admirable
arch. If he had been the son of a beggar, he would
still have women swooning after him.

She recovered enough from her astonished perusal
of his appearance to remember why she had desired
to speak alone with him.

"Sit down, please," she requested, taking a seat herself. "I will be brief so your sister does not have a
lengthy wait in the carriage." She shifted uncomfort-
ably, unable to meet his open gaze. "It has occurred
to me that when I introduce you tonight I cannot very
well say we are acquaintances because you relieved
my family of debt."

He oozed confidence when he responded. "No, not
at all. Have you an idea as to how we have become
acquainted, Mrs. Harrison?"

She folded her hands in her lap. "Actually, yes. I
thought perhaps I could say that your aunt, who is a
very good friend of mine, sent me a letter of intro-
duction to you."

He nodded, but a coldness in his eyes told her he was not completely in accord with her scheme.

"Clever of you," he said. "My nonexistent aunt, by virtue of being friends with you, should add rank and respectability to the merchant from India."

She raised her shoulders and dropped them in exaggerated fashion, then spoke sharply. "One would think you'd be pleased, Mr. Moreland."

"Pleased that you will lie for me?"

He did it again. He made her feel embarrassed and ashamed. And she disliked him excessively.

"Think you I should be pleased that you find me so low you have to invent relatives of rank for me?"

"Very well, Mr. Moreland," she hissed through gritted teeth. "I shall tell everyone you are merely a merchant who desires to foist his sister into a higher class."

His eyes flared in anger. "You will do no such thing."

"Then what do you desire that I say?"

His voice was low, and something in his manner evoked sorrow when he spoke. "You can say I am renewing an acquaintance begun many years ago."

What a paradox the man was! First, not wanting her to lie about the aunt, then encouraging her to lie about their friendship. She fleetingly wondered if they actually *had* met before, but she recalled names as a mother remembers her offsprings' birthdays, and she was sure she had never met a Mr. Thomas Moreland. "Very well," she snapped, rising and stomping from the room.

Stanton informed them Glee had already come downstairs and rushed to the carriage.

A still-angered Felicity found her sister happily

seated beside Dianna in a front-facing carriage seat, chatting as rapidly and unflappably as a hen's cackle.

Felicity became more enraged. *She* would have to sit beside the odious Mr. Moreland. Sighing, she plopped onto the velvet seat and scooted as close as she could to the outer side of the carriage.

Thomas sat next to her, his eyes jutting to Glee. "You are beauty and innocence and all that should rob young men of their ability to speak tonight, Miss Pembroke."

A huge smile brightened Glee's pretty face as she cast her long lashes down. "How very kind you are, Mr. Moreland."

Felicity felt her own anger toward Thomas softening. It *was* very kind of him to sense Glee's fears over her first assembly and very considerate of him to take notice of the young girl.

It was not consideration, however, that caused Felicity to commend Dianna on her appearance. "And you look quite lovely, Miss Moreland. You two shall be the most sought-after dancers of the night, to be sure," Felicity said.

Dianna wore white, too. The pristine stiffness of her elaborate gown should have cast Glee's simple dress into shabbiness, but it did not. While Dianna's gown signaled wealth and breeding and extraordinary taste, Glee's soft gown spoke of sweetness and quiet elegance.

Though the light was dim and infrequent, Felicity studied her sister on the short ride to the Assembly Rooms. Lettie, whom the two sisters now shared, had outdone herself with the challenge of Glee's thick, unruly auburn spirals. Though swept back from her oval face, coppery-colored, curly tendrils framed her sweet features. Felicity could not remember Glee's lips ever appearing so red. Had the scamp colored them? She smiled to herself at her younger sister's unaccountable penchant for stretching and pushing rules.

He should be bursting with confidence and good-will, Thomas thought. He was about to launch into society in the company of the three undoubtedly most beautiful young women in the social hub of Bath. To him, Felicity was loveliest of all despite her absence of sparkling jewels and her drab mourning gown. She was actually quite striking in black with her fair hair and pale butterscotch skin. But then, she would be striking in pauper's rags. How he loved to see her dimples pierce her solemn face. If only she could soften toward him. He wondered if she would consent to dance with him tonight.

The thought of dancing brought a twinge of fear. He had never danced on English soil. He had bought the services of a qualified fop to teach him dancing, and as with everything, it came easily to him. Would that he could remember the steps if Felicity would do him the honor of dancing with him.

Thomas was learning to sense Felicity's feelings and moods, and he knew by the way she edged herself into the bitterly cold side of the carriage that she was angry with him.

But she had met her match in him. He turned toward her and spoke. "You know, Mrs. Harrison, I am not ashamed that my father was merely the proprietor of a bookshop. He was the most noble man I've ever known. I hold far more respect for a man who builds his own position than for one who is given it."

"It is a difficult concept for me to understand self-made men since you are the first I have ever encountered," Felicity said. "Your satisfaction with your rank I do find commendable. Even noble."

She seemed to soften, he noticed. Her shoulders relaxed, and she edged away from the chilly side of the carriage. He found himself reacting to her nearness in a profound way. He fought the urge to draw her hand into his own, and as much as he desired to hold her in his arms during a soothing waltz, he did not want this intimacy in the carriage to come to an end.

Five

Though she had probably been to the Assembly Rooms a hundred times before and knew every last soul there, Felicity felt utterly self-conscious tonight. It was as if a second nose protruded from her face, the way everyone watched her. That they were watching her entire group, she had already taken into account. Glee and Dianna did indeed draw a great deal of attention from young bucks, and no doubt a man as tall and handsome as Mr. Moreland was bound to be the recipient of admiring stares.

Carlotta, for one, wasted no time in swooping upon Felicity and her *friend,* like a predator in the jungle.

"Felicity, dear, you simply must make me acquainted with this tall, dark, and handsome man," the black-haired beauty purred once Felicity had settled on the side of the room where peers took their seats.

Not bothering to sit down, Felicity turned to Carlotta. "Do me the goodness of welcoming my friend Mr. Moreland of Winston Hall and his sister, Dianna," Felicity said with newly summoned grace. Turning to Thomas, she said, "May I present you to my friend, Mrs. Ennis?"

Carlotta moved her head ever so slightly toward Dianna and nodded before turning her full attention on Thomas. "How good it is to meet you," she said, gushing with enthusiasm. "I cannot pretend that I haven't heard about you as well as the wonderful things you've done to Winston Hall. Pray, you must allow me to see the improvements there."

He took her proffered hand and pressed a flat-lipped kiss to it. "Whenever you would like, I should be happy for you and Mrs. Harrison to pay a call."

Felicity scowled. Why did she have to be included in all his schemes? Accompanying him at social functions was compensation enough for his services. Surely he could not force her to dance attendance upon him at Winston Hall.

Carlotta seductively raised her lengthy black lashes at him. "It is refreshing, indeed, to have new blood here, Mr. Moreland. I daresay the regular company grows quite tedious." She turned to Felicity. "Why did you not tell me you were acquainted with Mr. Moreland?"

Felicity could not meet her friend's gaze. "It had been such a very long time since I had seen Mr. Moreland, I simply did not realize he was the one who had taken Winston Hall."

"I knew Mrs. Harrison before I went to India," Thomas explained.

Why did the insufferable man keep saying that? an agitated Felicity wondered.

"Then you must have known Felicity when she was still Miss Pembroke," Carlotta said.

He nodded slightly, his mouth firm. "Yes."

An authoritative man's voice cut in. "I would happily trade my medals and my wealth to have known the delightful Mrs. Harrison before she lost her heart to Captain Harrison."

Felicity looked up at Colonel Gordon and felt her

face coloring. She glanced quickly at Thomas, who held the colonel in his scathing gaze.

"Allow me to introduce you to Colonel Gordon, Mr. Moreland," she said.

The two men eyed each other like circling lions.

Colonel Gordon threw his head back. "Ah, yes, the man who *purchased* Winston Hall."

Felicity felt awkward over the extreme coolness in the heretofore pleasant colonel's tone. Could he be jealous of the nabob? What a ridiculous notion! Surely the colonel knew by now that no man would ever again own her heart. Every time the colonel had begged her hand, she had reminded him of her undying feelings for Michael.

Thomas bowed curtly to Gordon. "I have found, Colonel Gordon, there is little in the kingdom that cannot be purchased, provided one has a large enough purse."

"And from what has come to my ears, you most certainly have the purse," Carlotta said in her soothing voice, her eyes dancing.

The colonel steered the conversation away from Thomas's hefty purse. "I understand you spent some time in India, Mr. Moreland."

Thomas nodded. "Nearly six years."

"Did you come in contact with Colonel Armstrong there? I believe he was in Bombay."

"I did, though we were not well acquainted."

The colonel began to impart his memories of Colonel Armstrong when he was a young officer, which afforded Felicity the opportunity to watch her sister enjoy her first assembly.

By this time, a sizable group of ogling young men had gathered around Dianna and Glee, clamoring for a dance.

Felicity was well pleased. She watched with satisfaction as both girls filled their dance cards. Glee not only looked lovely, but she had dressed with quiet good taste and thus far had conducted herself with genteel deportment. Felicity had feared her little sister would be unable to repress her vibrant, giggly nature. She also feared that Glee would be entirely too flirtatious. More than likely, Miss Moreland could be thanked for Glee's subdued behavior.

The orchestra began to play, and for some unaccountable reason, Felicity felt her heartbeat accelerating. Knowing Mr. Moreland would ask her to dance, she refused to look in his direction.

It did not matter.

"Tell me, Mrs. Harrison," Thomas said, edging closer to her, his back to Carlotta, "does your mourning prohibit you from dancing?"

She felt small and unaccountably feminine standing next to the overpoweringly strong Mr. Moreland. Her gaze swept upward into his hopeful black eyes. "I am no longer in mourning, Mr. Moreland. I live a full and satisfactory life, and yes, I can dance."

"Then I must beg you to stand up with me," he said.

Why did she have the distinct feeling he did not doubt that she would comply? That very afternoon the odious man had told her he always got what he wanted. "Now?" she asked mockingly.

"It's as good a time as any," he stated flatly, offering her his crooked arm.

It was a country dance that afforded little opportunity for intimacy. In fact, Felicity rather enjoyed the dance because she was close enough to Glee to appreciate her sister's flawless dance steps as she stood

up with a swarthy young man who appeared to be the
age of George.

Flawless, too, were Mr. Moreland's steps. Must the
man succeed at everything? When they reached the
head of the line and had to hold each other's hands
for more than a second as they moved down the longway, Felicity fought the tremblings rumbling deep
within her.

Judging from the rattling effects of his touch, it had
obviously been too long since an attractive man had
held her hand. But Colonel Gordon *was* good looking.
His touch, though, had certainly never caused the unexpected reaction Mr. Moreland's touch provoked.

As she was thinking about the colonel, she saw him
from the corner of her line of vision. He glowered at
Mr. Moreland. Before she had time to ponder this,
Mr. Moreland settled her at the end of the line and
faced her contentedly. And before she realized what
she was doing, she favored him with a beaming smile.
He really had done awfully well, especially for one
not born to such a life.

When the dance was finished, Felicity led Thomas
to the opposite side of the room from where they had
started. She had at first automatically gone to the peerage side of the ballroom from a lifelong habit, but
such a seating situation obviously excluded Mr. Moreland. She whispered to him. "I had forgotten the far
wall is reserved for members of the peerage." She
wanted to prevent him from embarrassing himself by
sitting down in the elite section.

"It troubles me that my presence prohibits you from
enjoying what is yours by birth."

"Pooh!" she said. "It does not signify in the least."

He actually believed her. Now she reminded him of
the Felicity he had fallen in love with six years ago,

the Felicity who had compassion for others regardless of their rank. He was also touched that she warned him about the peerage section so that he would avoid what could be an embarrassing situation. It occurred to him that Felicity was at her most lovable when she initiated the kindness. He would have to remember that.

When she issued another warning, he was even more delighted.

"I am not sure the extent of your social education, Mr. Moreland," she whispered, "but I thought it best to tell you one simply does not dance more than two or at the most three times with the same partner."

"And I had hoped to dance every dance with you," he said with exaggeration.

A self-conscious smile turned up the corners of Felicity's mouth. "In case you are deaf, dumb, and blind and have failed to notice, my friend Carlotta appears to be most anxious to dance with you."

"The raven-haired beauty?"

Felicity nodded.

"What of her husband?"

"I am surprised your surveillance of me did not ferret out that information," she said with agitation.

He shrugged. "I daresay before the night is out, the ravishing Mrs. Ennis will make her marital situation known to me." He was half ashamed of himself for his arrogant reply, but he had come to expect beautiful women to push themselves on him. Not that he for a moment believed he was sought after for anything other than his fortune. He watched Felicity as her eyes narrowed with displeasure.

"You are positively odious," she said.

The skin around his dark eyes crinkled when he responded. "Yes, you've told me before."

"Oh, there you are," Carlotta greeted Thomas breathlessly. "How very well you dance, Mr. Moreland. I daresay you brought to mind my dear departed husband, who was tall like you."

Thomas threw a mischievous glance at Felicity, who could not avoid smiling cynically. Then he quickly regained his manners and thanked Carlotta for the compliment. "You must do me the goodness of standing up with me, Mrs. Ennis."

Her lush black lashes slowly peeled away from her lavender eyes and her voice crooned seductively. "But most certainly. I am all yours, Mr. Moreland."

As soon as she spoke, the orchestra began to play another set.

Thomas paid little attention to Carlotta as they went through the steps of the dance. His gaze stayed on Felicity and the colonel, who were sitting down. Thomas did not like the colonel, and he prided himself on his ability to evaluate other men. The runner's report had told him that Colonel Gordon was a frequent visitor at Felicity's town house. A single look at the lame military man confirmed that he was in love with Felicity. No, Thomas thought, his neck muscle tightening, he did not at all like the man.

The rest of the evening Thomas hovered near Felicity. He wanted to be at her side when a waltz was played. Detecting the first violin strains, he made eye contact with her. "May I depend on you, Mrs. Harrison, to suffer through a waltz with me? Perhaps you can impart instruction that will render me an agreeable waltzing partner." He held out his hand, and she took it.

Truth be told, Thomas thought the waltz his best dance. How fortunate he was that he no longer limped. Felicity's doctor had been most skillful. With confidence, he drew Felicity into his loose embrace, reminded that he owed everything to this woman he held in his arms. God's eyes, but she felt even smaller than she looked. And despite his confidence, her nearness caused him to forget the steps, to forget where he was, to forget everything save that his cherished Felicity was in his arms. He trembled. He grew hot. He could not find his voice.

"Mr. Moreland," she said softly and not without affection, "you are forgetting to count and are scarcely moving your feet at all."

"I must confess that dancing with a living, breathing woman is a great deal different than dancing with my previous waltzing partner."

She threw her head back and laughed. "You have brought to mind *my* first actual waltz and how utterly mortified and scandalized I was. I daresay, I feel five years younger just remembering it."

"You are still a very young woman, far too lean of years to speak like one in her dotage."

"You sound exactly like my abigail, who really is in her dotage!"

"It's very kind of you to help me and Dianna," he said. *And to save me from dying,* he wanted to say.

"It has nothing to do with kindness, Mr. Moreland," she snapped.

The magic was gone. The remainder of the dance passed in silence, his only satisfaction coming from the tortured feel of holding her in his embrace. He disliked excessively the thought of another man waltzing with Felicity.

"Upon my word," she exclaimed, "there's George with Mr. Blankenship! George never graces the Assembly Rooms, except to play cards, which he has sworn off. I cannot imagine what he is doing here."

"Perhaps he wishes to assure that his little sister is not a wallflower," Thomas offered.

"That does not sound one bit like George. He's rather self-absorbed, which you must be aware of."

"As are all men of three and twenty years." Thomas's stomach jerked as she peered into his eyes.

"Somehow, Mr. Moreland, I cannot picture you as an idle young man. Were you once?"

He smiled and shook his head. "Actually, no, but you must own that my circumstances are not of the ordinary."

"To be sure."

He was very sorry when the dance came to an end and he had to relinquish his hold on the fair widow. As they removed from the dance floor, her brother joined them.

Felicity looked upon George with smiles and cordial greetings. "You will be happy to know Glee is a great success."

But it was not Glee whom George was watching. He could not remove his eyes from Miss Moreland. When Dianna finished dancing with a young man who was her own height, George greeted her as one would an old friend. "May I hope there is room on your dance card for me, Miss Moreland?" he asked.

She glanced nervously at her brother. "I was not sure what Thomas would think of me waltzing, so there is but the next waltz left open on my card."

"I have no objection to your waltzing with Lord Sedgewick," Thomas said, nodding to George.

"Then I shall look forward immensely to the next waltz," George informed Dianna as he and his friend strolled away.

Carlotta snapped her fan shut as she watched the two young men depart.

Thomas saw Lady Catherine Bullin enter the room and stroll past him.

"Good evening, my lady," he said.

She kept on going, giving no sign she had heard him. Then Thomas realized she *had* heard him. He had been given the cut direct by the lady who formerly inhabited Winston Hall.

Colonel Gordon, who had been acutely aware of every move made by Felicity, now crossed the room to her. "Since I am unable to dance," he said, "I was hoping you would sit with me for a moment."

She smiled wanly and walked to a nearby set of chairs. He sat beside her, propping his cane against his knee.

"I was not aware," he said, "that you were friends with Mr. Moreland."

"I quite forgot the connection, I assure you. It was so very long ago," she said.

He detected an unfamiliar nervousness in her voice. He could not like the encroachment of the big man of even bigger fortune. The colonel had waited too long and risked too much for Felicity Harrison.

"Just when was this, my dear?"

"Oh, it must have been just before I married Michael."

Must have been? Either it was or it wasn't. "But as I understand it, he would not have been wealthy then. How was it that he came within your circle?"

"You must admit he is very handsome."

"To be sure," he said, containing his fury. How skillfully she had evaded answering his question! "I shall be very jealous of him."

"You have nothing to be jealous of, Colonel. The man is really quite arrogant. I suffer his company in order for Glee to reap the influences of his sweet sister."

"I must admit I found the girl to be possessed of the quality I am sure her brother lacks."

Felicity stiffened. "He has been from English soil many years whereas his sister has enjoyed the tutors and masters that her brother's wealth could furnish."

"His own clothes, I will admit, are very fine. A pity he can do nothing about his hideously dark skin," the colonel said.

"Yes, quite a pity," Felicity said.

Her voice lacked sincerity, Gordon thought. A frown furrowed his angular face. Throughout the dance, he found himself watching the nabob. Though the man could probably have any woman he desired, Mr. Moreland chose not to dance this time. Instead, he hungrily watched Felicity. Gordon knew the signs. He knew what it was to lust after the beautiful widow until his very loins ached.

And he could gladly kill Moreland. What was the man about? He had a strong desire to learn more about the enormously wealthy Mr. Thomas Moreland.

Six

"Thank you so much," a jubilant Glee said to Felicity as they left the mantua maker's shop. "Never did I dream I would get so many new dresses."

Seeing her sister's happiness was more than enough thanks for Felicity. That Glee did not ask how they had come up with such money surprised Felicity, who had been fretting for hours how she would explain their newfound wealth to her sister.

Indeed, Felicity was surprised when her solicitor informed her that morning the generous quarterly allowances were already available. Mr. Moreland was clearly a man of his word. A man who would never allow grass to grow under his feet. No wonder he had amassed a great fortune through his own cunning.

Though she had no desire to rush out and purchase finery for herself, she was ever so glad to be able to settle accounts with the tradesmen who were owed sizable sums of money.

Felicity came to a halt and waited for a cart to pass along the busy street. "I think we'll cross here and go to the milliner's," she told Glee.

Glee's emerald eyes sparkled. "Do you mean I get a new hat, too?"

"No. I mean you get more than one." Felicity stepped onto the stone street.

"I can't accept so much when you're not getting anything for yourself," Glee protested.

They quickened their steps to get to the other side before they collided with a pair of oncoming horses. "I don't need new clothes since I'm not on the market," Felicity said.

"I do love the sound of that," Glee said. "On the market . . . Think you I will find a husband this season?"

"Only if you comport yourself with more maturity than you've shown heretofore."

Now they were on the sidewalk teeming with pedestrians and lined with fashionable shops on either side of the street. "Did I not conduct myself with deportment last night?" Glee challenged.

"You did. I am completely puzzled over your exemplary behavior. I must admit it was nothing like your usual manner. And today, you have not once proclaimed yourself to be in love."

Glee frowned and thrust one hand to her hip. "I will have you know I do not fall in love with every young man I meet. In fact, not one of the men last night caught my fancy. They were all rather . . . well, rather insipid. The whole lot of them so much the same. Dressed the same, talking the same. They all looked the same, fair and very British."

"You, my dear, are British."

Glee stomped her softly booted foot. "You just don't understand. I long for a man who is dark and mysterious."

"Perhaps you're not ready for marriage, after all," Felicity said with displeasure. "Such a comment shows gross lack of maturity. One does not select a life's mate based on the color of his hair."

"I will show you that I am ready," Glee said with irritation.

"I hope you do. A pity it would be to waste all this money," Felicity said with intentional dramatic flair.

Glee glowered at her sister as they rounded the next corner to Cheap Street, where their milliner was located.

Felicity saw the lad who was always in front of Mrs. Simmons's millinery shop, and her heart lurched. He was maybe half a dozen years and had great brown eyes set in a small angelic face. He was small for his age, and unable to walk. But he seemed cheerful enough, always playing marbles by himself.

"Good afternoon, young sir," Felicity said to the boy.

He looked up from his game and smiled, and her heart melted anew, for he was missing his front teeth. Like other boys his age. Only the other boys could walk and run and play any manner of boyish games. "Hello," he said shyly.

That his hair was the same shade of red as Glee's must have tugged on Glee's heartstrings, too, for she leaned down and asked him what his name was.

"Jamie," he whispered.

"I am guessing you must be a very good boy," Glee said.

"How did you know?" he asked, warming to her.

"Because you are always in the same place. I believe your mama has told you to stay put in this very spot."

His red head nodded.

Glee straightened up. "I am going to go see your mama and tell her what a good lad you are."

He favored her with his toothless grin and returned to his game.

As they entered the shop lined with bonnets and headdresses of every color and style, Felicity could not rid herself of the vision of little Jamie and his toothless smile.

Mrs. Simmons greeted them and was only too happy to assist Glee in selecting her new head wear.

"Is Jamie your lad?" Felicity asked the milliner.

The stodgy woman shook her head. "His mum— Mrs. Campbell—is my seamstress. She came here from Aberdeen, hoping the waters would help her lad." Mrs. Simmons shook her head and whispered. "Poor tot. Not a bit better."

Felicity and Glee frowned. "How sad," Felicity said.

"He's a very good lad," Glee added. "Please tell his mama we said so."

Felicity noticed a smile cross the face of a red-haired seamstress at the rear of the shop.

With Mrs. Simmons's help, Glee selected an olive green velvet bonnet to go with one of her new pelisses, and a straw bonnet with a variety of colored flowers that could be switched out to go with several dresses. The selection of a white feathered headdress for evenings completed their purchases.

As they left the shop, said farewell to Jamie, and were walking back down the sidewalk, a phaeton slowed beside them, and they turned to see Mr. Moreland and his sister.

"What a pleasant coincidence," Dianna said, "we were on our way to call on you."

Glee eyed her new friend. "Since your brother's phaeton is not large enough for the four of us, why do you not come and walk the rest of the way with me while Felicity rides ahead with Mr. Moreland?"

Dianna moved to disembark, but her brother jumped down to assist her. Then he turned to Felicity and offered her his hand. "Allow me." His smooth gallantry did not reflect his disappointment in the unhappy expression on Felicity's face.

As they rode down Milsom Street, he felt intoxicated from the feel of her so close to him. Why was it, he wondered, when he was with Felicity he felt a bumbling greenhorn once again? Never mind that each governor of India had treated him as exalted guest. Never mind that he held wealth enough to possess the finest manor on English soil. Never mind that any woman in Bath would gladly find room in her bed for him.

He did not want *any* woman. He wanted Felicity. Always had. Always would. Even when there had been no hope, when he had thought her married to her paragon, he could never purge her from his thoughts. Or from the numbing desire her very memory aroused, a desire that no other woman had ever been able to slake.

All his successes would be nothing if he failed at the conquest that mattered most. With a sickening jolt of reality, he realized he might never possess Felicity. He stole a glance at her perfect profile, at the metallic white highlights in her spun-gold hair. His lids lowered as his glance swept over her slim body and softly rounded breasts. And he knew if this was all he would ever be granted, it would have to be enough.

He attempted conversation with the icy beauty. "You and your sister have no doubt been purchasing finery."

"I do not know why you bother to ask," Felicity snapped, "when you already know everything there is to know about us—including the amount of funds so recently made available to the members of my family."

A smile curved his lips. "Perhaps I need to procure the services of informants in the various shops."

Felicity haughtily stuck out her chin. "I daresay you could, given your propensity for throwing around your money on foolish pursuits."

"But I beg to differ," he replied, "none of my pursuits are foolish. For everything I do, there is a sound reason."

He turned onto Monmouth Street. "May I hope you purchased a dress of color for yourself?"

She kept her gaze straightforward. "You may hope for anything you want, Mr. Moreland, but I fear your hopes are uncharacteristically thwarted this time."

"Alas, I will not have the pleasure of seeing you in a dress the color of your lovely eyes."

"I am sure it is a disappointment from which you will recover." She smiled coyly. "It's not as if your stocks decreased in value."

" 'Tis true," he said, turning to gaze at her, a crooked grin on his face. "How disappointing it would be to have reduced stacks of money to count."

Her eyes inadvertently met his, and he detected a mirth she tried to suppress.

She folded her gloved hands in her lap and turned to him. "How are you liking Bath, Mr. Moreland?"

He looked straight ahead. "Some aspects of it I find . . ." He thought of the exhilaration of sitting next to her at this moment. ". . . most satisfactory. But I cannot say it a pleasant matter to behold so many invalids who have come to Bath for the waters."

She nodded her agreement. "I know what you mean," she said softly. "A seamstress at the milliner's brought her little boy here from Aberdeen for the cures, and the poor little mite is no better. He must be around six years old and still unable to walk. Sits alone in front of the shop day in and day out."

Now, Thomas thought, Felicity demonstrated the compassion she had revealed six years ago, the compassion that separated her from the other Bath matrons who entered the millinery shop every day without a thought for the lame boy. He winced. "It's hard enough on adults, but for a mere lad . . ."

"It's heartbreaking."

"I can't have your heart broken, Mrs. Harrison. Should you like seeing the new production of *Taming of the Shrew* at the theater? It is said to be quite good."

"I should enjoy it excessively. I confess to a preference for Shakespeare's comedies."

"Most women do," he said with authority. "They deal with love and happy endings."

"And what's wrong with that?"

He smiled. "Nothing."

"It will be delightful to see *Taming of the Shrew* live. I've not seen it before."

"Tomorrow night?" He was afraid to glance at her, afraid of being rejected. He flicked the ribbons and looked straight ahead.

"Yes," she said self-consciously.

They pulled in front of her house at the same time Carlotta did. Thomas whisked Felicity down from the seat, and as he turned toward a door caught a wave of heavy lavender scent that emanated from the woman in lavender. He ran his eyes approvingly over Carlotta. "May I say it is refreshing to be in the company of at least one widow who graces us with beautiful color."

Felicity's sulking expression did not escape his notice.

As Felicity opened the door, she said, "Mr. Moreland happened by as Glee and I finished shopping." She held the door open for the others.

"And Miss Pembroke and my sister chose to walk home together while Mrs. Harrison did me the goodness of riding home with me," Thomas added. He came to halt in the entry foyer and spoke to Felicity. "Since you have the companionship of the gracious Mrs. Ennis, I believe I'll extricate myself from the hen party that is sure to follow once our sisters arrive. I have only just recalled something that demands my immediate attention. Please tell Dianna I will call for her in an hour." That said, Thomas departed to the cooing disappointment of Carlotta and the quiet resignation of Felicity.

Once he was gone Felicity ordered tea, and she and Carlotta shared a sofa in the drawing room.

"Really, Felicity, I do not know how you suffer the man's company. He positively reeks of new money."

Although Mr. Moreland certainly held no place close to Felicity's heart, somehow she did not like to find him maligned by someone other than herself. "Well, he is very rich."

"Wasn't it you who cautioned me to hold out for good birth?" Carlotta challenged.

"I don't know why we're having this perfectly obtuse conversation. It's not as if I'm going to marry the man. I don't even like him." As soon as she uttered the words, Felicity was sorry. It was one thing to impugn him to his face, quite another to do so when he was unable to defend himself. To soften her words, she added, "I must admit there is nothing offensive in his or his sister's manners, and Mr. Moreland *is* a very fine-looking man."

Carlotta did not meet Felicity's gaze as she brushed

lint from her gown. "I daresay he's much too big for my taste."

Felicity did not believe her for a moment.

Thomas had no trouble finding Jamie. After tethering his phaeton, he walked to the boy and squatted beside him. "I used to play marbles when I was a lad about your size. How old are you?"

"Sixth," Jamie lisped through the gap in his teeth.

"What's your name?"

"Jamie." Framed by rich red curls, the boy's face was almost too pretty, Thomas thought, with its fair skin the color of country cream, its great eyes as brown as fresh humus. There was a slight hollowing in his slender cheeks. Thomas's eyes traveled the folded-up length of the lad, and his stomach twisted at the sight of the ill-formed legs. "You are from Bath?"

Jamie shook his head. "No, thir, we're from Aberdeen."

"Aye, I hear the sun rarely shines in those parts."

"Not often, thir."

Thomas remembered the ill-formed bones of young sailors he had observed as a younger man. Was not the disease of rickets associated with lack of sunshine and lack of the sunshine fruits? "Tell me, Jamie, do you like oranges?"

The boy nodded. "Mum says they're much too dear."

"As it happens, I have a place where they grow oranges on my property. It's called an orangery. I've got more oranges than ever I can eat. I'll send some to you and your mother." He glanced toward Mrs. Simmons's establishment. "Your mother works here?"

Jamie nodded.

Thomas stood up, tipped his hat to the boy, and entered the milliner's shop. "I should like to speak to Jamie's mother," he said.

From the rear of the shop a frail, redheaded woman raised her head from sewing at a table piled with threads, ribands, feathers, and flowers of every color. Her eyes darted to Mrs. Simmons, who nodded her assent. The young mother rose and walked to Thomas. "I'm Jamie's mother," she said timidly.

"Has he seen a doctor since you've come to Bath?"

She shook her head. "No. I had to find work, and find a home. Haven't had the time nor the money." Her green eyes brightened. "But he's had the waters," she defended.

Thomas nodded. "I would like for you to take him to Dr. Langston, whose office is just on the next street." He took a guinea from his pocket and gave it to her. "This should cover the charges as well as your lost wages."

He turned to Mrs. Simmons, whose eyes darted to another shiny guinea in his hand. He gave it to her. "For the temporary loss of your employee."

Jamie's mother's eyes misted. "Thank you, kind sir."

" 'Tis nothing," Thomas muttered. "The ingestion of oranges could benefit the lad. Expect some." He doffed his hat and left.

"Who was that man?" Jamie's mother asked.

"I've never seen him before," Mrs. Simmons said. "A gentleman of quality, to be sure. And ever so handsome."

Thomas's handsomeness held him in good stead when he collected his sister at Felicity's home and found himself the only male in a drawing room filled with a dozen young women. Though Felicity was sure he did not remember half of them from the Assembly Rooms, his geniality belied the fact. He had a knack for making each of the maidens blush and giggle at being addressed by him. The only maiden inured to his charms was Lady Catherine Bullin, who completely ignored him.

And Carlotta, more than any of the others, openly flirted with him. Why had Felicity never before noticed how vulgarly low-cut Carlotta's daytime dresses were? Had the woman no concept of propriety? To Felicity's dismay, Mr. Moreland seemed not to object to the lavender-hued widow. In fact, he flirted right back with the raven-haired beauty.

"How is it such a beautiful woman has not remarried?" he asked Carlotta. "How long has it been?"

"My dear Captain Ennis died four years ago," Carlotta said, reverently lowering her long lashes.

Pooh! thought Felicity. *Her dear captain, my foot. If he were so very dear she would still be wearing black, like me.* Then she was reminded of Mr. Moreland's desire to see her wear colors. And she blushed at the memory of his seductive glance at her own body, clad in the eternal black. She found herself wondering how Mr. Moreland would respond to her were she to don a low-cut purple dress like Carlotta.

Then she was angry at herself for harboring such thoughts. She clutched Michael's locket tightly, as if the action would remind her of the fidelity she had pledged.

Despite being the center of attention, Thomas stayed but a short time before making his excuses. Directing his attention to Felicity, he said, "Would you and your sister do me the goodness of accompanying Dianna and me to the Pump Room in the morning?"

How could she refuse? She had already spent his money. "It would be our pleasure, Mr. Moreland," she said, refusing to look at him.

Seven

It had been a very long time since Felicity had allowed a man to escort her into society. Perhaps that was why she and Mr. Moreland seemed to be drawing an inordinate amount of curious stares as they made their way across the stone floors of the Pump Room to get their obligatory glass of foul-tasting water. Or perhaps it was Mr. Moreland's dark good looks that drew the attention. He was so very tall. Much taller than Michael had been, she thought as she fingered her husband's locket. She directed her gaze at Thomas's finely crafted face. A lock of black hair swept over his stern brow. Guilty over her admiration of his looks, she lowered her lashes, only to be presented a view of his muscled thighs.

She looked up quickly and into the face of Colonel Gordon. He was not looking at her but at Mr. Moreland, anger flaring in his green eyes. He seemed to catch himself and shifted his gaze to Felicity, a feeble smile playing at his lips.

"Ah, Mrs. Harrison, you're about early this morning," he said, recovering his usual air of gallantry as he took her hand and pressed his lips lightly over her gloved fingers.

She had never thought the colonel a small man, but

now he seemed rather frail. Now that she compared him to the ruggedness of Mr. Moreland.

"I am showing the splendors of Bath to its newest resident," she said. "You remember Mr. Moreland?" She took a drink of the nasty-tasting water.

The colonel nodded at Thomas. "Moreland," he said brusquely.

"Do you find, Colonel, the waters beneficial to your affliction?" Thomas asked, casting a glance at the colonel's cane.

Felicity observed the colonel stiffen. How utterly insensitive Mr. Moreland was! Colonel Gordon, who rarely referred to his injury, preferred to believe that no one noticed it.

"I'm as fit as I was when I led a thousand men into battle," he testified, then turned to address Felicity. "How did you find last night's musicale?"

"I suffered through it tolerably," she said, giving her glass back to the attendant, a grimace on her face.

"Ah, the things one does for one's siblings," the colonel said.

She smiled and glanced at Glee, who was taking a turn about the large room with Dianna. "Having nothing to compare it to, Glee did enjoy it excessively."

"I believe Miss Pembroke has taken well," Colonel Gordon said. "The young bucks fairly clamor to be near her, as well as Miss Moreland."

Felicity looked up at Mr. Moreland, her eyes sparkling. "See, you had no reason to worry over Dianna."

He looked pleased as his eyes followed his sister, who was dressed in a mint green promenade gown.

"I believe Glee's as delighted over her new friend as she is over her debut into society," Felicity said.

Carlotta entered the room and joined her friends, her ever-present lavender scent too strong for Felicity's tastes. "I cannot recall seeing the Widow Harrison out this early before," Carlotta said in her rich voice.

"I assure all of you I am an early riser," Felicity protested. "But having no taste for the waters, I had no reason to be about in the mornings before Glee was out."

Carlotta slipped herself between Felicity and Thomas. "Is this your first visit to the Pump Room, Mr. Moreland?" she asked.

"Indeed, it is," he answered.

She hooked her arm into his. "Come, let us take a spin about the room."

Felicity watched as they walked away. She was struck by what a handsome couple they made. Two manes of lustrous black hair. Two perfect bodies. But something was wrong. Despite their beauty, they did not belong together. Not that Carlotta did not deserve to find a mate. It was just that Mr. Moreland was not the man for her.

Even if Carlotta did not know it.

Colonel Gordon offered Felicity his arm. "Come, my dear, a walk will do you good."

She slipped her arm through his. Why would a walk do her good? Was something wrong with her?

"I must confess I am worried about you," he began.

"About me?" Felicity asked.

He nodded gravely. "I cannot approve of your alliance with Mr. Moreland. You must remember your sister. You owe it to your dear papa to secure for her an equal match."

"That is precisely what my intentions are, Colonel."

"Then I need not inform you that friendship with a merchant could drive away men of good birth."

"From Glee?"

He nodded.

"I do not believe a *good* man would be shallow enough to shun Glee because of her family's friendship with Mr. Moreland." She quickened her step, watching Glee's back, concentrating on her sister's bouncing red curls.

He sighed. "I hope you're right, my dear."

Why did the man always refer to her as *my dear?* She had never particularly noticed it before, and now it annoyed her excessively.

He patted her hand. "I have written to an officer friend of mine in India to inquire about Mr. Moreland."

She wheeled at him, anger flashing in her eyes. "I fail to see how Mr. Moreland's affairs connect to you, Colonel."

"Oh, but they do." He covered her hand with his and spoke as one would to an underling or a child. "Since you have no father or husband to look out for you, I must take it upon myself to protect you from unsavory persons."

Her eyes narrowed. "I hardly think Mr. Moreland an unsavory person. I have dined at Winston Hall and assure you both Mr. Moreland and his sister conduct themselves as do those who were born to such wealth."

She detected a slowing in his uneven step. "I had not realized you had been a guest at Winston Hall."

Because she had not wanted anyone to know. She lifted her chin, met his quizzing gaze, and spoke in a frigid voice. "I do not apprise you of all my movements, Colonel." She saw Mr. Moreland walking toward her, his black eyes on hers, Carlotta still clinging to his arm.

"I believe it's my turn to take a stroll around the

room with Mrs. Harrison," Thomas said, shooting a steely look at the colonel.

Felicity was grateful to be rescued from the colonel. He had become so possessive lately. Annoyingly so. In fact, he was driving her away with his prying and cynicism. She gave Mr. Moreland a weak smile and took his proffered arm.

Neither of them said anything when they first started walking. Then, Felicity spoke. "What is your opinion of the water, Mr. Moreland?"

"As nasty as reported."

"And the Pump Room?"

He looked down at her. "Quite nice, actually. What I have seen of Bath so far is favorable."

"I am told that only London exceeds it for variety of fine shops," she offered.

"And the architecture, too, is impressive—on a much smaller scale than London, of course," he added.

"Have you been to the Royal Crescent?"

"Not yet. I'd like to very much. Would I be presuming on your generosity, Mrs. Harrison, to ask you to walk there with me this morning?"

She looked up at his hopeful expression and did not have the heart to refuse him. After all, he was paying handsomely for her time. Besides, she loved to stroll through Bath, and today was perfect for enjoying Crescent Fields. "It's a fine day for a walk," she said.

Just feet outside the Pump Room, Felicity's chiding started. "I believe, Mr. Moreland, you are overdue a lesson in good manners."

"Have I not been amiable to you?" he asked lightly.

"To me, yes. But your conduct toward Colonel Gordon was abominable!"

"Because I referred to his affliction?"

"Yes. It was totally insensitive."

Thomas didn't believe the colonel had a sensitive bone in his body. "I will be the soul of compassion if you can truthfully tell me Colonel Gordon did not malign me during your stroll about the room." He gazed down into the golden loveliness of her face.

She didn't speak for a moment, nor did she meet his gaze. When she spoke, she smoothly shifted the conversation. "And your conduct toward Mrs. Ennis lacks gallantry." Though her words held censure, her tone was teasing.

"I beg to differ. I pay appropriate homage to her beauty." He purposely walked on the opposite side of Cheap Street from Mrs. Simmons's millinery establishment to avoid being recognized by Jamie. A glance toward the boy, who sat in front of the shop eating an orange, brought a smile to Thomas's lips. One of his footmen had already begun his assignment of bringing the lad fresh oranges daily.

"I can't argue with that," Felicity said. "But what of you ignoring her hints that she wanted to accompany us to the Royal Crescent?"

"Hints? I did not know Mrs. Ennis could be subtle about anything."

Felicity tossed back her head and laughed. "You are quite wicked, you know."

Laughter emanating from her somber person was balm to his soul. He looked down at her with smiling eyes and was rewarded with a view of her deep dimples, which of late had too often been hidden in her somberness. "Yes, I know," he said.

She swatted at his arm, and he answered by placing his big hand over hers. Sweet heaven! but her hand was tiny. And warm. A strange, ethereal feeling washed over him, leaving his heart light.

They walked past Theater Royal, and he was disappointed she did not mention the play she had agreed to attend with him.

"Since you are so well acquainted with the sins of my family," Felicity began, "I must tell you I have been most pleased with George's behavior—at least in the past few days. Despite that you've made generous funds available to him, he has not gone near the gaming tables. And did you notice him coming to the Pump Room as we were leaving?"

"Most uncharacteristic, getting up before midafternoon."

She frowned. "I forgot. You *would* know all of our habits only too well. I suppose you employed a Bow Street Runner to follow us about."

"But, of course. Only the best, you know."

She heaved an exasperated sigh, then once again shifted the conversation. "I wonder if George fancies himself in love."

Thomas shrugged. "About your brother's gambling, don't get your hopes up too much, the quarter is young yet."

She nodded, but her mind was clearly elsewhere. "Has your sister remarked on George?"

So Felicity had been aware of her brother's infatuation with Dianna. "Being reticent, Dianna shares little with me."

"If only Glee could be more like her." Felicity shook her head. "I know the color of eyes of every young man Glee has ever found handsome, for she endlessly enumerates each man's merits. And, of course, the problem is they all have merit, and there are far too many of them. I do wish she could be more constant."

That Felicity chose to share her views with him sent deep waves of contentment over him. Friendship was the first rung on the climb to love. "She's young yet," he murmured, patting the top of Felicity's hand.

He watched as her other hand darted toward the locket she always wore at her neck. He started to ask if her husband had given her the locket, but changed his mind. He didn't want to hear the answer. He had only to gaze upon her black dress to know where her heart lay. He kicked the cobblestone. Damn Captain Michael Harrison!

"Do we go to the play tonight?" she asked.

His heart soared. "We do. Dianna is also looking forward to seeing her first Shakespeare production."

"And, being a lady, she prefers comedy too, no doubt?"

"But of course."

"And you, oh lofty thinker, what do you prefer?"

"The histories."

She nodded. "And if they have a battle in them, so much the better, I suppose."

"I perceive you say that because I'm a male."

"As you say all women prefer the comedies."

"Touché."

"Do you really suppose Richard III said, 'My kingdom for a horse'?" she asked.

"Not for a minute. It's just the genius of Shakespeare."

"I'm sure you're right," she said thoughtfully. "I suppose it's the same for *'Et tu, Brute.'* "

He nodded. "I expect Julius Caesar's actual words not only lacked poignancy but were likely unmentionable."

By now they had reached the Royal Crescent and strolled along the half-moon-shaped block of fine town houses, talking comfortably all the while, then stopping to rest at Crescent Fields.

"Since you're not bashful over instructing me on proper etiquette, I have a question for you, Mrs. Harrison."

Felicity arched her brows.

His heart thudded. "Would it be acceptable for me to send you flowers?"

With a sick feeling in the pit of his stomach, he watched as her hand leaped to the locket and fingered it. Then she looked up at him, an unreadable expression on her face. Was it embarrassment? "If you want to waste your precious money on flowers for me, I have no objection."

Rung two, he thought.

Colonel Gordon had not seen Felicity lift her laughing face to a man since Captain Michael Harrison was alive. Watching it then was painful, but not as painful as it was now. Now that Felicity's dimples creased for the Upstart of Winston Hall. Was Gordon going to have to eliminate one more man before he could claim his beautiful Felicity? Nothing would give him greater pleasure.

After she left the Pump Room with the Upstart, the colonel hurried to Lady Catherine Bullin. "You would bring me great honor if you would stroll about the room with me, my lady," he said.

Since not a single man had so honored her, Lady Catherine smiled widely and took his proffered arm.

The woman, who was but a pair of years older than Felicity, repulsed him. A homelier woman of quality he had never beheld. 'Twas no wonder she had never married.

He waited until they had passed the orchestra, then he broached the subject that had forced him to tolerate Lady Catherine's company. "It has come to my attention you have no love for Mr. Moreland."

"I loathe him."

He liked her more already. Even if her weak chin promised to sink into her fleshy neck. A smile curled at his lips. "As do I. That's what I want to talk to you about." He hoped she wasn't disappointed he had not sought her out for herself. After all, he knew himself to be an uncommonly good-looking man, even if he did have to use a cane to walk. "I have had a distressing communication from my friend in India, Colonel Armstrong, who has a rather juicy bit of gossip about Moreland."

Her brows arched.

"Normally, I wouldn't repeat such, but since the Upstart of Winston Hall has lavished his attentions upon Mrs. Harrison—whom I am quite close to—I fear for her well-being."

A smile tweaked at Lady Catherine's lips. "You must tell me what the odious man has done."

The colonel cleared his throat. "Armstrong told me while the Upstart was in India he lived out of wedlock with a dark-skinned Indian woman."

"That's disgusting," she said, "but I'm hardly surprised."

He lowered his voice as a pair of young ladies strolled past them. "The pity of it is, several children were born of the alliance—children he left unprovided for when he came back to England."

"At least the men of our class make settlements for their by-blows," she said with indignation.

Gordon nodded. "I desire to protect Mrs. Harrison from the dishonorable man, but I can hardly repeat such gossip to her. Because of my feelings for her, she would think I was merely jealous of the Upstart."

Lady Catherine's gloved hand patted his arm. "Leave it to me, Colonel. We ladies of nobility must watch out for one another."

Eight

Glee and Dianna, accompanied by George and Blanks, exited the box amidst the rustle of swishing silks. Felicity turned to Thomas, who sat beside her in the dimly lit theater. "Do you not want to have a cigar during intermission?"

" 'Tis one bad habit I never acquired," he answered.

"Let me see, you don't smoke. You don't gamble. Surely you have acquired at least one vice," Felicity teased.

"Much more than one, I am sure." His eyes dropped to the flowers she wore. A gift from him. That she wore them sent a possessive thrill humming through him. He settled back in his plush seat and directed his full attention at her. "And how have you enjoyed the play thus far?"

She didn't answer right away, but the happy expression on her face assured him she was collecting her thoughts. "It's so much more than I had hoped for. The language, of course, is beautiful. The costumes are wonderful. And the cast is superb." She gave Thomas an animated look. "As you can see, I'm in raptures."

"The night is all I hoped it would be," he said, his meaning encompassing more than the play.

She shot him a mischievous glance. "It has struck

me that Petruchio bears a certain resemblance to a Mr. Thomas Moreland."

"You malign me," he protested, the glimmer in his eyes belying his indignation. "I'm nothing like Petruchio. I don't have to marry for a dowry."

She could not mask the amusement in her voice. "Has it not struck you that he *does* get what he wants?"

"But, my lady, I only gain what money can buy. You must admit there is much that cannot be procured by riches alone."

" 'Tis true, but I believe you were born under a lucky star. Does not everything come easily for you?"

What could she be referring to? He had worked hard for everything that had ever come his way. And the one thing he wanted most was still far from his grasp. Might not ever be within his reach, he thought as his eyes swept over the black of her dress. The black she wore for her captain. Thomas's jaw tightened. " 'I am not merry; but I do beguile the thing I am by seeming otherwise.' "

A curious expression passed over her face, and she whispered, *"Othello."*

He nodded as his eyes swept across the theater. Damn, but he hadn't meant to allow her that glimpse into his innermost self.

Carlotta sat with the colonel in a box opposite them. She nodded at Thomas, a sensuous smile on her face as she leaned toward the colonel and said something in his ear. Thomas returned the silent greeting, leaning to Felicity. "I see your colonel and Mrs. Ennis across from us."

"He is not my colonel," Felicity snapped. She, too, nodded across the rounded theater. "Carlotta will be a positive lioness tomorrow. Really, Mr. Moreland, it would not have hurt you to have invited her to share our box tonight. Her regard in Bath, you must know, is as good as mine."

"Ah, but Mrs. Ennis is not the daughter of a viscount."

"I daresay if she were, it would be she sharing your box and not me."

"And how dull it would be not to have you to spar with, Mrs. Harrison."

A smug smile stole across her face. "We do seem to clash rather well."

The curtain behind them opened, and the four young persons noisily reentered the box.

It rained the next day. All day. With the exception of George, who refused to allow bad weather to interfere with his shooting expedition at Winston Hall, no one else stirred outdoors. Hampered by darkened skies, Felicity and Glee bent over their embroidery, aided by candles even though it was still afternoon.

"I didn't think to be saying this so soon," Felicity began, "but you have shown remarkable maturity as of late, my sweet."

"In what way?" Glee asked.

"You have not once extolled the perfection of a single buck. And not once have you declared yourself to be in love with a man you've scarcely met. Quite a departure for you."

"That's because none of the young men I've seen in society have captured my heart. They're all so . . . so bland, so immature. I declare, they're all so much the same."

Felicity's brows lowered. How could her little sister have changed so rapidly? Felicity could not remember a time when Glee had not found something to swoon over in every male she met. Just a few short weeks ago Glee had begged to attend assemblies, and now that she did, she adopted a cavalier attitude toward them.

On the other hand, Dianna Moreland, though reserved in manner, appeared to relish her public outings. She was gracious to all the young men who hovered near her and Glee, and forever wore a smile on her lovely face. However, a complete metamorphosis occurred in Dianna whenever George was near. Her natural poise and gracious charm abandoned her, replaced by acute shyness. Only when she looked into George's eyes, Felicity thought, did Dianna reveal a tender affection.

"A pity," Felicity said. "Perhaps you'll not be wed, after all."

Pricked by a stab from her needle, Glee issued an exclamation, then glared at Felicity. "I believe I wish to wed an older man."

An older man? Felicity could not remember Glee ever having been attracted to older men. And what did she mean by old? When one was seventeen, seven-and-twenty seemed ancient. All of a sudden, a thud spiraled through her insides. *Could Glee have developed a crush on Mr. Moreland?* That would explain her sister's resentful glances at Felicity. Sweet heaven, such a match would never succeed. Glee would be bored to distraction with Mr. Moreland's love of Shakespeare. They were totally unsuited in every way.

And not because of his lack of rank. Mr. Moreland would no doubt make some fashionable lady a good husband.

But Glee was not that fashionable lady.

"I wonder if Mr. Salvado will come today in this dreadful rain?" Glee said.

"I've been meaning to talk to you about him. Now that you're out, you no longer need Mr. Salvado's services. He's done a commendable job teaching you to dance."

"Oh! but . . ." Glee protested, then faltered. "Though he's a fine instructor, I'm a most poor student. I tend to execute the right steps to the wrong dances, or some such stupidity. Please allow him to continue for another few weeks."

Felicity met her sister's imploring green eyes. "Three weeks. And that's all."

The door burst open, and George entered the room, rivulets of water pouring from his greatcoat, his darkened gold hair dripping down his face. Despite his sodden state, a smile stretched nearly ear to ear.

"Winston Hall is a veritable haven for fowl," he exclaimed. "I bagged half a dozen."

"I'm sure that's very good, but you'll have to tell us about it *after* you change into dry clothing," Felicity said. "You'll ruin the carpet."

Five minutes later he was back in the drawing room, intent on describing in detail his and Mr. Moreland's good fortune shooting. "Makes me long for Hornsby Manor," he concluded.

His words stung Felicity. The letting of their ancestral home had always saddened Felicity, but she had been able to endure it because George had so stoically accepted the loss. His loss.

"Did you see Dianna?" Glee inquired.

He took the hot cup of tea Felicity had poured, then sat down. "As a matter of fact, I had tea with her before returning to Bath."

Glee flung down her embroidery. "Tell me, did she

have on still another dress? I've not seen her wear the same thing twice."

"How would I know?" George said. "Don't know about such."

"What color was her dress?" Glee asked.

He thought for a moment. "Pink!" he finally exclaimed with pride.

"See," Glee said to no one in particular, "I've not seen her in a pink day dress before. Another dress. I'd give my new straw bonnet to see her wardrobe. I wager she's got a hundred dresses."

"A young lady doesn't wager," Felicity scolded.

"You place too much emphasis on dresses, pet," George told Glee. "Miss Moreland would be just as pretty if she wore the same dress every day."

He is smitten, Felicity thought. And she did not know how to react. Of course, nothing disparaging could be found in Miss Moreland. And George did need to settle down. But he was still rather immature. She could not imagine him running a household, having a wife . . . fathering a child. Though it was exactly what he needed.

Glee sighed. "Mr. Moreland must be unbelievably rich."

"And he'd be as likable if he were poor," George said. "I'll be the first to admit my reluctance at bringing him into our circle. But now I find him just as much one of us as Blanks. Though he's nothing like Blanks." He eyed Felicity. "Doesn't know how to enjoy life as Blanks does. Reminds me of you."

"Me?" Felicity questioned.

He nodded. "Always somber. Acts far older than his nine-and-twenty years. The two of you are bent on seeing to others' happiness while sacrificing your own."

George *was* more mature, Felicity thought, a sadness settling over her for the loss of her brother's rattled youth. "I hardly sacrifice myself. I expect the similarity between Mr. Moreland and me arises because we're both the firstborn."

"Mr. Moreland is only nine-and-twenty?" Glee questioned. "He seems so much older. To think, he's already made more money than ever he can spend."

Felicity watched her sister intently, searching for a spark of affection toward Mr. Moreland. The only thing Glee revealed was her belief that nine-and-twenty was not such an old age after all.

In the weeks that followed, easy intimacy flourished between the members of Felicity's family and Dianna and Thomas Moreland. Mornings and afternoons were spent at the Pump Room. Wednesdays were set aside for musicales, which Felicity barely tolerated. Twice a week, assemblies provided still another opportunity to mingle in society. Felicity wondered why Mr. Moreland still accompanied her as frequently as he did. His own credit was firmly established. Women were reduced to blathering, admiring idiots when in his company. It seemed no woman in Bath was immune to his charm. Or his rugged good looks.

Thomas hoarded Felicity's companionship, but not to the exclusion of Colonel Gordon and Carlotta, both of whom were quick with a critical word against him. Colonel Gordon turned frigid whenever Mr. Moreland entered his circle, whereas the opposite was true with Carlotta Ennis. When in his company she gave no evidence of holding him in dislike, as she did when speaking of him to Felicity.

"Really, Felicity," she would say, "the man is such

a flirt. I daresay you cannot believe a word he utters." Or she would feign disinterest in him while professing his keen interest in herself.

When she was with Thomas, however, the raven-haired beauty treated him as if he were the only man in the room. She persisted in linking her arm through his for a walk around the Pump Room, and she boldly asked him to dance with her at assemblies. And whenever an occasion called for his impressive carriage, Carlotta always managed to be seated next to Thomas.

On another dreary, rainy day in which Felicity had decided not to leave the comfort of her home, Stanton informed her Lady Catherine Bullin wished to see her. As Stanton led the lady into the drawing room, Felicity ordered tea and asked her to take a seat.

Felicity was puzzled that Lady Catherine was paying her a call. Though they were acquainted, the two women had never been close.

The grave look on Lady Catherine's face did not escape Felicity's attention, but she chose not to remark on it.

"Your friendship with Mr. Moreland has not gone unnoticed," Lady Catherine began. "And since we are both of the upper class, I felt compelled to come here today to warn you about the man."

Felicity shot her a curious glance.

"I must tell you of Mr. Moreland's sordid past."

The allusion set Felicity's heart to hammering as if some tragedy had befallen her. Had Mr. Moreland stolen his fortune? No, not that. Instinctively, she knew he was incapable of such an action. "Do share your grievous news with me?" she asked.

Lady Catherine sighed. "During the years he lived

in India, Mr. Moreland developed a . . . an intimate relationship with an Indian woman. A very dark complected person, you understand. Terribly bad *ton,* you know. And during the course of their . . . ah, association, several children were born of the union."

Felicity's heart hammered harder. She could not remove her eyes from Lady Catherine's.

"I have learned that when Mr. Moreland left India, he made no provisions for his . . . his family."

"I hardly see how this concerns me," Felicity snapped. "It's not as if he were marrying Glee." Her words belied the tumultuous quaking within her.

"It's not Miss Pembroke who concerns me."

For an instant, Felicity's eyes locked with hers, tension between them as tight as a bowstring.

"If you think I mean to marry him, you don't know me. I plan to stay true to my Michael's memory."

Lady Catherine rose. "Then I am most relieved." Her eyes narrowed. "I would hate to think of the wretched man attempting to use any friend of mine."

Then the former owner of Winston Hall swept from the room, leaving Felicity shaking in disbelief.

Nine

Fine lines crinkled Dr. Langston's face when he frowned. "Some of the damage is irreparable," he said.

Thomas winced and leaned into the doctor's desk, directing still another question at the patient man. "But will he ever walk?"

Langston nodded, his spectacles slipping farther down the bridge of his ruddy nose. "With proper diet and braces, perhaps."

"Do whatever's necessary. No matter what the cost," Thomas said.

The doctor removed his glasses and set them on his cluttered desk. "You understand the boy will be lame for the rest of his life?"

"For one who's never been able to walk, lameness is but a slight hindrance." Thomas rose. "All the bills can be sent to me at Winston Hall." He walked to the door, then turned back toward the doctor, who sat writing at his desk beside the tall window, its draperies ruffled by a breeze. "I'm depending on your discretion. No one is to know I am helping the lad."

Her skirts spread out on the lush grass, Felicity lounged in the shade and watched her brother and sister ride off into the thicket with Dianna. The grounds here at Winston Hall could grace a Turner landscape, she thought. The verdant land sloped to bridle trails thick with centuries-old trees, canopied with cerulean skies and speckled with shimmering lakes. Her own recent paces with Mr. Moreland's fine horse left her exhausted. Her host, too, sought a respite from the brisk activity, reclining in the shade, while Felicity—bonnet shadowing her face—basked in the sun a few feet away. The mellow breeze tempered the sun's penetrating warmth.

"Your sister rides well. Were you her teacher?" Felicity asked.

Thomas nodded. "I was horse-mad as a lad. Quite a disappointment to my father, who wanted me to work in his bookshop. Even though I loved books, I loved horses more and took a job as a groom."

Felicity ran her eyes along his well-clothed, muscled limbs spread out on the grass and had difficulty picturing him as an ill-dressed boy smelling of horses. His breeches of rich buff-colored superfine molded to his powerful thighs, and his chocolate frock coat hugged his huge shoulders, tapering down to the solid V of his waist. His boots bespoke a good hour of preening care from his valet. "I can understand your father's disappointment," she said.

He smiled and brought his bulk up to rest on his elbows. "It turned out to be the best thing that could have happened to me. Seeing firsthand how the nobility lived ignited in me a strong desire to emulate their lifestyle. I saved my paltry few shillings, determined to make my fortune. I knew it couldn't be done through a bookshop or other such enterprise. My fortune lay in a far-off land. Either the Colonies or India.

Enamored of exotic silks and spices, I decided on India."

"How old were you?"

"Just over twenty."

"How brave you were to forsake the familiar for worlds unknown."

" 'Our doubts are traitors and make us lose the good we oft might win by fearing to attempt.' "

His fund of Shakespeare awed her. *"Two Gentlemen of Verona,"* she whispered.

"Ah, a woman after my own heart." The long, glazed look he gave her belied his jesting tone. She felt uncomfortable being so close to him. So vulnerable to his undeniable virility. The thought of him making love to an Indian woman crowded into her thoughts. She thought of them together, and her own body was acutely affected by the idea of Mr. Moreland lying with a woman. She wondered if the poor Indian woman had been in love with him. Had the woman crumbled beneath his touch? Felicity's breath grew short as her anger mounted.

Her back stiffened, and she rearranged her bonnet. "How did you get on in a strange country?"

"Before I went, I read every word that had ever been written about India, and I taught myself Hindi—as well as one can without benefit of the native tongue."

She willed herself to concentrate on his words, not his unsettling presence. "And it was beneficial?"

"It was." He sat up, planting his shiny black boots in the soft grass. His legs were as powerful as the trunk of the mighty oak that shaded him. "I have a plan for everything I do. My plan was to live among the people, to learn their ways. In that way, I could better discover the sources for the riches I sought."

"And you were obviously successful."

A rustle of wind caught his coal black hair as he nodded. "By the time I'd been there two years, I had made enough money to buy my own ship. Once I had reduced my shipping costs, the wealth followed."

"So I presume you now own a fleet of ships." She kept her tone light to mask the direction of her thoughts. For ever since he had confessed that he had lived among the Indian people, she could think of nothing save what Lady Catherine had told her about him. Mr. Moreland had had an Indian mistress. He had fathered Indian children. Children he had left behind.

"And mills both here and in India."

He was close enough for her to touch. She could smell his sandalwood scent. She found herself wondering how the Indian woman had felt about him. Had she loved him? Had she been drawn to his undeniable masculinity? Then Felicity wondered what it was like sharing a bed with him, the bronze hardness of his body stretched beside her. Her hand flew to the locket, and she caressed it. *I'm sorry, Michael.* She could not be disloyal to her husband's memory. Why was she thinking about lying with another man?

Thomas's black eyes followed her movement, a somber look replacing his mirth. "I picture you in a blue dress," he said solemnly.

She swallowed and fingered the locket even tighter. "Black suits the person I am." She looked away from his probing eyes. "Do you know George said you are always serious, that you are just like me? I told him such sobriety must come from being the firstborn."

"Were you always so serious?" His voice was gentle. "Before you were wed?"

"Not really," she said. "But then I married. I was

a morose bride, always fearing for Michael." She looked into her lap. "It seems my fears were founded. Then—after Michael was killed—I returned to England to learn that Papa had lost everything except Hornsby Manor, which was entailed, but we couldn't afford to live there." She looked back at him and laughed an insincere laugh. "And since then I've had to be the ogre with George and Glee."

"You're not an ogre," he said in a soothing voice. "As the firstborn, we must wear the mantel of authority."

She favored him with a smile. "You once told me you never were an idle lad. Did you never have any vices, Mr. Moreland?" As soon as she uttered the words, she thought of the Indian woman.

He thought a moment before he answered. "Greed, I suppose. But I've always tried to be fair to those I've dealt with."

"And generous, as you've been to my family." Now why did she go and say that? The man hadn't been generous to his own Indian family.

He was looking at her with an overpowering tenderness. "You really should wear color," he said throatily.

She wished he would stop looking at her like that. And why did he continue to refer to her mourning? "I owe it to Michael—"

" 'What's gone and what's past help should be past grief.' "

She glared at him. "How conveniently you quote Shakespeare, Mr. Moreland."

"There are no feelings or occasions that he has not addressed far more eloquently than ever I could."

She simply had to get him to stop looking at her as if he would ravish her. "I'm very concerned over

Glee," she began. "She has not at all been herself
lately. At first I was glad, but now . . ." She wondered
once more if Glee could be in love with Mr. Moreland.
And, more than that, she wondered at her own ease
in sharing family worries with Thomas Moreland. After all, she had only known him a few weeks.

His brows lowered. "I've been meaning to speak to
you about her."

Had the two of them an agreement? Her heart
pounded frantically.

"She has been having clandestine meetings with an
unsuitable gentleman."

Relief rushed over her. *Then it wasn't Mr. Moreland.*
"Who?" she demanded.

Thomas frowned. "Would that I could tell you his
name."

"You have seen him?"

"Yes, I saw the two of them on a bench at Sydney
Gardens."

The insufferable, arrogant, conniving upstart persisted in spying on her family! She whirled at him.
"So you still spy on my family! I know Glee is impetuous, but she would not conduct herself with such
impropriety. She's a lady, the daughter of a viscount.
I'm sure you only thought the girl was Glee." Felicity
shot him a haughty look.

He took up a blade of grass. "I don't mean to pry.
I just thought you should be aware."

The sound of laughter and the drumming of hooves
was a welcome respite from her confrontation with
Mr. Moreland. She turned to watch her brother and
sister and their newly cherished friend reign in and
dismount. George leaped to assist Dianna, leaving
Glee to get down on her own. His hands cinched about
Dianna's tiny waist, George looked down at her with

laughing eyes. "I say, this has been great fun, Miss Moreland. We must do it again. Only next time, don't allow me to win."

She looked up at him, wonder in her porcelain perfect face. "I assure you, Lord Sedgewick, you bested me with no help."

He offered her his arm and guided her to the shade of the tree where her brother and Felicity sat. "Drat, Miss Moreland, I do wish you'd call me George, as much time as we spend together."

Before sitting down, she met her brother's gaze with a questioning look.

"I have no objections to you calling Lord Sedgewick by his first name, though I'd as lief he didn't address you by your Christian name in society."

"How glad I am not to be the only ogre," Felicity said to Thomas.

Glee threw herself on the grass, tossed off her bonnet, and glared at her sister. "You are such a positive stickler for propriety."

What had come over Glee of late? She never used to speak to Felicity with such resentment. It was as if the bond that united them had suddenly snapped.

Her thoughts flitting to Thomas Moreland, Felicity told herself she should see less of him. After all, she had kept her part of the bargain. He and his sister were accepted everywhere. Even without Felicity, their standing in society was assuredly secure.

Then why did he continue to spend every free moment with Felicity? Were it not for his respect and gentlemanly conduct toward her, she might almost believe him enamored of her. But his desire for her companionship bore no resemblance to Colonel Gordon's naked lust for her.

Most likely, it was just as he had said. She was the

daughter of a viscount. Having a friend on the fringes of aristocracy could certainly boost his credit. Hadn't that been the whole point to their unusual bargain? But now—knowing him as she was beginning to—his hunger for social standing was at odds with the man she knew him to be, though she supposed he did long for Dianna's acceptance in the *haute ton.*

She smiled as she thought of what a kind brother he was to his younger sister, of the lengths he had gone to assure her a gentleman for a husband.

But he continued to spy on Felicity's family.

Once again, she remembered the poor Indian woman. And she grew even angrier. Another juxtaposition of the man she knew him to be and the man he was.

Thomas had mistakenly hoped George could keep the younger girls occupied longer and was disappointed when they returned before he had been able to penetrate Felicity's armor. Not only had he not penetrated it, he seemed to have thickened it with his well-intentioned remark about Glee's clandestine meetings with a man who could not be worthy of her since he was exposing her to scandal.

Just when Thomas was beginning to thaw the ice around Felicity's heart, he had once again managed to anger her. And instead of gaining a hungered-for kiss from her, Thomas had drawn her ire.

One remark that had slipped from her lovely lips cut him deep and wide. *She's a lady, the daughter of a viscount.* Would he ever be able to cross the gulf that separated his kind from hers?

He got to his feet, brushing grass from his breeches.

"We had best take the ladies back before they get too much sun."

Disappointment flashed across George's face, but he, too, stood up, then assisted Dianna. As had become the pattern now, Thomas helped first Felicity, then Glee, mount the horses he had provided them. He watched with favor as George rode ahead next to Dianna and Glee while he held back several feet with Felicity next to him. Her bonnet shaded her face from the sun's brightness but did nothing to prevent her hair from bowing to the direction of the stirring breeze.

Birds chirped from nearby trees and the sun warmed him. It should be a glorious day. It had begun with so much promise. He'd run his eyes over a reclining Felicity and been nearly debilitated with want. He had longed to stretch out beside her, to feel her softness pressed to him, to feel his lips on hers. Then he had sabotaged himself, and it was no longer a splendid day.

Before, when he'd ridden his vast acreage, he'd swelled with the pride of ownership. These fertile orchards and sweeping pastures and nurturing lakes all belonged to him. Bought and paid for with money earned as a result of his own cunning. But today, there was no pride. What good was all this without the woman he loved and his own progeny to hold it all in trust for generations to come?

The sound of laughter ahead cheered him. Dianna, at least, was enjoying herself. "Please don't laugh over your horse, I beg you," Dianna implored George, "for my brother bought him specifically for you. In fact, the horses the three of you ride were purchased as gifts for you."

He hadn't wanted them to know that. At least not

yet. He glanced at Felicity and was sickened over the outrage that blazed on her face.

"If you think to buy us," she said through clenched teeth, "you are grossly inept." With that remark, she dug in her heels and rode like the wind toward Winston Hall.

Ten

Dressed all in black, save for the snow white linen of his shirt, Thomas stood before the open carriage door and offered Felicity his hand. She felt utterly self-conscious. Her unease increased when she gave him her hand. Must he hold it so firmly?

Once in the carriage, she saw Dianna sitting alone, and a wicked smile alighted on Felicity's face as she seated herself next to Miss Moreland while Thomas instructed the coachman to take them to the Upper Assembly Rooms. *I'll show him,* Felicity thought. Mr. Moreland had grown smugly used to having Felicity always by his side in the carriage. In fact, the man was used to having whatever he wanted, she thought with anger. Did he think to add her to his lists of conquests? Did he think to purchase her? His latest bribe—the gift of the horses—she had been unable to refuse because her siblings had been so thrilled over them. She had wished to refuse them with all the haughtiness her mother had taught her to use with up-starts. Unfortunately, she couldn't crush his preten-sions. To do so would hurt his lovely sister. Dianna didn't deserve the pain such an event would cause. But somehow Felicity would thwart him.

Dianna looked lovely in a saffron-colored gown, Fe-licity thought. "I regret that Glee will not be able to accompany us tonight," Felicity said to Dianna. "I fear she has gone to bed with a bad head." Felicity felt guilty leaving Glee. Her sister had to be very sick to miss an assembly. Why, Glee had never had a headache before.

Miss Moreland expressed her sympathies as her brother climbed into the carriage, saw that Felicity chose not to sit by him, then tossed a chilly glance at Felicity.

A pity Miss Moreland would not have Glee to keep her company tonight, but Felicity brightened upon remembering that ogling young bucks would keep Dianna so busy standing up with her that she would scarcely have time to realize Glee's absence.

Which proved to be the case. Dianna had barely set her well-shod foot into the Assembly Rooms when a circle of admirers formed around her. Felicity and Thomas, standing ten feet away, watched with amusement, and Felicity was pleased when one or two young men inquired about Glee's absence.

Felicity caught a whiff of lavender water and stiffened. *Carlotta.*

"So good to see you here, Mr. Moreland," Carlotta said to Thomas, then nodding at Felicity, "and you too, Mrs. Harrison."

Mrs. Harrison! Since when had Carlotta called her by that name? Not in the past five years, to be sure. While Carlotta made every effort to capture Thomas's attention, Felicity pondered Carlotta's attraction to Mr. Moreland. For it was an attraction, despite Carlotta's attempts to disparage him to Felicity. Could it be she was afraid Felicity sought to snare him for herself? That *could* explain why her friend referred to her as Mrs. Harrison. Carlotta most likely wished to remind Mr. Moreland of Felicity's matrimonial state.

For even though Michael was dead, Felicity would always think of herself as his wife. Surely Carlotta realized Felicity had no interest in any other man.

Thomas attempted to draw Felicity into the conversation. "Mrs. Ennis has remarked on your sister's absence, Mrs. Harrison."

"Yes," Felicity said, agonizingly aware that Mr. Moreland would not remove his eyes from her. "Poor dear has a dreadful headache. She went to bed immediately after dinner."

Carlotta actually looked at her, which she rarely did when Mr. Moreland was present. The raven-haired beauty's eyes, like all the gowns she wore, shone in lavender. Why couldn't they be brown? Felicity lamented. "I would have wagered your sister would have dragged herself here—headache or not," Carlotta said. "The girl absolutely thrives on the company of gentlemen."

Must Carlotta reveal Glee's impetuous nature to Mr. Moreland? "It is my belief," Felicity countered, "that Glee is beginning to show remarkable maturity. Methinks you will find that she has become much more levelheaded." She glanced at Thomas as if to demand his agreement. "My sister is far less flighty of late." She felt a compunction to defend her sister, especially to Mr. Moreland, who had implied that Glee might be involved in an unequal relationship. He, of course, had to be mistaken. Despite her immaturity, Glee was a lady and simply would not act with such impropriety.

The memory of his accusation against Glee sent Felicity's stomach dropping while an unexplainable sense of fear gripped her.

"I daresay you're right," Thomas said. He moved closer to Felicity and lowered his voice. "I believe the orchestra is playing a waltz. Would you do me the goodness of standing up with me?"

She had an odd feeling there was no one else in the noisy room save the two of them. The way he gazed at her only reinforced this feeling.

Though her first instinct had been to refuse to dance with him—to prevent any further intimacy—she could not. Because of the man's kindness to her family, Felicity put her hand in his. She dared not glance at Carlotta, who was sure to be livid.

Now that Mr. Moreland was used to dancing with a real live woman instead of a foppish dancing master, his steps were smooth and unfaltering. And Felicity confessed that if she had to dance with a man, Thomas Moreland was her preferred partner. After all, he was surely the tallest man in the room and undoubtedly the most handsome.

What Felicity could not understand was why the man persisted in seeking her out—knowing she was completely unattainable—while snubbing the exotic-looking Carlotta, who was equally as pretty as she knew herself to be. And decidedly attainable. Felicity decided the man must aspire to the coattails of nobility.

She pondered Mr. Moreland's hunger for nobility a moment but was not at all convinced of her accuracy. Other than his aspirations for his sister, Mr. Moreland was surely the most unaffected man of her acquaintance. He, more than anyone she knew, never pretended to be something he was not.

Her flat hand barely touching his sleeve as they danced, she was keenly aware of the solid feel of his well-muscled body. She did not doubt he could seduce some poor Indian woman out of her virtue. Men of her class also fathered illegitimate children on their mistresses, but it was a practice Felicity abhorred.

Michael would never . . . but he had died so young, she could not say for a certainty what he would have done given a long life. Nevertheless, men of quality provided for their indiscretions. They didn't just abandon them.

I must not think on Mr. Moreland's virility, Felicity willed herself. *Think of something else.* "Why must you persist in snubbing Mrs. Ennis?" she asked.

Felicity gazed up into his sun-burnished face and noted the twinkle of amusement in his eyes. "Me? Snubbing Mrs. Ennis? Are you telling me I am not behaving as a gentleman ought to? For, of course, I should like to be a lump of clay for you to mold appropriately."

She whacked him with her free hand. "You know very well what I'm speaking of, Mr. Moreland. Why could you not waltz with Carlotta?"

"I prefer to waltz with you."

"Pray tell, why?"

"You are shorter, and therefore make me feel taller and stronger."

The corners of her mouth lifted in mirth. "I do not believe you for a moment, Mr. Moreland. It has been my observation your self-confidence needs nothing further to inflate it. You must know half the women in this ballroom—and indeed all the maidens—would not hesitate to dance to your bidding."

"I did not come to Bath to launch myself," he said seriously.

Felicity glanced at Dianna, who was dancing with a naval officer. "You must be delighted, then, with how well your sister has taken."

"I am, though I am cognizant that such success

could not have been attained without your sponsorship."

How could Felicity be angry with him when he behaved with such humility? She started to respond to him but decided she did not want to acknowledge the covert bond that united them. She was beginning to think she would have befriended the Morelands even without the generous inducement. "I would be proud to call Miss Moreland my friend had I never met you." She felt compelled to change the subject. "Pray, you must ask Mrs. Ennis for the next set."

"It will be my pleasure."

It suddenly struck Felicity that Mr. Moreland always managed to seek her—never Carlotta—for the waltz. *How very odd.* Carlotta's buxom beauty rendered her a far more desirable dance partner, especially for the waltz.

Another odd thing occurred to her as they swept from the dance floor at the conclusion of the waltz. Mr. Moreland held her hand the entire distance from the dance floor to the spot where they had left Carlotta, then he brought her hand to his lips and kissed it. His touch was unexpectedly sensuous. Shocked, she gazed up at the intensity on his face, and she quickly withdrew her hand. She was so shaken, she barely heard it when he asked Carlotta to join him for the next set.

A surging quake overtook Felicity's body as she watched them walk onto the dance floor. He did not hold Carlotta's hand as he had held hers. For some unexplainable reason, she was happy that he did not.

When the colonel joined her several minutes later, the inner quaking in her body had not subsided.

"Ah, Mrs. Harrison," he said, "how fortunate I am

that you are not dancing. Please do me the goodness of sitting with me."

The prospect of sitting with him held no allure. "Of course, Colonel," she said, giving him her hand as he hobbled—assisted by his ever-present cane—to some nearby chairs.

She sat beside him, then noticed that George and his chum Blanks had entered the room. She smiled at how handsome the pair of them were. George was scanning the crowd, then he scowled. Felicity followed his line of vision and saw that he was displeased to see Dianna dancing with another naval officer, this one taller than George but not as good-looking.

Though George had avoided the Assembly Rooms for most of the two years they had resided in Bath, something in them now attracted him most heartily, and Felicity knew without a doubt the attraction was the lovely Miss Moreland.

Felicity rejoiced that her brother had found something to keep him away from the gaming table. She liked Miss Moreland excessively and only hoped her brother would be good enough for the lovely Dianna.

When the dance was finished, Felicity watched with satisfaction as George met Dianna coming off the dance floor. The open welcome on Dianna's face pleased Felicity excessively. Then Felicity turned to greet Mr. Moreland and Carlotta. That Carlotta's arm tucked possessively into Thomas's somehow irritated Felicity.

The four of them—Felicity and Carlotta, along with Thomas and Colonel Gordon—attempted to converse amiably, though, as always, there was a perceptible chill between Thomas and the colonel.

"You must be extremely proud, Mr. Moreland, at

how well your sister has taken despite her unfortunate birth," the colonel said.

"Actually," Thomas replied, "I remember her birth quite well, and there was nothing at all unfortunate about it. I daresay you're remembering your own mother's words."

Carlotta coughed.

"Oh look," Felicity said, "here is Mr. Blankenship."

George's friend Mr. Blankenship had little taste for these affairs and was now abandoned by George while he danced with Dianna.

"I say," Blanks said, "where's Miss Pembroke tonight?"

"I fear she is abed with a troubling headache," Felicity answered. Once again, that feeling of unexplained fear settled within her. She was unaccountably worried about her sister. Could Glee's illness be more than a headache? Felicity began to think of all the afflictions a headache might signal, and her worry mounted.

Even when she waltzed with Mr. Moreland later in the evening, she felt no sense of ease as she had recently begun to feel in his presence.

He held one hand while resting his other hand securely about her waist. She no longer felt ill at ease when he touched her. His touch elicited warmth and contentment. And even something more. She stiffened when she realized what that something more was. *It was desire.* How could she allow another man to evoke such feelings? That deepest of intimacy was something she could only give to one man. And he was dead.

She should feel dreadfully guilty. What would Michael think? She was convinced Michael stood in heaven looking down at her. She had often communicated to him during the four years since his death. Only lately those one-sided conversations had grown farther and farther apart.

"Are you pleased that I danced thrice with Mrs. Ennis?" Thomas asked Felicity.

And this was only the second time he had danced with her. That it was a waltz, though, oddly comforted her. For some unexplained reason, she would not at all like for him to waltz with Carlotta. Felicity smiled at him. "You did very well. Now if you would only be civil to Colonel Gordon."

"Do you find that I am an honest man?"

She thought on it for a moment. He would not allow her to lie about his nonexistent aunt though it would have increased his favor. "I believe you to be an honest man though there is much about you that I don't know." She thought of him living with an Indian woman and siring children with her. Her feeling of unease, which had started with worry over Glee, grew.

"I abhor liars," he said. "I cannot feign fondness for Colonel Gordon, because I cannot like the man."

She could not defend the colonel. After all, he treated Mr. Moreland with great malice. "I beg that for my sake you will be civil to him."

"If it pleases you, I will," he said coldly.

With his words, a deep contentment rushed through her. Could Mr. Moreland really be interested in her and not in what she could do for his sister and for him?

She thought on this for a moment but decided there were many more eligible women than she. She looked around the dance floor at all the women in beautiful gowns and lamented her own dreariness in black silk. And, of course, Carlotta was the prettiest woman she had ever seen. *Even if she did wear the neckline of her dresses too low.* Why, tonight her breasts spilled into the bodice of a rather indecent purple silk gown. Carlotta's tastes were so flamboyant, Felicity wondered why Carlotta had not set her cap for the colonel. His loud taste—which extended to a bright red carriage—more closely mirrored Carlotta's than Felicity's.

Felicity decided Mr. Moreland's interest in her was a result of his alliance with her family. If he were the honest man he purported to be, he would be bound to respect her above all others. And that, she thought decisively, explained why he focused his attentions on her. Certainly she had made it clear she had no interest in developing a more intimate relationship with *any* man.

They were silent the rest of the waltz though not detached. For the second time tonight she felt almost a oneness with him, a sense that no others shared the room. Her consciousness was totally unaware of the hum of voices, the strains of the orchestra, the rainbow of lovely gowns swishing around them. When the music faded away, she experienced a deep disappointment.

As he had done after the last waltz, Thomas enclosed her hand in his as they strolled across the dance floor to rejoin their companions.

When the assembly came to an end, Felicity accepted her cloak from Thomas and bid goodnight to a scowling Colonel Gordon as she walked off with Thomas and got in his stately carriage. She thought of the colonel's flashy carriage. Perhaps Mr. Moreland had the innate good breeding Colonel Gordon lacked.

As she had done on the way to the Upper Assembly

Rooms, Felicity sat next to Dianna while Thomas sat across from them.

"I cannot believe that your brother has only just started coming to the Assembly Rooms," Dianna exclaimed. "He is quite the best dancer in all of Bath, I declare."

At least Miss Moreland did not hold George in disfavor. Which was very good. As far as Felicity knew, it had now been a month since George had been to the gaming rooms. "I believe you're a good influence on both my brother and my sister," Felicity replied. "It appears George comes to the Assembly Rooms only to dance with you, Miss Moreland."

It was far too dark in the carriage to see whether Dianna blushed or not, but Felicity was certain she did.

"Tell me, Mrs. Harrison, will you allow me to fetch you in the morning for a trip to the Pump Room?" Thomas asked.

Her heart pounding for an unexplained reason, Felicity thought again of Glee. "Yes. A pity my sister is ill. I daresay the water there would do her good." Felicity did not know if she could trust herself around Mr. Moreland. He had a positively unsettling effect on her.

"You will have to bring her along, then," Thomas said.

When they got to her house, Thomas stepped down from the carriage, assisted Felicity down, then walked her to the door. He took her hand into his and brought it to his lips. *Warm, soft lips,* Felicity thought, her knees growing weak.

Her face flaming, she mumbled good night then scurried into the house. With the door firmly closed behind her, she flipped the locket open. She had to see Michael's face. She had already forgotten the sound of his voice. She could not allow herself to forget his smiling face. She took a long look at his miniature. Her eyes scanned the portrait from his chestnut hair to his military dress.

Then with sadness, she closed the locket and rushed up the stairs. On the one hand, Mr. Moreland caused her anxiety; on the other hand, Glee summoned worry. Even if it would rob Glee of needed sleep, Felicity was determined to check on her sister. That was the only thing that would ease her mind.

Glee's door squeaked as Felicity opened it. The room was in total darkness and—despite the cold outside—the window was open. The floor creaked when Felicity walked to the window to close it, then tiptoed to Glee's bed. She reached out to feel her sister's forehead to see if Glee might be burning with fever.

But Felicity's hand came into contact with nothing but a pillow. Felicity's pulse sped up. She could not hear Glee's breathing. Her trembling hands moved along the empty pillow, then slapped at the smooth silk covering.

The bed was empty.

Eleven

A trembling Felicity tried to assure herself her sister had merely gone down to the kitchen to get a cup of warm milk. She felt at Glee's bedside table for a candle and lit it from the lighted sconce on the wall outside her sister's chamber door.

But why hadn't Glee summoned Lettie? Their abigail would have been only too happy to wait on an infirm Glee, Felicity realized as she trod down two flights of stairs, only to walk into a black kitchen.

Now shaking with fear, Felicity raced upstairs and threw open the door to Glee's room. Her eyes fell on the smooth silken spread over her sister's bed. The bed had not been slept in.

Could the open window mean that Glee had escaped from her room that way? Felicity ran to the linen press and held her candle close to see what dress was missing. And her heart thudded.

All of Glee's new dresses were gone. Which could only mean one thing. Her sister did not intend to return.

Felicity's mind raced back to the unwelcome words Mr. Moreland had uttered about Glee. Had he been right? Was Glee meeting an unsuitable man in stealth?

Good God! They could be on the road to Gretna Green this very moment. Tears began to stream down

Felicity's cheeks, and her breath grew short. Surely this couldn't be happening. 'Twas worse than a bad dream.

If only George were here. He would know what to do. But she had no idea how to find him. He and Blanks were known to associate with women of questionable morals, and Felicity did not know where such women could be found.

But there was someone who could help! Thomas Moreland. She ran down the stairs and called Stanton.

Buttoning his coat, the butler came upstairs from the basement. "Yes, ma'am?"

"I need you to rush to Winston Hall and tell Mr. Moreland it's imperative that he come here to Charles Street immediately."

He started back downstairs. "I'll just fetch my greatcoat and be off."

"Oh, Stanton, ask Mr. Moreland to come in his carriage."

During Stanton's absence, Felicity nervously paced the floor of the drawing room. Where was George? It should be him—not Mr. Moreland—who went after Glee. Why hadn't she believed Mr. Moreland when he had tried to warn her about Glee? Her pride had caused her to distrust him and, in turn, kept her from speaking to Glee, perhaps preventing her strong-willed sister from running off with a totally unsuitable man.

What manner of man would abduct a seventeen-year-old girl? Felicity clearly wished to strangle him. After she strangled Glee.

Felicity agonized over the time it took for Stanton and Thomas to return. How many more miles had Glee and the fiend gained on them during this time? If only a horse had been available to Stanton. He would have been able to make much better time. Her only hope lay in the fact that Mr. Moreland's grays were said to be extremely fast. Dare she hope they could catch up with her sister?

When Stanton and Mr. Moreland finally reached the house on Charles Street, Felicity quickly thanked and dismissed Stanton, then burst into sobs and threw herself into Thomas's arms.

"What's happened?" he asked in a worried voice as his arms closed around her.

"It's Glee. She's run off."

Thomas grabbed Felicity's shoulders and pried her off his chest. "When?"

"I don't know. The headache—"

He cut in. "There was no headache." Then he cursed under his breath.

Her eyes watery, Felicity solemnly nodded, then burst out crying again.

He strode to the liquor cabinet and poured a glass of sherry, then brought it to her. "Here, sit down and drink this. It will help calm your nerves."

He dropped to one knee before her chair and smoothed away her tears, speaking softly to her. "Felicity, I'll do everything in my power to bring her back." Then he moved to get up.

She reached for him. *"We'll* bring her back."

"You don't know what you're saying. The trip will be torturous. And what of your own reputation? You can't go off with me."

She set down the sherry glass and sprang to her feet. "How can you expect me to care for my own reputation when my innocent sister is being seduced by . . ."

He moved to Felicity and settled her against his chest, wrapping her firmly in his arms. "All right. Go get your coat. We're off to Scotland."

She ran upstairs to get her coat and scribbled a quick note to George.

Mr. Moreland and I have gone to Gretna Green, to prevent Glee from making a dreadful mistake.
—F.

She left the note in George's room, then hurried back downstairs. The sherry did seem to calm her nerves somewhat. That and Mr. Moreland's assurance he would bring Glee back.

Thomas told his coachman to go toward the North Road. "There's ten quid in it for you if you can make Coventry by daylight." Then Thomas assisted Felicity into his waiting carriage and sat next to her, taking her trembling hand into his. "Don't worry, Felicity," he said softly, "we'll find them before any harm is done." Would that he could believe his own words. A pity it was now past midnight. Glee could have as much as five hours on them.

Felicity looked up at him and squeezed his hand. "Have you any idea who the wretched man is?"

He cursed himself for not having the girl followed. Because of Felicity's anger at his interference, he had not. "No, but I believe he is not a man of means."

The coachman turned the corner so sharply and quickly Felicity fell against him. She stayed where she landed and looked up at him. "What makes you think so?"

"Had the man access to a carriage, he would not have been meeting openly with her in Sydney Gardens, thus exposing Glee to scandal."

"But she wouldn't have gotten into a carriage——"

A cold silence sliced into the dark carriage.

"Oh, Mr. Moreland, I'm so sorry I didn't believe you. Glee has a great deal more growing up to do than I realized." Her chest quivered as if she were holding back sobs. "I . . . I should not have let her go to the assemblies yet. It's all my fault."

He spoke sternly. "It's not your fault, Felicity. Going to the assemblies was the best thing you could have done for her. There, she was exposed to gentlemen. The man who has abducted her is undoubtedly no gentleman."

"I know you only saw him from a distance, but can you at all remember what he looked like?"

Thomas pictured Glee sitting on the park bench looking up at the man. "He was older—perhaps older than I."

"And you are?"

"Twenty-nine. The man appeared tall, and his hair was dark. That's all I can think of."

"Sweet heavens, I have been so very stupid. The signs were there but I ignored them."

"What signs?"

"She said the men at the assemblies were mere boys and all so terribly British."

"Which means she was already enamored of an older man with dark hair who most likely was not British."

"Exactly!" she said with enthusiasm. "I know who he is!"

Thomas bent toward her. "Who?"

"Her dancing master. Mr. Salvado."

"If you're right, the man must have let a carriage here in Bath!" He shouted to the coachman to stop.

As soon as the coach slowed down, Thomas leaped from the carriage and spoke to his driver. "Take us to the livery stable in the worst section of Bath." Then he got back in for the short ride to the livery stable, where he disembarked again, ordering Felicity to stay put.

A lantern lighted the wooden exterior of the livery stable, but the interior was in darkness. Thomas's calls roused a groom who was sleeping upstairs. The lad came downstairs and stumbled past Thomas to remove the lantern from the outside hook while tucking his shirt into his breeches.

"I believe Mr. Salvado has bespoken a coach here tonight," Thomas said, tossing him a coin.

The lad looked at it and rubbed his eyes. "Shocked I was since the foreigner don't even own a 'orse. But he 'ad money, all right."

"Was there a lady with him?"

The lad shook his head. "I thought it strange he needed a coach fer just 'imself."

"How long ago was this?"

" 'Twas just before I went to bed." The groom scratched at his chin. "Musta been 'bout ten of the clock."

"Did he say where he was going?"

The boy screwed up his lips. "All he said was he'd be gone for three or four days."

To Scotland. Thomas turned toward the door, then stopped. "What did the coach look like?"

" 'Twas the smallest we have. Black, of course. Had to take a driver, too. We mean to get our rigs back, if ye know what I mean."

"I do indeed."

Thomas had learned one positive thing. The coach was likely costing Salvado his life's savings. He would hardly be willing to pay extra to put up for the night after only an hour or two ride. No doubt the Italian expected to come into money from his bride's family.

Thomas conveyed all the information he had learned to Felicity. "I'll be damned before I allow him to marry Glee," he finished in a stern voice.

"How can we catch up with them if they have a start of two and a half hours?"

He took her hand within both of his. "My horses are very fine; his are not."

"I'm glad you thought to go to the livery stable. Now, we at least have some information."

He patted her hand. "Enough to know it will be many hours before we can catch up with him. I suggest you try to get some sleep."

"I'm far too upset to sleep."

"When we find Glee she will need you—bright and alert. I recommend you put your head on my shoulder. It's more comfortable than the side of the carriage."

"I'll try," she said softly, burying her face in the black jacket he had worn to the night's assembly.

He steadied her against him with an arm around her shoulder. Her softness and the light floral scent of her perfume reminded him he was with his precious Felicity. He had been so concerned for her sister he had quite forgotten how much he had to be thankful for. *It was to me she turned in her time of need.* He still could hardly believe she had sent for him, that she was comfortable enough with him to lay her head on his shoulder. She had allowed him to hold her hand. She had not bristled when he put his arm around her. And she had not even raised a brow when he had called her Felicity.

Twelve

Thomas counted himself fortunate the road from Bath was well traveled, broad, and relatively flat. It was not that bad a road to travel at night.

When they reached Chippenham, he asked the coachman to stop.

Felicity's head shot up.

He bent to her and spoke soothingly. "I'm just going to make inquiries at the inn." Then he left the carriage.

Face-to-face with the innkeeper, he gave the man a shilling. "Tell me, if you will, if a dark-complected man who speaks with a foreign accent has been here tonight in the company of a lovely young redheaded lady."

"I'm sure he 'asn't," the ruddy-faced man replied, pocketing the coin.

When he got back to the carriage, Thomas tried to reassure Felicity. "They haven't stopped here. Though we'll have to inquire at each inn along the way, I would be surprised if they stop before daylight. Then, they'll likely be hungry and will stop for a respite. That's when we'll catch up with them."

"I wish I could believe you," she said.

He lifted her chin. "Have I ever lied to you?"

Even in the dim carriage, he saw her shake her head. "I wish I had your confidence," she said shakily.

"I have a bit of an advantage over them. I will not stop until I find them. They will feel free to stop whenever they like."

"But surely Glee knows George and I would rent a hack if we had to in order to find her."

"Let's hope she's not thinking logically."

Felicity gave a bitter laugh. "No hoping is needed. The girl positively exasperates me. I keep wondering where I went wrong. Why can't she be more like your sister?"

"You forget Dianna is two years Miss Pembroke's senior."

"Even when Miss Moreland was Glee's age, I'm sure she would never have conducted herself as does my sister."

He spoke solemnly, almost as if he were thinking aloud. "I know how worried you must be. If it were Dianna . . ."

"Dianna's so fortunate to have you for a brother."

Was she referring to his so-called sacrifice to launch his sister? God's eyes, he felt guilty. There had been no sacrifice whatsoever. A bonus to being able to spend time with his beloved Felicity was that Dianna's acceptance into the gentry was assured. He only hoped she did not lose her heart to Felicity's scoundrel brother.

'Twas George who should have been going after his own sister, but George was likely at one of the gaming establishments he still frequented. "I'm sure Sedgewick is just as good a brother to you and Miss Pembroke." He would never tell Felicity her brother was still gaming.

"He is becoming much steadier," she answered. "I suppose he's maturing. Miss Moreland has been a welcome presence to our family. I *had* thought her a good influence on both Glee and George, but I see now Glee has a long way to go to become the lady your sister is."

He was overwhelmed. He truly did not care if the *ton* accepted him, but Dianna's acceptance delighted him. "It is kind of you to say—and to feel—that. She *is* very dear to me."

Felicity stomped her slippered foot. "I wish George was half the brother you are."

"You're overwrought, that's all. You're angry because he wasn't home tonight and because you don't have him to lean on. I assure you he would have acted with authority had he been apprised first of his sister's actions." He paused. "Though I'm happy he was from home. Had he been at Charles Street I wouldn't have the pleasure of sitting here with you right now."

"How gallant you are. I'm sure you would much rather be home in your bed than on this country road on so cold a night." Her voice raised in concern. "Why you don't even have a coat! And you're hardly dressed in traveling clothes. I fear I have greatly imposed on you."

He took her hand again. "It's not an imposition, Felicity. It's an honor. I'm flattered that you turned to me in a crisis. I only hope I merit your confidence."

Sweet heavens, but she needed to look inside Michael's locket, lest Thomas Moreland make her completely forget him. Had she ever felt this light when Michael had held her hand? She had long been conscious of Mr. Moreland's physical attributes. And sitting so close to him, smelling his sandalwood scent, feeling his large hand take possession of hers, rammed all his masculinity at her with the fury of a tidal wave.

And now, his strength of character forced her to admire him as a demigod.

All these thoughts had the effect of making her feel guilty that she could be thinking erotically about Mr. Moreland when her sister's very future was at stake.

"Would you not like to sleep now?" she asked him.

"I'm used to grueling schedules."

Why couldn't he be less a man? He was making it terribly difficult for her to remember Michael.

They grudgingly continued to stop at every inn to make inquiries, cursing the time being lost. But it was imperative they prevent the dancing master from compromising Glee. Neither of them had to voice their fears for Glee. There was a peculiar bond between Felicity and Mr. Moreland, Felicity had to acknowledge. It was rooted far deeper than their shared love of Shakespeare.

When he patted his shoulder for her to put down her head on it, she silently complied.

The next morning when the coach slowed, Felicity raised her head. Dawn's feeble light had squeezed into the carriage. She was surprised she had been able to sleep. If Glee's disappearance wasn't troubling enough, Mr. Moreland's presence surely was. "Where are we?"

"I'm not really sure of the village name," Thomas answered. "But we're forced to change horses. Will you be able to continue on without eating? I promise you a feast when we find Miss Pembroke."

"I couldn't possibly stop to eat."

"I'll go make inquiries while the coachman selects our mounts."

He returned a moment later with no news to report, and the carriage took off at a breakneck pace.

Three hours passed before they came to another inn. His inquiries there netted him the information that a coach carrying a lady and a dark-complected man who spoke with a foreign accent had, indeed, stopped to change horses nearly an hour before.

When he conveyed this to Felicity, she smiled so deeply, her dimples creased her face. "We've gained more than an hour on them!"

"See," he said, "it's as I told you it would be. We'll catch up with them as they stop to eat."

"Don't talk about food. I'm ever so hungry."

"I thought you said you *couldn't possibly eat,*" he said playfully.

She narrowed her eyes in mock irritation. "Would that you had a poorer memory, Mr. Moreland." The trouble was, he did have a good memory. He had a good . . . everything. Drat! Michael must be looking down at her with displeasure.

Three hours later they came to another posting inn. This time the coachman made inquiries in the stableyard.

She and Thomas watched him out the window. They saw him smile and hurry toward the coach. Thomas leaped out and rushed to the man. "Are they here?" he asked hopefully.

The coachman nodded.

"How long ago did they arrive?" asked Felicity, who had scurried from the coach after Thomas. She trembled with dread.

"Less than half an hour ago."

She and Thomas ran toward the inn.

There, at a table in the private parlor, they saw them. Mr. Salvado, still wearing his greatcoat, had his back to the fire. A weary-looking Glee sat across from him.

Thomas stormed to the table and grabbed Salvado by his coat, bringing him to his feet, each of them uttering oaths under their breath.

Salvado's brown eyes widened with fear. "But Miss

Pembroke and I we share-a a deep-a love," he protested as Thomas slung him into the nearest wall.

"You know, don't you, that Miss Pembroke's family has lost everything. They have no more money."

The thin man's eyes widened, and he swallowed hard as he wiped away the blood that trickled from the corner of his mouth. "I don't-a care. I love Miss Pembroke."

Thomas's big hands gripped the man's shoulders as Thomas moved his face to within inches of the dancing master's. "The girl you have abducted is not of the age of consent. She is barely more than a child. Do you know what the penalty is for kidnapping children?"

Now the man swallowed even harder, prominently displaying his large Adam's apple.

Watching with trepidation, Felicity saw fear on the man's face, but she felt no pity for him.

"Get the hell out of here, Salvado," Thomas growled. "If you value your life, you will never set foot in Bath again. Do you understand?"

The dancing master opened his mouth to speak, but no words came. He gave a frightened nod.

When Thomas released him, Salvado ran from the room, not pausing even to look at Glee.

Tears running down her pale cheeks, Glee gazed up at her sister.

"I know you're mad at me now," Felicity began, "but one day you'll realize that what Mr. Moreland and I have done today is for your benefit."

As the serving woman brought two plates of steaming food, Glee broke into sobs. Felicity gathered her sister into her arms. "I'm not mad," Glee managed between sobs. "I'm so very glad you came."

Over the meal, which Thomas had instructed be increased, Glee explained. "As soon as I climbed from my window, I knew I had made a grave mistake; but by then Mr. Salvado had whisked me into the carriage, proclaiming his undying love. And I was too great a coward to tell him of my change of heart."

She took a bite of potatoes, and her crying stopped. "Though it wasn't actually a change of heart. I don't believe I ever truly loved him. I loved the idea of being a married lady and of having a man who loved me. Though I don't believe now Mr. Salvado really loved me at all. I expect you were right, Mr. Moreland. He thought because my brother was a viscount my family was in possession of great wealth."

"Whether he loved you or not is irrelevant," Felicity said with tenderness. "What matters is that you be allowed to mix in society until you find a fine man who will be happy to make you his wife. When you marry, you will do so in a church surrounded by your loved ones. And that's why last night's actions must never be revealed to anyone. If scandal were to attach to your name, all hopes for your future would be robbed."

Glee looked remorseful.

It tore at Felicity's heart to see her sister look so unkempt with curls matted to her head, her eyes red from crying, and her clothing a mass of wrinkles.

Then it occurred to Felicity she must look equally as bad. And she wished ever so much to look good for Mr. Moreland.

It was nearly midnight when Thomas's coach pulled up at Felicity's house on Charles Street. The door whipped open, and George darted out to greet them. When he saw Glee, he sighed deeply. He helped them from the carriage. Glee departed last. "You are to go straight to your room, young lady. I'll be there presently to talk to you."

Glee scurried off.

George turned to Thomas. "Words fail to express my profound thanks, Moreland."

Pride over her brother's maturity filled Felicity's heart.

George turned to Felicity. "Who was the fellow?"

"Her dancing master."

George started for the door. "I think I'm about to wring my little sister's neck."

Thomas saw Felicity to the door. When she made eye contact with him, she raised her face to his for a kiss.

Thirteen

"You have done me an immeasurable service," she said softly, releasing her arms from around him and looking up into his weary face.

His head bent to hers.

Her breath short and ragged, she stood on her toes to receive another kiss.

The hungry intensity of the kiss that followed nearly overpowered him. For her passion exceeded anything attributed to mere gratitude. Her arms linked behind the muscles of his back, and her lips parted intimately to receive his tongue.

He drew her closer, crushing her into his chest as his arms came around her even more tightly. He only barely managed to terminate the kiss some time later but could not bring himself to release his cherished Felicity. He felt compelled to savor the soul-numbing pleasure of feeling her within his arms. Nothing had ever felt so good. This giving, breathing, caring Felicity—not the stiff woman in black—was the same woman he had fallen in love with six years ago. Thank God, she still resided beneath the black silk.

That she had been as willing as he, sent his heart soaring. A woman did not kiss a man she hated as Felicity had just kissed him.

God in heaven, he was the luckiest man in the world.

He held her until his breath returned to normal, chiding himself for being the opportunist who would take advantage of Felicity's gratitude. Some gentleman he had made.

With great reluctance, he released her. "I beg your forgiveness," he said, gazing into her misty blue eyes. Pray that she was not lamenting he was not her precious Captain Michael Harrison.

She rigidly brought her arms to her sides, a dazed expression on her face.

His gentle finger trailed along her smooth cheek, and he forced himself to speak of something besides the intimacy that had just occurred between them. "I hope your brother's not too hard on Miss Pembroke," he said.

Felicity gave an exasperated shrug. "I fear we both may strangle her! Why in heaven's name did she jeopardize her whole future over such a worthless man?"

He shrugged.

"It is to be hoped she finds a far more worthy man than one who has so little regard for her that he would steal her away to Gretna Green."

"Many girls of her age are just as foolish," he defended.

He backed away, then bowed. "I shall take my leave. You must be quite tired."

She held out her arm to stop him. "I cannot adequately tell you how grateful I am to you for all you have done."

"That you sought me in your time of stress is more payment than ever I could hope for." He inclined his head, then left.

* * *

As soon as he was gone, she moved toward the street. She had forgotten to ask that he tell no one of Glee's transgression. Then Felicity came to a halt, realizing there was no need. Thomas Moreland needed no such warning. He was as true a gentleman as she had ever known.

She entered the house and mounted the narrow stairway, oddly puzzled that her thoughts were on the enigmatic Mr. Moreland rather than the wayward Glee. Felicity was shocked over her own wanton behavior with Thomas Moreland. He had certainly not forced his kiss on her. She had risen hungrily to meet his lips!

She had never thought to ever kiss another man. Perhaps she *had* been too long without affection. The kind of affection a woman shared with a man she cared about, a man to whom she would pledge her life.

Her thoughts engaged on Mr. Moreland, Felicity walked past Glee's closed chamber door. From within, she heard George's raised voice and continued to her own chamber, pleased that George was finally taking his role as head of their household.

Still wearing the gown she had worn the night of Glee's flight, she finally took it off, donned a warm night shift and climbed beneath the covers of her bed, her muddled thoughts on the peculiar intimacy that had occurred between Mr. Moreland and herself moments before. Though she should be ashamed of her actions, quite oddly she was not. She had actually reveled in Mr. Moreland's warmth. It *had* been far too long since she had known love.

Not that Thomas Moreland loved her, of course. But since the day he had first come here, she had sensed that he found her . . . desirable. The thought brought a smile to her lips. A smile she was utterly ashamed of.

The memories of Michael and the love they shared had sustained her for the past four years. And now, she thought bitterly, she could not even remember the sound of his voice. Until Thomas Moreland, she had forgotten what if felt like to desire a man so keenly she ached to be held in his arms.

Perhaps she had been wrong to act as if she were still Michael's wife. *He is dead.* Time had lessened her grief and vanquished his memory more with each passing day.

Everyone who loved her told her she was too young to throw herself into a Portuguese grave. Even Michael, sensing his early demise, had urged her not to mourn him. He had known how badly she wanted children and told her to marry again. "I can't bear to think of you growing old without children," he had told her.

Had they all been right? Should she put her mourning behind her? *Oh, Michael, if only you could tell me what to do.*

With such thoughts, she drifted off into a deep sleep.

When she awoke to a sunny morning, her first thoughts were of Thomas Moreland. She had a strong desire to see how Thomas would react if she were to wear color. Had he not expressed his wish to see her in blue? Her thoughts flitted to her meager premourning wardrobe. She did possess a blue wool . . .

Good Lord! Was this track of thought a sign from Michael? Was he urging her to live again?

She went to her linen press and flung open the door. At the far end she found the pale blue wool and removed it from the peg. She would wear it.

Then she wept for the demise of Michael's memory.

* * *

As if two days had not elapsed since the night Mr. Moreland had asked Felicity to take the morning water at the Pump Room, he showed up the following morning.

As Felicity came down the stairs to meet him, Thomas nearly lost his breath. She wore a pale blue wool dress, covered by a pelisse in the same shade of blue. He swallowed hard. It was the same dress she had worn the night she rescued him six years before. Never, though, had she been more beautiful than she was right now. Her silvery white hair shimmered around her face like a halo, the same way it had done that long-ago night. Her periwinkle eyes now met his, a smile deepening her dimples.

He was nearly speechless as he moved to meet her. "You . . . you look more lovely than ever, Felicity."

"Wearing color was the least I could do to show you how much I am indebted to you. I cannot forget that you have beseeched me to do so at least a dozen times." At the foot of the stairs, she offered him her hand, and taking it in his own hands, he bent to kiss it.

When he rose again, his sparkling eyes met hers. "It is I who am profoundly grateful."

Not wanting to share her with any other companions, he had come in his phaeton, which had seating for two and no more. As she sat next to him on the short drive to the Pump Room, he commended himself on his decision. He very much liked the feel of her sitting this closely to him. When her leg brushed against his, his pulse raced like a lad's who was still wet behind the ears.

A number of people on the pavement looked at her,

their jaws dropping. He fancied they were as pleased as he to see the beautiful blond widow wear color.

In the Pump Room, company was thin. He and Felicity made their way toward the fountain, where an attendant handed each of them a glass of the water that they quickly downed, looks of displeasure on their faces.

Felicity handed Thomas her glass, an amused smile on her face. "Please assure me that, having drunk the odious water, I shall enjoy remarkable health for the rest of my days, Mr. Moreland."

He tossed back his head and laughed. "Would that I could." He offered his arm, and Felicity laughingly linked hers through his as they set off to circle the room.

'Twas good that he was a large man, Thomas reflected. Were he lighter, he would have soared to the heavens. Such happiness as he now felt was alien indeed. The love of his life had shed her widow's weeds for him, and at that moment possessively hooked her arm into his, pressing his arm into the soft side of her breast. Thomas was swamped in strong emotions and physical pleasure almost as powerful as last night's kiss. The very thought of the kiss stirred him to his core—and had a levitating effect below his waist as well.

"You are drawing rather a lot of stares," he told her as they continued to make the circle around the room.

"I had no idea that many people had ever taken notice of me," she said with wonderment. "You must admit I was enormously drab."

"I cannot agree with you. Even dressed as a scullery maid, you would be beautiful."

He could tell his comment embarrassed her for she was quick to change the topic of conversation.

"I must say I was most surprised to see you this morning, Mr. Moreland. I thought you would be catching up on your sleep because you had not slept since . . . since that awful night."

He patted her hand. "And you slept well during that time?"

"Of course I didn't," she said. "Except for a couple of hours. But not so with my wayward sister. Shortly before you came, I looked in on her, and the sound didn't rouse her in the least."

"Don't be surprised if she sleeps all day," he warned.

"Under normal circumstances, she does that!" Felicity said with a smile.

He nodded. "As do most youths of her age."

Felicity looked up into his face. "Except Thomas Moreland when he was a youth. You were driven by an unquenchable thirst to succeed."

"Ah! You remember."

"My dear Mr. Moreland, I am hardly likely to forget anything about you, for I have never before known anyone even remotely like you."

"I shall take that as a compliment," he said.

She was quiet for a moment, then said in a voice barely above a whisper, "I suppose it was."

He soared even higher.

He could not have said how many times they had circled the room. He had no desire to share his precious Felicity with anyone else, which had prompted him to encourage his sister to stay in this morning.

So it was with reluctance he saw Carlotta of the Lilac Gown enter the room, though he ignored her presence.

Only Felicity could bring this stroll to a stop. He

hoped she was so lost in conversation with him that her friend's entrance had escaped her.

But here his luck ended. Felicity got a glimpse of the lady in lilac and stopped in order to greet her friend.

This was the first time Carlotta Ennis did not greet him first. "Felicity! You are wearing color! Pray, what has come over you?" A look of concern swept across Carlotta's face.

Then Carlotta looked up at Thomas, the features on her face hardening.

"I have decided you were right to encourage me to put my mourning behind me—as you have so wisely done," Felicity said.

"How nice." Carlotta's voice lacked sincerity.

"Does she not look lovely in blue?" Thomas asked, hoping that now the raven-haired beauty would understand Felicity's unique pull on his affections and would abandon her designs on him.

"Blue is a very good color on Mrs. Harrison," Carlotta said stiffly.

How he wished Carlotta Ennis had avoided the Pump Room today.

Not only did Carlotta not avoid the Pump Room, but neither did Colonel Gordon. With anger, Thomas watched the tall man with a cane limping toward them.

Felicity had been perfectly content with only Mr. Moreland for company. She was coming to realize he was not only more handsome than other men of her acquaintance but also more interesting.

His dark good looks alone could never have assured her acceptance of him. Only a man of noble actions was capable of releasing her from her bondage to Mi-

chael's memory. In so many ways, Thomas Moreland
was proving his worth.

She thought of her brother and other idle men of
his class and realized how poorly they compared to
Mr. Moreland.

With great reluctance, she had greeted Carlotta—
steeling herself against her friend's onslaught of outrageous flirting with Mr. Moreland.

Felicity was greatly surprised over Carlotta's hostility to Thomas Moreland and her. Did Carlotta think
they had an understanding? It wouldn't do at all for
such nonsense to be spread over Bath.

"I see you two have managed to slip away from
your young sisters," Carlotta observed wryly.

"You must know from Tuesday night at the Assembly Rooms that Glee is not feeling well," Felicity
snapped.

"And my sister is like a fish from water without
her bosom friend," Thomas added.

From the corner of her eye, Felicity saw Colonel
Gordon enter from the antechamber, and for some odd
reason she grew nervous.

Dressed immaculately, the colonel came straight to
her and bowed. "You dazzle me, Mrs. Harrison. How
very good it is to see you in color." Not acknowl-
edging Thomas, he turned to Carlotta. "You must
agree, Mrs. Ennis, your friend looks lovely in blue."

"So I've been told," Carlotta replied icily.

"I suggest you and Mrs. Ennis take the water,"
Thomas said to Colonel Gordon. "You don't look at
all well today, Colonel."

"Do, let's," Carlotta said, tucking her arm into the
older man's.

Thomas offered Felicity his arm, and they began to

walk again. "I am most displeased over your comment to Colonel Gordon," she scolded.

"You must admit he ignored my presence first."

"His rudeness is no excuse for yours."

"Yes, madam. I am deeply repentful. And do not forget, 'Sweet mercy is nobility's true badge.' "

"So you think to soften me by spouting Shakespeare. This once, I will show you mercy, but you really must be kinder to the colonel."

Though she spoke glowingly of Colonel Gordon, unexplainable ill feelings toward him lurked within her. Wherever she walked in the room, she found Colonel Gordon's glaring eyes on her.

And she felt excessively uncomfortable.

Fourteen

Colonel Gordon's throat was so constricted in anger, he could barely drink. He was losing Felicity to that damned upstart from India. After being in love with Felicity for five years, the colonel was not about to lose her now. Not after all the things he had done for her. Things that could send him to the gallows.

Without being summoned, a vision of the dying Captain Harrison sprang to the colonel's thoughts. He remembered standing over Harrison as he'd pulled the sword from Harrison's belly.

"Why?" the captain had asked with his dying breath.

The colonel had smiled down at him. "For Felicity. Now she'll be mine."

"I've always refused this odious stuff," Carlotta told Gordon as she took a long sip and winced. "But I thought perhaps I needed it today."

He nodded solemnly, clearly understanding her meaning. "You have desired Mr. Moreland for only a matter of weeks. I have loved Felicity for many years."

She looked at him sympathetically. "A pity we cannot force them to love us."

There was no room in his life for pity. He would let nothing stand in the way of his possessing Felicity

Harrison, especially not a big oaf recently returned from India. Obviously his lie about Moreland's illegitimate family had failed to dampen Felicity's interest in the Upstart.

The devil of it was that it was damned hard to compete with the man. Not only was he enormously wealthy, he was also a man women found incredibly handsome. The colonel looked down at his own useless leg, and anger roiled within him. *I did this for you, Felicity.*

He and Carlotta stood watching Felicity and Moreland stroll about the room. Felicity spoke to the Upstart as if no one else existed. The colonel swallowed hard. Never before—not even when Captain Harrison was alive—had he seen her glow so happily.

Nor could he remember ever feeling lower.

He meant to have Felicity Harrison even if it meant killing Moreland. He had already killed once for her, and he would gladly do it again.

Now, to devise a scheme . . .

"You are not wearing your locket today," Thomas said, ignoring the colonel and Mrs. Ennis, who seemed to be waiting for them. *To hell with them.* He was intent in his resolve not to share Felicity.

"You are far too observant."

"What was in the locket?" he asked.

Her lashes swept low, as did her voice when she replied. " 'Twas my husband's picture and a lock of his hair."

The sadness in her voice prevented him from rejoicing. Victory was so close he could almost taste it. That would have to be enough.

"It's good you have finally cast off your mourning.

You are young and beautiful—and far too alive to deny yourself a family. Not many women as young as you would have mourned so long and faithfully. 'Tis a tribute to what must have been a happy marriage."

"I cannot pretend that I haven't heard the same words a thousand times. I suppose four years *is* long enough to mourn Michael—not that I will ever stop loving him."

"Of course," Thomas said, his stomach sinking.

They were silent for a moment, then she began, "There is something troubling me about you, Mr. Moreland."

His heart thumped. "What, pray tell?"

"I have learned something of your past in India that is deeply at odds with the man I know you to be."

His step did not falter. "I did nothing in India for which I must apologize."

She came to a stop and gazed at him with flashing eyes. "What of the children you fathered there and left behind?"

Anger flared in his eyes. "What the devil are you talking about?" he asked with outrage.

"Are you telling me you did not live as husband and wife with an Indian woman?"

"I am indeed telling you that," he replied angrily. "First, I didn't have the time. I was a very busy man. And, second, you know nothing of India if you think it permissible for a Hindi woman to live with an Englishman. The woman would have been killed by her own kind for an action such as that."

Felicity nodded solemnly and began walking again. "It did not sound like something you would do."

"I don't have to ask who told such lies about me. It had to be Gordon."

"I cannot say who, but it wasn't Colonel Gordon."

Thomas gave a bitter laugh. If Gordon hadn't told the lie himself, then he had someone else do it. Carlotta perhaps? He would put nothing past Gordon. It wouldn't surprise him to find out the man had shot himself to get out of combat.

Good manners dictated they rejoin the colonel and Carlotta, though the conversation that followed was sadly flat. At least until George and Blanks showed up.

"I say, Moreland," George said, "where's your sister today?"

Thomas was surprised to see the young cad about so early. The fellow must not have gone to the gaming establishments after he dealt with Glee the night before. That was a good sign. "I regret to inform you she's back at Winston Hall," Thomas answered.

It was becoming more obvious by the day that young Lord Sedgewick was enamored of Dianna. Hadn't Thomas hoped for so good a match for his only sister? To think, the daughter of a bookseller to become the wife of a viscount. *Lady Sedgewick.*

But he did not like to think of the man's foolish ways. The heavy gaming. His excessive lifestyle that exceeded his means. His taste for women of dubious morals. Though Thomas had to admit Sedgewick had improved since meeting Dianna, he was not at all assured such stability would last.

And he was not at all sure that George Pembroke, the viscount Sedgewick, was good enough for his sweet sister.

"Miss Moreland had no interest in coming here without Glee," Felicity said. "And, as you know, Glee is still recovering from her illness."

"Oh, yes, quite," George said awkwardly.

"I did not know you were such an early riser, Lord Sedgewick," Carlotta teased George good-naturedly.

"Oh, I've changed all my habits as of late," he said. "For the better, I hope." He cast a nervous glance at Thomas.

"Bloody dull he is," Blanks muttered.

George patted his friend on the back. "You'll understand, old chap, when you're more mature. Gaming tables and sleeping one's days away will shorten a man's life and reduce his capacity for enjoying simpler pleasures."

Felicity nodded. "Indeed. Papa was scarcely more than forty when he died, and I needn't hide from any of you Papa's affection for gaming."

"Lived a long, happy life, it seems to me," Blanks said.

"Then by your standards," Thomas said to Blanks, "I have but ten more years to live."

"You are thirty?" Carlotta asked, her lavender eyes wide.

"I will be soon. I am nine-and-twenty for but two more months."

The colonel gave a wicked laugh. "A mere babe. I am nine-and-thirty and except for my bad leg, as fit as an eighteen-year-old. Not to mention that I'm far wiser."

And free of humility, Thomas thought, though he did have to admit the man had not gone to fat as had other men his age. However, he suspected Colonel Gordon was rather slender by nature.

"Tell me," Blanks said to the colonel, "since you're older and wiser, what does a man do around here for amusement in the daylight?"

Everyone in their circle burst out laughing.

"My good man, you need only find a young lass to make everything interesting," Colonel Gordon said.

Blanks shook his head vehemently. "I'm not about to get caught in the parson's mousetrap."

George rolled his eyes. "Blanks insists he will never marry."

" 'Tis because the women whose company he keeps are not the kind men of quality marry," Carlotta interjected.

Felicity angrily faced Carlotta. "Carlotta! I beg that you don't speak of such."

"Please forgive me, Mr. Blankenship," Carlotta murmured in her husky voice.

"Nothing to forgive, Mrs. Ennis," he said.

Thomas found himself wondering why Dianna had never been attracted to Gregory Blankenship. He was as handsome a man as Thomas had ever seen. That he was a man of great fortune, though, would matter little to Dianna.

All of this was not to say that George wasn't handsome. He was rather shorter than Blankenship and far more fair. Perhaps that is what Dianna found attractive about him. Was it not true that opposites attracted? And Dianna was nearly as dark as her brother. Of course she would be attracted to George's golden good looks.

There was also the fact that George treated Dianna with the reverence one would reserve for the queen, while Blankenship beheld her with indifference. Thomas wondered if his indifference was because George had clearly marked his spot, or was Blankenship simply not attracted to Dianna?

As dearly as he loved Felicity, Thomas was not sure he could bless a union between her brother and his sister.

Anxious to be alone with Felicity again, he said, "Mrs. Harrison is surely worried about her ailing sister. I had best take her home."

They said their farewells, and he and Felicity rode home in his phaeton.

"I realize you must come by horse or conveyance because the distance from Winston Hall to my house is quite far," Felicity said to Thomas, "but I beg you next time to leave your phaeton at my house. I prefer walking the streets of Bath. Everything is so close at hand here, not at all like in London."

"As you wish, Felicity."

"Pray, do not call me by my Christian name while we are in company."

"I have not done so."

"I know," she said.

At least she had not forbidden him to address her by her first name. Another victory, he thought with delight. His six-year quest neared a fruitful conclusion.

He would have preferred to drive along every street in Bath to keep Felicity with him—so close that she touched him—but he knew he could not.

When he reached her house, he drew his rig to a stop, leaped from his seat, then lifted Felicity down. He walked her to the door and tenderly kissed her hand. "Thank you for making me the happiest of men."

She gave him an odd look, then slid in the door's opening.

Felicity had no more shut the door when Glee came flying into her arms, crying. "Can you ever forgive me, Felicity?" she sobbed, blotting her tears on the sleeve of her sprigged muslin gown.

Felicity clasped her arms around Glee, stroking her sister's slender back. "I'm just so happy you're not forced to spend the rest of your life with Mr. Salvado," Felicity whispered tearfully.

Glee released her, and they began to mount the stairs. "What did George say to you last night?" Felicity asked.

They entered Glee's chamber and shut the door.

"He had me utterly trembling. I've never seen George act so . . . grown-up."

"Nor have I," Felicity said, beginning to hang up her sister's garments that had been stuffed in a cloth bag.

"George said he blamed himself for not being around more. He acted as if he plans to accompany me whenever I go out."

Felicity raised her brows. Did this mean George was finally behaving as a viscount who was head of a household ought?

"I can't believe I ever found Mr. Salvado handsome," Glee said, shaking her head and plopping on her bed. "He's terribly old. He must be five-and-thirty. And I did not at all like the smell that lingered about him in the carriage."

"I daresay it was garlic," Felicity commented. "Italians, I am told, sprinkle it about all their food." She wrinkled her nose. "It has a most foul odor."

The two of them burst into giggles.

"Thank your lucky stars—and Mr. Moreland—you aren't shackled to Mr. Salvado for the rest of your life."

Fifteen

Glee ran her eyes over Felicity, taking in the pale merino dress her sister wore. "I am so very pleased you have thrown off your mourning, though I am most jealous. Now you will sadly outshine me."

"Pooh! We are different types, that is all."

"Yes, you're the elegant blonde, and I'm merely a perky redhead."

"I don't know how elegant I am," Felicity countered, "but, pray, what's wrong with being perky? And you forgot to mention you are lovely and petite."

Glee shrugged, cocked her head, and studied her sister. "As pretty as your dress once was, you must own it is now sadly outdated. How many years have you had it?"

Felicity thought on it a moment. "It was part of my wedding trousseau, which would make it——"

"Six-and-a-half years old," Glee answered.

"Does our newfound money not run to purchasing a few new things for yourself?" Glee asked.

Felicity looked down at her gown and realized her sister was correct. The dress even smelled old. "Perhaps I could do with one or two new dresses." The money *had* come from Thomas; and with smug satisfaction, Felicity knew he would heartily approve of her getting new clothing. In fact, Mr. Moreland would likely rejoice.

The knowledge caused her insides to flutter. She had felt unaccountably light all day. Thomas Moreland brought her to life as no other person had ever done. Not even her beloved Michael. 'Twas time she allow herself to live again.

Felicity stood up and began to don her pelisse. "You must come with me. I believe I'm going to make some frivolous purchases."

A smile arched across Glee's face.

They went first to Gay Street, to the same mantua maker who had fashioned Glee's new dresses. There, Felicity and Glee bent over pattern books and fingered expensive silks. After nearly two hours, Felicity selected patterns for two evening gowns and three promenade dresses. Remembering how well Thomas liked her in blue, she chose two of her dresses in that hue, one for day and one for night.

"I feel terribly selfish you are only getting yourself five when you allowed me twice as many," Glee said.

"As I told you before, pet, I am not the one seeking a husband."

After leaving the mantua makers, the sisters walked along Cheap Street to the milliner's; but before going in the shop, they stooped to speak with Jamie.

He happily showed them his new toy soldiers. Felicity was most surprised for the toys were very costly. How had the lad gotten them? Surely his mother's limited funds would not spread so far. Felicity had been told that some seamstresses worked for just two pennies a day. She supposed one of the shop's wealthy patrons must have bestowed the toy soldiers on the boy.

Bless her.

"I say, Jamie," Glee said sweetly, "your coloring is ever so much better than it was the last time we saw you. The waters of Bath must be doing you good."

"Oh, 'tis not the waters. 'Tis the sunshine—and the oranges. My benefactor sees to it that I ride a pony in the open air every day of the week. Told me mum that oranges would make me walk. Sends 'em to me every day."

What a kind woman the benefactor must be, Felicity thought.

In the shop, Felicity selected a straw bonnet for daytime. Why buy several when she could easily make this one complement each of her dresses merely by adding different colored flowers and ribbons? For evenings, she chose an ivory plumed band. Though they were the height of fashion, Felicity admitted the bands were actually quite foolish looking. What was wrong with being crowned by one's own shining hair?

Before she left, Felicity nodded at the seamstress who worked in the back of the shop. Jamie's mother. "Your lad is ever so much healthier looking than when we last saw him."

A huge smile crossed the woman's face. "Oh, he is! With the help of his benefactor's groom, who brings the pony to him each day, Jamie has even taken a few steps." A tear slipped from her brightened eyes.

"How wonderful! May I know the name of the benefactor?" Felicity queried.

"I wish I knew it. He's the finest gentleman I've ever seen."

A gentleman? How odd. Men never came to these shops.

"He sends oranges to Jamie each day. Says he has his own orangery. He must be a fine lord. And he's ever so handsome. Young, and tall and dark."

Good God, the woman was describing Thomas Moreland! He had an orangery. And he was certainly tall and dark and dangerously handsome. Now that she thought on it, Felicity remembered mentioning poor little Jamie to him. The day he had suddenly excused himself from her morning room, only to return for Dianna an hour later. That had been a month ago.

Felicity addressed the lad's mother again. "How long now has Jamie's benefactor been helping him?"

"Funny you should ask," the woman said. "He came the very day when last you and your sister were here."

Mrs. Simmons, the shop owner, nodded. "Such a fine lord he is. He paid me handsomely to allow Mrs. Campbell to take the little tyke to the doctor." She harrumphed. "As if I wouldn't have been happy to help the sweet little lad."

"And," Jamie's mother piped in, "the kind benefactor has paid for Jamie to have the best doctor in all of Bath, Doctor Langston."

"How very kind," Glee marveled.

"Does the doctor believe Jamie will ever walk?" Felicity asked.

Mrs. Campbell shrugged. "He's not willing to commit himself, but the benefactor is sure. His groom works with Jamie every day."

"The benefactor comes here no more?" Felicity asked.

Mrs. Campbell now made no pretense of working on the green velvet that had occupied her when Felicity and Glee entered the shop. "No, it's my belief he doesn't want anyone to recognize him and know of his good works. He refused any praises—"

"And absolutely refused to tell us his name," Mrs. Simmons added.

"It's really quite exciting, is it not, Felicity?" Glee said.

Felicity smiled smugly. "Indeed, it is."

Soon after leaving the milliner's shop, Felicity and Glee came upon their brother walking with Miss Moreland, who was accompanied by her French maid.

Dianna's face lit up when she saw Glee. "I am happy your health is so improved," she exclaimed.

Glee held out her arms. "Fit as a fiddle."

Felicity glanced from her brother to Dianna Moreland. "We are much indebted to you, Miss Moreland, for keeping our brother out of mischief."

George scowled, but Miss Moreland smiled. "How can you say that of Lord Sedgewick?" Dianna said. "He is everything that is gentlemanly."

Felicity could have sworn George's chest puffed out with pride. *Dianna is just what he needs.* Felicity's whole family had been saved by the dark, dashing man who'd recently returned from India. Thomas Moreland. Everyone's benefactor, it seemed. *Perhaps Mr. Moreland is just what I need, too,* she thought.

"Say, Sis," George said to Felicity, "just noticed you are wearing color again. Deuced becoming on you, it is."

"Why, thank you, George." Felicity smiled as she watched him pat Dianna's hand, which rested on his arm; then they moved along.

Felicity suddenly became impatient to see Mr. Moreland. He would call for her at seven to take her to tonight's musicale. She wished the hours would fly by; she could hardly wait to see him.

Not that she would have even a moment's private time with him, for joining them would be his sister and her brother and sister.

That night five of them squeezed into Thomas's carriage. Fortunately, Felicity thought, George was not nearly as large as Thomas, wedged as he was between the tiny Glee and the slender Miss Moreland, who gave no indication she was at all uncomfortable.

And Felicity cherished sitting beside Thomas, even though they would not be afforded any private conversation. She wondered when she would get the courage to address him by his Christian name, as he sometimes did her. Already, in her mind, she had begun to think of him as *Thomas*. The name suited him. It was solid. And sensible. And it harkened back to biblical times. All in all, a most satisfactory name for a most satisfactory man.

"I don't see why Blanks doesn't come," Glee protested to her brother.

How awkward it must be for Glee, Felicity thought, to be a fifth wheel. She really did wish Mr. Blankenship would have come, though she had no idea where they would have put him. Of course, Mr. Blankenship had his own carriage, and a nice one it was, too.

At the music hall, they all claimed seats on the same row, and once again Felicity found herself seated next to her paragon.

As the pianist began his number, several candles were snuffed to darken the room. To her surprise and delight, Felicity felt Thomas draw her hand into his—and he gave no sign of letting it go.

She could scarcely attend to the performer. Only the man beside her held her attention. She thought of Thomas's many kindnesses to her, of how he had not hesitated to go after Glee and bring her home, saving her from an unthinkable mistake. She remembered the pleasure that brightened his face when he beheld her wearing color, and she recalled his stillness when she told him that she had finally managed to put Michael's locket away. She thought, too, of fragile little Jamie, the frail lad who had no father, and of how Thomas had helped the boy and given him hope that he would walk one day.

From the corner of her eye, she saw that George had drawn Dianna's hand into his own. Felicity realized George had fallen in love with Dianna Moreland.

The offspring of a viscount should not be feeling so very comfortable with the offspring of a lowly bookseller, but she—they—did. Of course, no one meeting the Morelands would guess they had not been born to privilege.

Would that she could take credit for Thomas's unerring sense of rightness, but, most assuredly, the credit must lie with his parents for raising such exemplary offspring. Thomas had no more needed her tutelage than he needed another thousand pounds.

He was always successful. Always the victor. And he had done it through intelligence, fairness, and honesty.

Why would such a paragon be interested in a drab widow? Surely, he could have any woman he wanted. Yet, she knew instinctively, he wanted her.

After the first tune was finished and the next begun, she wondered what the other women he had been with were like. Having been a married woman, Felicity knew of men's sexual appetites. As a man of nine-

and-twenty summers, Thomas Moreland had likely enjoyed the sexual favors of many women. She did not like to think on that at all.

Her beloved Michael had confessed to bedding many a courtesan in the days before he married. Were there courtesans in India? she wondered. Were they English or Indian women? Had Thomas been attracted to blondes before? Or had he preferred dark-haired women?

By the end of the performance, she was trying to convince herself she was merely a novelty to Thomas Moreland. The man couldn't be attracted to her. The idea of wooing a viscount's daughter, no doubt, held appeal for him.

But when the candles were lit again and he turned to her with genuine warmth in his black eyes, she questioned her recent conclusion. If Thomas was one thing, he was honest. And his expression told her she was special to him. He had eyes for no other woman.

Including the dazzling Carlotta Ennis, who had fairly thrown herself in Thomas's path. Indeed, Thomas and the colonel, who was thankfully absent from the musicale, were the only men Felicity had ever known who preferred her over the exotic-looking Carlotta.

"You found the performance commendable?" Thomas asked Felicity.

"Yes, very," she replied. Truth be told, she could not have said if the pianist had hair of black or of white. Not for one moment had the man engaged her attention.

She turned to her other side to address Glee. "How did you find the performance, pet?"

"Let me say that I shall be most happy to return to the Upper Assembly Rooms."

"One cannot dance seven nights a week," Felicity chided.

"Then perhaps I could be fortunate enough to capture the heart of a dashing young officer so I would not have to go to the assemblies at all," Glee said.

"You will, in time. When last we were at the Assembly Rooms—you'll remember the night you were abed with the headache—Miss Moreland was completely surrounded by dashing officers."

Glee sighed. "Drat! I would have to pick that night to . . . to be sick."

Felicity chuckled.

"I beg that you tell me what you find so amusing," Thomas said to Felicity.

She faced him and spoke gently. "It was really nothing you'd be interested in."

He stood and offered her his hand. "I regret that the night nears its end, and I must take you home."

He led her from the hall and through the darkness toward his waiting carriage. How he saw the coach through the dense fog was a mystery to her. The five of them were damp from the mist.

They had gone but a short distance when Thomas straightened his arm in front of Felicity and came to a halt.

A menacing-looking man stepped out of the fog, a knife glinting in his hand.

"Give me yer purse," he shouted.

Thomas stepped forward as a gasping Felicity tugged at his coat in a vain effort to stop him.

Thomas tossed the man a purse bulging with coin. "Pray let the others go," Thomas said. "This night has been most profitable for you."

The robber shook the full purse and laughed a

wicked laugh, then he sliced open Thomas's shirt. Blood quickly gathered on his chest.

Thomas cursed and watched helplessly as the robber mounted his horse and sprinted into the murky fog.

Tears welling in her eyes, Felicity rushed to see to Thomas's wound.

"He merely scratched me," Thomas said.

His carriage was now just steps away.

"But you're bleeding!" she shrieked. She watched as the red stain spread on his white shirt.

Then she fainted.

Sixteen

When Felicity came to, the five of them were in the dark carriage, going full speed ahead. Her head, she knew, rested in Thomas's lap. She opened one eye and saw her brother, sister, and Dianna across from her. Then, remembering Thomas's injury, she jolted upright, whirling to see him sitting next to her, blood staining his clothing. Then she remembered something altogether different . . .

It had been a chilly night like this so long ago. She was on her way to London to marry Michael before he had to leave for Portugal. Then there was that poor young man lying near death beside the road. He was covered in blood. She remembered them bringing him into her carriage and how impossible it was to fit his long legs into a reclining position.

He was much the size of Thomas. And his hair was black. Like Thomas's. Her breath seized in mid chest.

And he was going to India.

"You gave us a frightful scare," Glee said. "I can't recall you ever fainting before."

"Save your concern for Mr. Moreland," Felicity said. "I am fine. I daresay it was the sight of all that blood that made me reel."

She turned to Thomas. "Are you sure your wound is but a scratch?"

"I've survived far worse," he said.

I'll wager you have. "I still think we should call for a doctor."

"No," he protested. "A cleansing with whiskey and a bandage are all that's required. The coachman can fetch me a change of clothes from Winston Hall, and I'll be as good as new."

George bent toward Thomas. "I'd feel better, old boy, if you'd stay with us tonight. Don't need to jostle around a fresh wound by riding in a coach."

Felicity sat ramrod straight and faced Thomas, her voice stern. "You're going nowhere until *I* see to the wound and judge you fit."

"Felicity attended injured soldiers in the Peninsula," Glee added proudly.

"Then we are fortunate to have her," Dianna said in a shaky voice, "for I admit to being wholly unable even to look at wounds without losing the contents of my stomach."

" 'Tis because you're so delicate and sensitive," George murmured.

Her little brother was really besotted, Felicity decided. And he couldn't have found a nicer girl.

The coach tore around the final corner to Charles Street. It had barely pulled to a stop in front of her house before the coachman, in a jumble of concern for his employer, leaped from the box and threw open the door.

Thomas stepped down from the coach with no assistance. "I assure you, I'm fine," he told the coachman. Then he turned back to offer assistance to Felicity and the others.

From that point on, Felicity took over. She sped through the front door barking orders to the servants.

"We'll put you in George's room," she called over her shoulder to Thomas as she mounted the stairs.

"Really, it's not necessary," he protested.

"I think you'd better, old chap," George said, setting a reassuring hand on his friend's shoulder.

"Please, Thomas," Dianna pleaded, her palm against his arm, her eyes watery. "I'd feel ever so much better if you would allow Mrs. Harrison to dress your wound and determine the extent of your injury."

Felicity looked down at them from the top of the stairs. "And I'd feel ever so much better if you two ladies would stay in Glee's room or in the drawing room."

The girls nodded.

Thomas shrugged, then started up the stairs. "I can see I'm seriously outnumbered."

Felicity awaited him in George's chamber, where she had already thrown back the bedcovers. "If you will just sit here, Mr. Moreland," she said, pointing to the bed.

"In these bloody clothes?"

"Yes," she answered sternly. "The linens can easily be washed."

"I feel most foolish allowing you to trouble yourself over so trifling an injury."

"Let me judge if your wound is trifling," Felicity said and turned to George. "Please assist Mr. Moreland in removing his coat and shirt."

George moved to the bedside and bent over Thomas, helping him take off the bloodstained coat, then the bloody shirt.

A maid bearing a pitcher of water and basin entered the room and set the water on the table next to the bed. Bubbling with excitement over the robbery, the maid watched Thomas for a long moment before taking her leave when George gave her Thomas's ruined shirt to dispose of.

Felicity hurried to the bed, not removing her eyes from the wound. "You're still bleeding." She winced with concern. "I think you'd best lie back."

Her chest tightening, she watched as he reclined. Except for that which was stained by his blood, the skin on his upper torso was pale like Dianna's, not dark like his face. Yet the hair that curled on his great barreled chest was black. Her eyes traveled over his rock-hard chest, which sloped toward a slender waist.

Felicity noted that blood discolored the gray breeches he still wore. George could help remove those later.

She dipped a clean cloth into the water basin, took a deep breath, and began to clean away the blood. The cut that sliced between his chest muscles was no more than an inch from top to bottom. Now she had to determine how deeply the knife had entered.

Except for the open wound, his chest was clean. She used a dry cloth to blot the fresh blood. Then, when the flow slowed to a trickle, she took another piece of clean cloth, pressed it into the wound, and held it there.

"Let's see if this will stop the flow of blood and allow the wound to close," she told Thomas. "If it does, then your wound is not deep." Smiling, she added, "But it is certainly *not* a mere scratch."

Her eyes examined him for scars from previous wounds, such as a stabbing to the chest. Her stomach plummeted when she saw the mangled flesh, now healed, on his left side. *He had been the injured man on the dark road to London that night!* She could not think on that now. Not while he was suffering from still another wound—this one received while defending her and her loved ones.

She and George made small talk with Thomas while Felicity continued to press the cloth over the injured area.

"Tell me," Thomas asked, "why did you faint at the sight of blood, when your sister tells me you assisted the surgeons on battlefields in Portugal."

She shrugged. " 'Twas the unexpectedness, I suppose."

"I expect, too," George added, "it's a shock when it's someone you care about."

Thomas's black eyes held hers.

She briefly met his gaze, felt her cheeks blaze, then quickly looked away.

After a few minutes, she removed the sodden cloth and watched the injured area. No more blood oozed from it. "Good, it's not a deep wound" she said. "We can bandage it now."

She proceeded to wrap his chest in strips of clean linen, with a thick square of linen directly over the site of the gash.

"Now," she said when she'd finished, "you must lie still on your back tonight. If there's no more bleeding by morning, I will allow you to go home—but only in a carriage. No horseback riding until the cut has completely healed."

Thomas watched her with amused eyes, barely capable of holding back his teasing smile. "Whatever you say, Doctor Harrison."

"What's he supposed to do now?" George asked. "It's too bloody early to go to sleep, and playing a game would require him to move his upper body."

Felicity thought on this a moment, then her eyes

brightened. "I believe I'll lull Mr. Moreland to sleep with Shakespeare's sonnets."

"You mean you're going to be alone in here with a gentleman?" George asked in surprise. "Don't know if I can allow that, Sis."

Felicity put her hands to her hips and tossed her brother an impatient glance. "I am not a maiden, George. I've been a married woman, you know."

Her eyes unexpectedly lit on Thomas's somber ones and, with tremors rocking her insides, she wondered if he was thinking of what it would be like to take her into his bed.

George shot an apologetic glance at Thomas. "I'd read to you myself, but I daresay Felicity's much better at it than I am."

"I shall look forward to her reading, then," Thomas said.

George fetched one of Felicity's volumes of Shakespeare, and Felicity settled in a chair a foot from the bed, close to the bedside candle. She began to turn the pages. "Is there a particular sonnet you'd like to hear?"

" 'Shall I compare thee to a summer's day?' "

It took her a moment to realize he was reciting the first line of a sonnet. She had the oddest feeling Thomas was speaking to her, not requesting a poem. She flipped through the pages until she came to the verse he requested, then she settled back and began to read, " 'Shall I compare thee to a summer day?' "

Midway through the poem, Thomas said the words with her: " 'But thy eternal summer shall not fade, Nor lose possession of that fair thou ow'st.' "

It *was* as if Thomas were saying the words especially to her.

When she finished, she met his gaze. "Is there another sonnet you would particularly like to hear?"

"I feel like an idiot," Thomas snapped. "You know
I'm perfectly all right."

"I know. It's just that moving your arms could cause
the cut to open, and we don't want that to happen.
I've seen all the blood I care to tonight."

" 'Those lips that love's own hand did make,' " he
said.

Color rising to her cheeks, Felicity settled back once
more and thumbed through the pages until she found
the sonnet about a lover's lips; then she began to read.

Again, she felt embarrassed as she read because she
was sure Thomas meant the poem for her.

"Now I shall select one," she said, narrowing her
eyes in mock displeasure. Soon she began to read
" 'Thou art as tyrannous, so as thou art.' " She finished that and read another, then another still. She
would not allow him to select one again, for it was
far too embarrassing.

She could see that her voice was lulling Thomas
into sleepiness. After the last sonnet, she got to her
feet. "I'll leave you to sleep now, Mr. Moreland.
Should you like your candle out?"

"Only if you promise me one kiss in the dark." His
voice was low and manly, and she could almost forget
that he was infirm.

"Only if you promise *not* to put your arms around
me." Now why had she gone and answered him like
that? It would have been just as easy to tell him no.
Or did she want the kiss as he did?

" 'Twill be a most difficult promise to keep," he
said.

"Give me your word."

"You have my word."

She blew out the candle and leaned toward him in the darkness. She thought to kiss him as one would kiss a brother, but Thomas had other ideas.

He met her lips with gentle passion that would not be doused. She was powerless to pull away from the wet, swirling openness of the kiss for she wanted it as much as he did. She tasted the ratafia he had drunk and convulsed at the sound and feel of his labored breathing.

Then she remembered something, and she broke away. She waited for her breath to slow. "You must sleep now, Mr. Moreland."

"A pity the kiss had to end," he said with levity. "I was enjoying it a great deal."

He did not have to tell her. She knew from his breathlessness. "It wouldn't do to get so excited your wound reopens." In the darkness she found the door and hurried to her chamber, embarrassed over the boldness of her words, if not her actions.

Lettie, who wanted all the details of the robbery, helped Felicity get ready for bed. When she left, Felicity crawled beneath her covers, thankful Lettie had run a hot brick between the sheets. Then she blew out her candle.

Now Felicity was free to ponder what she had learned tonight about Thomas Moreland. There was no doubt about it. He was the young man highwaymen had left for dead on the road to London six years ago. The man had been going to India to make his fortune.

The young man's size and coloring matched Thomas's, and the scar on Thomas's chest gave her convincing proof. Also, there was the fact he had gone to India. She remembered asking Michael to arrange transport to that subcontinent for the injured man.

All of this added up to deliver her a most crushing

blow. Thomas Moreland had not sought her out merely to secure her help in presenting his sister to society. He had sought her out to repay her for saving his life.

The paying of her father's and George's debts was Thomas's way of showing appreciation for what she had done for him. Knowing of her family's long and proud lineage, Thomas must have realized how reluctant Felicity would have been to accept his charity.

So much was explained by this discovery. She had thought it odd that Thomas, who eschewed the idle rich, would want to embrace them. Never had he expressed an interest in assimilating into the higher classes. Nor had he attempted to hide his own heritage.

She remembered the day she had first met him downstairs and had felt there was something vaguely familiar about him. When she had asked him if they had met before, he had told her they had never before been introduced. Now she understood why he had answered her the way he did. That long-ago night, they had not been introduced. She had never known his name.

Now she knew how so honest a man—for she knew him to be honest—had skirted the truth without truly telling a lie, though to deceive was the same as telling a lie. *The beast.*

At last it hit her that his only interest in her had been to repay a debt. The realization left her sick inside. She had thought he cared for her as a man cares for a woman, when he only wanted to repay her for the kindness she had done him many years before.

Just as she had learned to be comfortable with him, to care for him as more than a mere acquaintance, she had discovered his deceit. And she grieved.

She cursed her own naïveté and the pride that al-

Introducing Ballad,
A LINE OF HISTORICAL ROMANCES

*A*s a lover of historical romance, you'll adore Ballad Romances. Written by today's most popular romance authors, every book in the Ballad line is not only an individual story, but part of a two to six book series as well. You can look forward to 4 new titles each month – each taking place at a different time and place in history.

But don't take our word for how wonderful these stories are! Accept our introductory shipment of 4 Ballad Romance novels – a $23.96 value – ABSOLUTELY FREE – and see for yourself!

*O*nce you've experienced your first 4 Ballad Romances, we're sure you'll want to continue receiving these wonderful historical romance novels each month – without ever having to leave your home – using our convenient and inexpensive home subscription service. Here's what you get for joining:

- *4 BRAND NEW Ballad Romances delivered to your door each month*
- *30% off the cover price with your home subscription.*
- *A FREE monthly newsletter filled with author interviews, book previews, special offers, and more!*
- *No risk or obligation…you're free to cancel whenever you wish… no questions asked.*

*T*o start your membership, simply complete and return the card provided. You'll receive your Introductory Shipment of 4 FREE Ballad Romances. Then, each month, as long as your account is in good standing, you will receive the 4 newest Ballad Romances. Each shipment will be yours to examine for 10 days. If you decide to keep the books, you'll pay the preferred home subscriber's price – a savings of 30% off the cover price! (plus shipping & handling) If you want us to stop sending books, just say the word…it's that simple.

Passion-
Adventure-
Excitement-
Romance-
Ballad!

A $23.96 value – **FREE** No obligation to buy anything – ever.
4 FREE BOOKS are waiting for you! Just mail in the certificate below!

Get 4
Ballad
Historical
Romance
Novels
FREE!

BOOK CERTIFICATE

Yes! Please send me 4 Ballad Romances ABSOLUTELY FREE! After my introductory shipment, I will receive 4 new Ballad Romances each month to preview FREE for 10 days (as long as my account is in good standing). If I decide to keep the books, I will pay the money-saving preferred publisher's price plus shipping and handling. That's 30% off the cover price. I may return the shipment within 10 days and owe nothing, and I may cancel my subscription at any time. The 4 FREE books will be mine to keep in any case.

Name _____

Address _____ Apt. _____

City _____ State _____ Zip _____

Telephone (____) _____

Signature _____

(If under 18, parent or guardian must sign)

All orders subject to approval by Zebra Home Subscription Service.
Terms and prices subject to change. Offer valid only in the U.S.

DN012A

If the certificate is
missing below, write to:

**Ballad Romances,
c/o Zebra Home
Subscription Service Inc.**

P.O. Box 5214,
**Clifton, New Jersey
07015-5214**

OR call **TOLL FREE
1-800-770-1963**

Passion...
Adventure...
Excitement...
Romance...

‖‖₁.₁.₁.‖‖..₁.‖₁.₁.₁.₁‖.₁.₁.₁.‖₁.₁.₁.‖‖.₁₁

BALLAD ROMANCES
Zebra Home Subscription Service, Inc.
P.O. Box 5214
Clifton NJ 07015-5214

PLACE
STAMP
HERE

lowed her to be flattered by his attentions. She condemned the man who likely sneered at how easy a conquest was this daughter of a viscount.

And she vowed revenge.

Seventeen

The St. George was a nice hotel, even luxurious, Colonel Gordon observed as he informed the clerk that he desired that Lady Catherine Bullin should meet him in the plushly furnished lobby. But still what a tremendous descent it was to have moved from Winston Hall to quarters in a Bath hotel. The blue-blooded woman must keenly feel her reduced circumstances.

The colonel limped to a leather chair and lowered himself into it, then propped up his cane on the chair's arm. A glance around the room told him they would have privacy. Which is what he needed for the proposal he was going to make. He was in luck. The French desk at which patrons could sit and write letters was empty. He commended himself on his cunning. Most of the elderly patrons of the hotel were sure to be taking their morning water at the Pump Room.

The note he had sent around last night had ensured that Lady Catherine would not be at the Pump Room. He had written that he had urgent business to discuss with her this morning, business that could be highly profitable for the titled lady.

The colonel fancied himself a keen observer of humanity. Such observations had convinced him he was losing Felicity to the rugged-looking—though very wealthy—commoner who now inhabited Winston Hall. Lady Catherine also could not tolerate the same commoner who now owned the house and lands that had been in her family for centuries. Together, he and Lady Catherine could destroy the Usurper.

Gordon impatiently tapped his cane while he studied the patterned carpet under his feet. He noted how its greens blended with the silken draperies that hung from a golden cornice at the room's tall windows.

The smell of rose water hit him, and he looked up to face Lady Catherine. A pity her family's fortune was as wasted as yesterday's wine, for there was no longer any hope of her attracting a husband as highly born as she. And Lady Catherine was a consummate snob who could accept no less.

She ran a tentative hand through her nondescript brown hair and smiled at him, revealing somewhat crooked teeth. "Good morning, Colonel Gordon. I see that, as are most military men, you are prompt."

He stood and bowed. "How good it is of you, my lady, to meet with me this morning." He eyed the desk and decided that since it hugged the window wall, it was in the part of the room that was farthest from passersby.

Also, since the lobby was chiefly used for writing letters, he must move to the desk in order to prevent anyone from disturbing their privacy. He had to be assured no others would be using the lobby during their sensitive discussion. "Please, my lady, take a seat at the desk."

Her brows elevated at the proposal, but she complied, sitting in the wooden chair and draping her muslin skirts beside her.

The colonel pulled up an upholstered armchair and

sat across from her. "You must be wondering why I wanted to meet with you today."

"You have to admit, Colonel, your missive was rather unusual. Especially the part about your proposal being profitable to me."

He looked around to assure himself no one was listening, then he leaned toward her. Now he would play into her hands. "I must tell you it grieves me to see a man so lowly born the new owner of Winston Hall. Has the Usurper no sense of honor? Does he not realize the Bullins have resided at Winston Hall for generations? How your ancestors must be turning in their graves to know a Usurper has stolen the family home from its true heir."

"I cannot bear to think what the big oaf has done to our lovely furnishings," she said, "for the man must be coarse beyond reason."

"To be sure." He leaned toward her again. "As you know, I am a wealthy man, though, of course, not nearly as rich as the Usurper."

She nodded, and he watched the meaty flesh beneath her chin jiggle.

"But I am prepared to pay you handsomely if you will help me expose the man for the evil person he is."

Her green eyes narrowed. "How handsomely?"

He smiled. "Let us say that if my plan meets with success, you may very well be able to regain possession of your Winston Hall."

Her lips curved into a smile. "Pray, tell me what I must do."

Leaning even closer, he began to whisper. "I propose that you ask the Usurper to meet you here at the hotel. You can say you wish to discuss some family portraits that have been left behind at Winston Hall."

She nodded.

"When he arrives, ask him if he will sell you the portrait of your dear grandmama. Once the matter is settled, you will say you're going to dash up to your room for a cloak in order that you can take a stroll about town. . . ." He paused. "Then . . ."

"What?" she asked.

"You will stand up and *pretend* to twist your ankle. The Usurper will attempt to act like the gentleman we know he is not, and you will beg him to go up to your rooms to fetch the cloak for you. You will give him the number to your room."

"Then?"

A wicked smile stretched across his face. "Then you will sneak up the stairs to your floor, surprise him in your rooms, and begin screaming."

She looked puzzled.

Still whispering, he continued. "You will say the man tried to force himself on you."

Her eyes brightened. "What a deliciously wicked plan, my dear Colonel."

He sat back in his chair and smiled broadly. "Yes, isn't it?"

Then a serious look came over her face. "But I don't understand where my money will come from."

"Don't you see," he said, "the man will be jailed, possibly hung. He will lose Winston Hall. At which time I am prepared to bestow upon you ten thousand pounds."

"Ten thousand pounds!" she exclaimed.

He put his index finger to his lips. "We must be discreet, Lady Catherine."

A look of complete satisfaction settled on her face. "I had no idea, Colonel, that you were *that* wealthy a man. I daresay with that much money I could live in the manner to which I have been accustomed."

"Then it is agreed?"

"Indeed, it is."

Clasping his cane and putting his weight on it, the colonel rose. "I will send word to you what day our plan is to take place." Then he bid her good morning and left the St. George, pleased with his day's mischief. This plan was really far better than killing the Upstart, though not nearly as much fun.

The colonel knew those who knew him, including Felicity, could not help but be aware of his great dislike for Thomas Moreland. If Moreland were to meet with an accident, he would be the only suspect. Now, though, with Lady Catherine's help, he could get rid of the Upstart without incriminating himself in any way.

He walked outside, and his Hessians came into immediate contact with a huge puddle from last night's rain. Though he abhorred boots that weren't perfect, he did not mind the soggy mess today. Today was a glorious day for Colonel Benchley Gordon. He allowed his coachman to let down the steps to his red carriage, and he happily rode off.

The morning after the robbery Felicity did her best to avoid seeing Mr. Moreland. In fact, she hoped she never saw him again. She and Glee busied themselves in the drawing room.

"Do you know, Felicity," Glee began, "I believe Mrs. Campbell's description of her son's benefactor sounds remarkably like Mr. Moreland."

Felicity shrugged. "I suppose it does."

"Don't you think it's him?"

"I suppose it could be." Felicity did not look up but continued at her sewing. "What does it matter to us? The benefactor asked for anonymity, and I mean to allow things to stay as they are."

Glee pouted. "You could at least say what a wonderful man Mr. Moreland is."

"Do you think he is?" Felicity said casually, running her needle into the cloth inside the embroidery hoop.

"You thought so as recently as yesterday," Glee said with agitation.

Felicity continued her sewing. "Did I?"

"Yes, you did! Even last night, you were terribly concerned over him."

Felicity looked up at her and smiled. "But now, my sweet, I realize the man was correct. 'Twas only a scratch."

"Then why did you forbid him to move or to go to his own home?"

"I suppose I thought the wound was deeper than it was," Felicity said.

"Will you allow him to go home today?"

"I wish him gone right now. A pity George hasn't sent him on his way."

"I suspect they await permission from you."

Felicity laughed. It would do the deceitful Mr. Moreland good to wait all morning long. She was not about to enter that chamber again so long as he remained there.

"George said Mr. Moreland's valet brought him a change of clothes this morning," Glee said.

"Then I heartily wish the man gone."

Looking puzzled, Glee searched her sister's face. "Yesterday—and especially last night—I was convinced you had given your heart to Mr. Moreland. I was so happy for you. What has happened?"

Felicity let out an insincere laugh. "I assure you, my wearing color again had absolutely nothing to do with Mr. Thomas Moreland."

"I don't believe you," Glee said. "What has Mr. Moreland done to you to bring about such a marked change?"

"Nothing."

"You can't lie to me, Felicity. I know you too well."

They heard male voices and looked up to see George and Mr. Moreland. Felicity hated that Thomas was so devastatingly handsome in his black coat and gray breeches, both of which looked as though they had come straight from the tailor. Was it just last night she had not only gazed at his manly chest but had also run her hands over its length as she cleaned away his blood? No wonder she had welcomed the opportunity to kiss him.

She couldn't allow herself to remember the kiss. There could be no more. No matter how painful it would be for her.

His valet must have shaved him, she thought, for Mr. Moreland's clean-shaved face looked rested, and his hair had been dressed.

"My nurse will be happy to know that I'm fully recovered," Thomas said to Felicity.

"Will I?" she said without emotion, not removing her gaze from her embroidery.

A flinch of distress passed across his face. "I hope I have not offended you, Mrs. Harrison."

"Why don't you tell my family the real reason you came to Bath, Mr. Moreland?" Felicity's eyes shot daggers at him.

He gave her a puzzled glance. "What do you mean?"

"Why do you not tell my brother and sister about

our first meeting? Our *real* first meeting. Tell them why you have been so generous to my family. Tell them that your kindnesses and attentions have merely been out of gratitude."

"What's she talking about, old boy?" George asked, a quizzical expression on his face.

Thomas ran a shaking hand through his dark hair and sank into a large velvet chair. "Your sister's partially right," he said, looking at George. "More than six years ago when your sister was on her way to London to marry Captain Harrison, she came upon me bleeding and near death on the side of a dark road."

"Good God! What had happened to you?" George asked.

"I had been robbed of the money I had saved to fund my passage to India. Highwaymen stabbed me and also stole my horse." He stopped for moment, his voice low and morose. "I broke my leg when I fell."

"I remember Lettie telling me about that!" Glee shrieked. "She said she warned Felicity not to take in the bleeding man, but Felicity was determined to save him."

Thomas lowered his gaze. "That she did. She even arranged—through her husband-to-be—a job for me in the ship's galley, where I could work sitting down until my leg healed."

"So you can see he feels compelled to repay me," Felicity said bitterly. "I daresay if it weren't for me, he would never have made his fortune, nor would he be standing here now."

"I say, that's quite a story," George exclaimed. "Fancy that. You knowing Felicity six years ago. When you were poor." He turned to Felicity. "Why did you not tell us this before?"

"It wasn't until I saw the blood on his shirt last night that I realized he was the same man."

"So when he said he was renewing an old acquaintance with you, he wasn't lying," George said.

Felicity laughed a bitter laugh. "Mr. Moreland never lies, he just deceeee—" A sob broke off her words as she leaped to her feet and ran from the room.

Eighteen

For the next few days, Felicity refused to see Thomas when he called. The letters he sent were tossed unopened on the fire. She encouraged Glee and George to go to the Assembly Rooms without her.

She could not face Thomas Moreland now that she had made a total cake of herself over him. To think, she had pushed aside dear Michael's memory for a man who had only pretended to care for her. She had foolishly mistaken indebtedness for romantic interest.

She tried to think back over the many ways she had embarrassed herself. It had to be obvious to Thomas there was no coincidence that she threw off mourning, as well as Michael's locket, the very day after they had kissed. She could not have made herself more available to him had she hung a sign around her neck.

Then there was the manner in which she had possessively tucked her arm into his at the Pump Room and the way she told him that he was the first person she would turn to in a crisis. That she believed him to be an honest, honorable man. The words fairly choked her now.

He must have pitied her greatly. She could never face him again. Why had she not stayed safely within her widow's garb and inured herself to pain forevermore?

She had a mind to take refuge in her black again; but once mourning was shed, there was no going back. She would only look more the fool.

Besides, when she had decided to wear color she had also firmly consented to bury her past with Michael and to embrace the future. But what kind of a future could she hope for now? Colonel Gordon and the other men who had made overtures to her held as much appeal as a case of leprosy.

For, despite his deceitfulness, Thomas Moreland stood head and shoulders above other men in more ways than just the physical. No other man could measure up to him. Even if she did despise him.

Felicity knew she could not spend the rest of her life feigning illness. Already, she had used every scrap of fabric and every inch of thread in the house on her needlework projects, and her fingers threatened to become permanently calloused. She had begun to reread the books in her library, except for the Shakespeare. That would remind her too much of Thomas. She longed to go to the lending library, but she refused to budge from her house on Charles Street.

After three days, Felicity decided she would have to face society—and Thomas—again. The trick was to act as if nothing had ever happened between them.Especially not the two kisses.

Tonight she would return to the Upper Assembly Rooms.

Thomas had grown to regret that when Felicity had told her siblings about the night she had really met him, he had not told them the whole truth—how he had dreamed of her for six years, how he worshiped the very earth she trod. If only he had, he would not be suffering as he now was.

For Felicity might as well be in India for the impossibility of communicating with her. She had refused to see him. He had waited in front of her house for a chance meeting for days, but she had never left the house. As a last resort, he had sent her long letters in which he had bared his soul; but she must not have read them. How could he make her see how truly he loved her?

He thought of all this now as he stood in the Assembly Rooms gazing at her for the first time in five days. Her appearance stole his breath. She had never looked lovelier. She wore a pale ivory gown he had not seen on her before. Her hair framed her face in spun-gold ringlets. Tonight, he decided, he would make her listen to him. He wasted no time in crossing the floor to her. "It is imperative I speak with you, Felicity."

Her gaze wandered somewhere above his head as she spoke haughtily. "I am sure I have nothing to say to you, Mr. Moreland." Then she turned, giving him the cut, and moved across the room to sit where the peers sat, though no others were present.

As he stood there pondering what to do next, Carlotta wandered up. "What have you done to make Felicity so angry?" Carlotta's eyes sparkled with mirth; there was no trace of concern in her voice.

The orchestra was beginning to play a waltz. He ignored Carlotta's comment while he reexamined his assault. He had tried to contact Felicity by all methods a gentleman would use, and none of them had met with any success. What about a more unorthodox method?

He turned to Carlotta, all smiles and interest. "You're just the one I was hoping to see, Mrs. Ennis."

Her brows raised. "Really?"

He took her hand. "You would make me the happiest of men if you would honor me by being my dance partner."

She gave him a quizzing expression. "But you've never wanted me for a waltz before."

If the woman had been less brazen, he would never have attempted to use her; but because of the way she had acted with him and Felicity since the first, he had no compunction about feigning a hearty interest. After all, she had done her best to keep Felicity and him apart. "Ah, but now I know what a wonderful dancer you are—not to mention that you are the most striking woman in the room." At least those words were not untruthful. She *was* the most striking. And Felicity was the most beautiful.

"Why this sudden change of interest?" Carlotta asked. "Won't Felicity have anything to do with you?"

"She will not, which has made me realize I have been overlooking one very lovely violet-eyed beauty." The part about the violet-eyed beauty was true.

He led her to the dance floor. In case Felicity was watching, he must appear to be having a good time with Mrs. Ennis. He set his left hand snugly about her waist while pulling her much closer to his chest than he ever had Felicity. "You dance the waltz as if you were born to it," he said with charm—and a broad smile.

He would have paid handsomely for the delighted expression Carlotta returned. "Why thank you, Mr. Moreland. You, also, are a most skilled dancer. However did you learn to dance so well when you were off making a fortune in India?"

He could tell she liked the part about the fortune. "My dear Mrs. Ennis, I have found there is nothing that cannot be had, provided one's pockets are deep enough."

Now, he could almost hear her purr. "And your pockets are very deep."

If Carlotta was purring, he hoped Felicity was sharpening her claws.

From the corner of his eye, he could see that Felicity was not unaware of Carlotta and him.

For the rest of the dance, he and Carlotta talked animatedly, even seductively. She spread her fingers over his shoulders throughout the dance and spoke in a lazy, low voice when she wasn't throwing her head back in laughter.

When the dance was finished, he made it a point to shadow Carlotta for the remainder of the night.

Felicity's only defense was to sit with the colonel, who was prevented from dancing by his bad leg. Thomas and Felicity glared across the room at each other like two prize-fighters before a match.

He didn't waste any time replacing me, a dejected Felicity thought as she grudgingly watched Thomas and Carlotta enjoy themselves. Had he run to Carlotta as soon as he no longer had to be gallant to her? Was Carlotta the one he had really desired all along?

Since the first time she had seen them dance together, Felicity had been struck by what a handsome couple they made. And now that she was no longer an encumbrance, the two could enjoy each other's company.

How many days now had Thomas been seeking out

Carlotta? Had they kissed? Felicity's stomach coiled at the memory of his hungry kisses.

She jerked her attention to the other side of the dance floor as George and a very bored-looking Blanks strolled into the room. George's eyes darted around the room until he saw Dianna on the dance floor with another naval officer. The easy expression on his face changed to a glare. Then his eyes alighted on Felicity, and he and his friend came to greet her and the colonel.

"Are you sure," the colonel said to George, "your sister is well enough to be out in the night air?"

George looked totally puzzled. "Ah, what sister would that be?"

The colonel placed a hand on Felicity's arm. "Mrs. Harrison, of course. It *has* come to your attention that she has not been in public for several days because of her infirmity."

"Oh, yes, quite," George said. "If you'll remember my sister Glee was, ah, sick before that."

The colonel nodded. "As happy as I am to see the lovely Mrs. Harrison out again, I cannot help but worry for her. I've encouraged her not to fatigue herself dancing tonight. There will be other nights for that."

"Quite right," George said, shooting impatient glances at Dianna. "Don't know why those navy blokes aren't off with Nelson sinking ships." He smiled when the dance was over, and Dianna had her partner escort her to where George stood.

"How good it is to see you about again, Mrs. Harrison," Dianna said. "Are you feeling up to attending an assembly so soon?"

"I am quite recovered, though you may notice I am not dancing."

Dianna smiled. "I declare, my brother has been beside himself with worry over you."

"I daresay your brother has quite forgotten Mrs. Harrison now," the colonel interjected, his gaze shooting to Thomas and Carlotta.

Before Dianna could reply, George begged her to stand up with him, and she accepted, a look of fresh pleasure on her face.

Now Glee came up, a cup of ratafia in her hand. "Well, Blanks," she said, "I see George has once again deserted you. You will be forced now to dance with me."

Though he had not noticed Glee until she spoke, he said, "That would be my greatest pleasure, Miss Pembroke." Then he led her out to the dance floor.

The colonel patted Felicity's hand. "Did you not see how coarse Mr. Moreland is? The way he held Mrs. Ennis's waist was most scandalous."

Felicity shrugged. "I hadn't noticed. I daresay whatever he does is at Carlotta's encouragement. She's never been shy in her persistent pursuit of him."

"What she sees in the Upstart is beyond me," Colonel Gordon said.

"I suppose there are those who might find Mr. Moreland handsome," Felicity said. "If one likes big men, that is. A woman would have a perpetual ache in her neck from simply kissing the man."

"I suppose she would," the colonel agreed.

Why did she have to mention kissing Thomas? She grew heated with longing to once more feel his lips on hers.

She shook off the thought. Now, she supposed, his kisses would only be for Carlotta. Felicity watched her rival, jealous of the way Carlotta's generous breasts spilled into her regal purple velvet dress. Despite that

Carlotta was flamboyant in her coloring and dress, the woman really was awfully beautiful.

Felicity's vision then swung to George and Dianna, who were dancing down a longway, their eyes bright with merriment. Yes, Felicity thought, her brother was smitten, and if she was not mistaken, Miss Moreland returned his ardor.

"You must allow me to take you home tonight," Colonel Gordon told Felicity. "My carriage will keep you out of the elements."

At first she didn't know what he was talking about. There was no rain or snow, and their house was just blocks away. Then she remembered he referred to her recent "indisposition."As much as she did not wish to ride home in the colonel's flashy red carriage, she did wish to make Thomas jealous. "How very kind of you, Colonel," she said, placing her hand on his sleeve.

A few minutes later the orchestra stopped playing, and chattering, laughing people began to file out the doors. She gathered up Glee, and the three of them left.

She had thought Glee's presence would protect her from Colonel Gordon's advances, but even in front of Glee, he said, "Now that you are no longer in mourning, Mrs. Harrison, you really must marry me. I could see to all your financial needs. I daresay you'd never want for anything again. We could even present Glee in London."

The lowlife! He was trying to sway Glee to favor his proposed arrangement. "You must know, Colonel, I care for you as a very dear friend. Nothing more."

"I have told you for four years now that I shall wait. And I mean to."

Glee attempted to change to subject. "Is there something wrong with your leg tonight?" Then she amended herself. "I mean, is your injured leg troubling you?"

"I daresay it's going to rain tomorrow," he said. "It always acts up when rain's in the air."

"How very interesting," an embarrassed Glee uttered.

The colonel's carriage came close to the front door of Felicity's home, and the coachman assisted the two ladies to their door while the colonel stayed within the coach, excusing himself because of the pain in his leg.

Felicity actually felt tired. This was, after all, the first time she had been from home all week. She yawned the whole time she was dressing for bed; then she blew out her candle and climbed atop her featherbed. But sleep would not come.

She kept picturing the handsome Thomas Moreland, a broad smile on his face, waltzing around the Assembly Rooms with Carlotta Ennis.

And despite her resolve to hate him, Felicity's eyes grew moist.

Nineteen

The colonel was wrong about the rain, Felicity thought. Despite the man's many kindnesses to her, she took a perverse pleasure in the idea of his fallibility. He was, after all, tediously pompous. She found herself wondering why she had tolerated him all these years but came to realize her mistrust of him had only recently crystallized. Not until Thomas Moreland had come to Bath had she been aware of the colonel's mean-spiritedness.

Because it was so lovely a day, she encouraged Glee to walk with her up to Crescent Fields. The two young women donned pelisses, gloves, and bonnets and strolled down Gay Street, the hills north of the city in the background.

"I declare, Felicity, the best part about today's walk is the opportunity it affords us to look into the shop-windows."

"That's because, pet, your favorite activity is spending money. I fear your happiness will be greatly thwarted if you do not marry a rich man."

" 'Twould be nice to marry a man of wealth," Glee agreed. "Speaking of marrying a rich man, I believe Carlotta has her sights on Mr. Moreland."

"Don't tell me you have only just now observed this!" Felicity said with a laugh. "I believe she was determined to make a match with him from the day she learned a nabob had taken Winston Hall."

"Before she ever saw him?" Glee asked incredulously.

"Yes. I daresay she would have desired a match with him had he been eighty."

"Then she must have been totally bowled over when she finally met him. He is ever so handsome," Glee said.

"A pity he couldn't have a wart on the end of his nose. The man has far too many assets."

"You're making a terrible mistake in letting him get away. Mark my words, Carlotta will stop at nothing until she has snared him for herself," Glee said. "Though I am certain he cares for you."

"Of course he cares for me! I saved his life."

"At what Lettie claims was great risk to yourself."

Felicity laughed. "You mustn't credit what Lettie says. You, of all people, know how she is."

Glee nodded. "I also know Mr. Moreland cares *romantically* for you."

"You mistake romance for sentiment. The man tolerates all of us purely from gratitude toward me."

Glee turned from looking in the window of a fine glove shop. "If you believe that, you are more the fool than ever I thought you could be."

"You've said yourself many times that Mr. Moreland is kindness itself. His actions toward me are merely a reflection of his amiability."

"I can see there's no reasoning with you," Glee said, shaking her head in dismay. She stepped down into the street in order to cross to the other side where a linen draper's shop caught her attention. They had to wait for a phaeton to pass. " 'Tis wonderful what Mr.

Moreland is doing for the poor little lad in front of the milliner's shop."

Felicity shrugged. "We don't know for certain Mr. Moreland is the lad's benefactor."

Glee came to a halt in front of the linen draper's. "Can you doubt it?"

"All I said is that we cannot be absolutely certain." Felicity shrugged. "What if he is the boy's benefactor? I agree that helping the lad is a very kind thing to do, but Mr. Moreland has a great deal of money. He has been extremely generous to our family."

Glee's eyes rounded. "Do you mean it was his generosity that paid for all my new gowns and hats?"

Felicity hadn't meant to let the cat out of the bag. "Surely you guessed as much when you learned of his indebtedness to me."

"I just never thought your pride would allow such . . . such charity."

"Of course, he didn't put it that way," Felicity defended. "He pretended to be repaying me for helping to launch Dianna into society, which you must own would have been difficult without our family's sponsorship."

"Oh," Glee said without expression.

"I was certainly a fool not to see through his ridiculous proposal."

"I wouldn't say that," Glee defended.

"I would!"

Now they both strolled into the shop and examined bolt after bolt of lovely fabric in every pastel color.

"A pity I already have a dress this color," Glee said as she fingered a light silk the color of dried oregano, "for this silk is even finer than what I have."

Felicity agreed. "Though really, pet, we don't need anything in here at present."

Glee sighed. "You're right."

They strolled from the shop. And saw Thomas with Carlotta, her arm draped possessively over his. Felicity's stomach plummeted.

Why were they not in his carriage or phaeton? Carlotta did not enjoy walking as Felicity did. To make matters even worse, they appeared to be going in the same direction as Felicity and Glee. Felicity had a good mind to turn back, but she decided if she and Thomas were to live in the same city she could not very well avoid seeing him.

Though Carlotta pretended she did not see them, Thomas caught sight of them. He halted, turning to watch the sisters as they came nearer.

"Good day, Miss Pembroke," he said first. Then, dropping his voice and his gaze, he added, "Mrs. Harrison."

"A lovely day, is it not?" Felicity said with false friendliness.

Carlotta smiled, revealing lovely white teeth. "To be sure," she said, moving closer to Thomas, the side of her generous breast brushing against his arm.

"What is your destination?" Thomas asked Felicity.

"Glee and I are going to Crescent Fields," Felicity said.

Thomas looked down at Carlotta. "Should you like to go there?"

A look of jealousy flashed in Carlotta's eyes for but a second, then she smiled, all amiable. "If it pleases you, my dear Mr. Moreland."

Mr. dear Mr. Moreland indeed! Felicity fought a strong urge to stuff a large handkerchief into Carlotta's mouth.

The foursome headed north toward the Royal Crescent. Felicity had the unwelcome view of Thomas and

Carlotta strolling in front of her. The two were engaged in casual conversation, which sent Carlotta into peals of laughter at every block.

Felicity longed even more for a handkerchief. A very big one.

The street they walked on intersected Cheap Street, and she glanced at the milliner's shop there. Little Jamie was in front of it; but instead of sitting as he usually did, he hobbled about on a crutch. For a moment she thought he could move his legs, then she realized his legs were still incapable of movement. Tears threatened to spill from her eyes. The poor little fellow had never known what it was to run and play as other boys did. She hoped, with Mr. Moreland's aid, one day he would. 'Twas just another example of Thomas's many acts of kindness. Genuine kindness.

She saw that Thomas ever so slightly checked on little Jamie with a quick glance; then he was careful to keep his head turned away from Jaime. Thomas obviously did not want the boy to recognize him. Felicity swallowed. Still another example of Thomas's nobility.

She really must remove her mind from him. "Tell me, Mr. Moreland," she said, "where is your sister today?"

"When I left Winston Hall she, too, was enjoying the lovely day. She and her maid were taking a turn about our gardens—with your brother and his friend Mr. Blankenship."

Glee pouted. "How I wish I were there."

"The trees must surely be filled with birds now," Felicity mused.

"Our brother appears totally besotted with your sister, Mr. Moreland," Glee said.

"What's there not to be besotted about?" Carlotta

added, smiling up at Miss Moreland's brother. "Miss Moreland is so lovely—and such a lady."

At the mention of George and Dianna, Thomas had noticeably stiffened—a fact that did not escape Felicity's notice. Did he object to George for his sister? Her stomach flipped. *Of course he would!* Hadn't he been the one who settled her brother's gambling debts and other debts accrued through George's irresponsibility? Didn't Mr. Moreland give haughty disdain to *idle lords?* But had he not wanted his sister to mingle in the society of our idle class? Now Felicity had another reason to detest Thomas Moreland. The nabob obviously thought his sister too good for George!

Had not Mr. Moreland observed George's constancy and maturity these past two months? He had sold his mount. He doted on Miss Moreland. And he had even managed to drag poor Blanks to any manner of somber activities, a difficult task, indeed. Couldn't Mr. Moreland understand that when George set his mind to settling down, he would make a most loyal husband for Dianna?

Which reminded Felicity of how constant her father had been to her mother. Even after she'd died, he'd never wanted another woman, for none could ever have measured up to his cherished wife. Then, Felicity's heart clenched. Her father's loyalty to his loved ones was not as great as was his desire to gamble. *And Mr. Moreland knew that, too.*

With every tap of her feet against the pavement, Felicity grew angrier with Thomas Moreland. He obviously felt superior to her family!

When they reached the Royal Crescent, Carlotta ogled over the fine town houses there, then said, "Of course nothing can compare to Winston Hall. You must be very proud of your home."

"Actually," he answered, "I find the house quite a bit too formal for my tastes, but the lovely park and wood more than compensate for the coziness the house lacks."

He put into words Felicity's exact impressions of Winston Hall, although she was certain she had never voiced them to him or to anyone before.

Another subject upon which she and Thomas Moreland were in complete agreement.

"Oh, Mr. Moreland, how *can* you say that about Winston Hall?" Carlotta implored. "It is one of the loveliest buildings in all of England. Why, the painted ceiling in the saloon is magnificent."

Had Carlotta been to Winston Hall recently, or was she remembering it from when Lady Catherine lived there? Felicity wondered.

"If one likes cherubs floating about on heavenly ceilings in one's saloon," Thomas quipped.

Felicity was unable to hold back her laughter.

He turned around and smiled at her. And she felt as if a pin had pricked her lungs, completely eliminating her ability to breathe. Why must the man have such an effect on her? Why didn't he leave his cold mausoleum of a house and live elsewhere? These meetings with him were entirely too painful for Felicity.

When he turned back, she found herself attending the conversation he conducted with Carlotta.

"Do you like Shakespeare, Mrs. Ennis?" he asked.

"I adored *Taming of the Shrew*. It was so terribly romantic."

Felicity watched the side of his face as he turned to Carlotta, raising his brow.

"What a clever take you have on it," he said.

Must he continue to find things to compliment Car-

lotta on? Felicity doubted her friend had ever read a single word of Shakespeare in her life. All Carlotta knew of the great author she had gleaned in the theater.

The foursome crossed the street to stroll through Crescent Fields, where the daffodils were beginning to bloom. Felicity dwelt on how ill suited were Thomas and Carlotta. The woman's superficiality would bore him within a week. Thomas was substance itself. He needed a woman equally as solid.

Felicity thought of Carlotta's refusal to care for her own son. Surely Thomas would not condone such lack of maternal devotion. But then she realized Carlotta had no doubt failed to mention the little boy who was being raised by her grandmother. Felicity was sure Thomas would not approve.

How was it she had learned so much of him in so short a time? It wasn't just that they had been together every day for a month. It was so much more. She had come to understand him in a way a woman understands the man who is her husband. She not only knew of and shared his love of Shakespeare, but she loved her siblings as he loved his. She knew he had had an affinity for horses since he was a lad, and she was aware of his facility for learning languages. She understood his urge to make a fortune and his disdain for idle men. She was keenly aware of his satisfaction with his own class. Now that she thought on it, she realized she and Thomas were close in so many ways. Or had been close, she amended with remorse.

Though Thomas had endeavored to draw Glee and Felicity into their conversation a number of times, not once did Carlotta. For the first time in her life, Felicity understood the expression "to scratch her eyes out," for she had a very strong desire to maim Carlotta in such a manner.

After she stuffed a huge handkerchief in her *former* friend's mouth.

Carlotta reached up and ran a seductive finger along the ridge of Thomas's nose. "I declare," she said, "even though you are so dark, I do believe the sun has made your nose pink!"

It was like flame to paper on Felicity's already bruised feelings. She wanted to shout, "Get your hands off him. I had him first."

Felicity snatched her sister's hand. "We must go home at once," she told Glee. "I just remembered something very important that requires my attention."

During the somber walk back to Charles Street, Felicity came to a daunting conclusion. She had fallen totally in love with Thomas Moreland.

Twenty

One would think him quite ill indeed, Thomas thought as he entered the Pump Room and strolled with his sister to receive his daily glass of water. Why else would he persist in drinking the obnoxious water?

The things he did for Felicity Harrison. Though by far the most distasteful thing he had done for her was to suffer Carlotta Ennis's company. His attempts at making Felicity jealous with Carlotta were taxing his patience. Carlotta was not his type in the least, but then no one was, save Felicity. Carlotta was a fortune hunter, pure and simple. She lacked intellect, maligned her dearest friend, and spoke in hyperbole. He detested every minute he spent with her.

As he waited for the water, Thomas gazed up at the orchestra. Once the attendant waited on him, Thomas handed the first glass to his sister; then he drank his, wrinkling his nose at the foul odor as he handed the glasses back to the attendant.

Still thinking about his plan to use Carlotta to make Felicity jealous, Thomas prided himself on how well the plan was working. Felicity had become so upset yesterday she had nearly run away from Carlotta and him at the park. And she had not made an appearance at the Pump Room last night, although her sister and brother did.

If he could just keep up his pretense with Carlotta a bit longer. Soon, he would make Felicity listen to him as he told her how deeply and for how long he had loved her.

Despite her coolness toward him the past month, Thomas believed Felicity cared about him. It was to him she had come for help when her sister attempted to elope. Felicity had relied on him as a woman relies on her husband. The very idea of being wed to Felicity sent his heart racing.

Then, too, there were her kisses. A woman who did not have the warmest feelings toward him could never have kissed him as Felicity had. The memory caused his breath to grow short.

He and Dianna had just finished drinking the water when he saw Carlotta shooting across the room toward him.

Without invitation to do so, she tucked her arm into his. "Shall we walk about the room, Mr. Moreland?" she asked, moving forward as if to the music without waiting for Thomas's reply.

He was amazed at how many different shades of lavender and lilac there were. For Carlotta wore no other color, and she seemed to wear a different dress every day.

By the time they had circled the room once, quite a few acquaintances had gathered around Dianna. Most important, Felicity. Then there were her siblings. And that damned colonel.

He forced Carlotta into the group, and they all began to speak of everyday topics. If the colonel referred to Felicity as *my dear* one more time, Thomas swore he would plant his fist into the man's face. Most of the talking was done by Carlotta and the colonel, the two he was certain had the least to say, but both of whom were intoxicated by the sound of their own voices.

Soon they were joined by one more, Lady Catherine Bullin, who formerly resided at Winston Hall. She had not spoken a word to him since the day he took possession of her ancestral home. It was as if she felt that a lowly born man like himself would defile her home. He found it odd that she went out of her way today to attract his notice.

She met his gaze, and to his surprise, spoke to him. "Mr. Moreland, I beg that you will call on me at noon tomorrow at the St. George Hotel. There is a personal matter I wish to discuss with you."

He swept into a bow. "You may consider it done, my lady."

Then she said her farewells and left the Pump Room entirely. So, he mused, she had come here only to see him. He wondered what personal matter she wished to discuss. Could she wish to regain some family possessions? They would, of course, be hers for the asking, though he doubted her lodgings at the hotel afforded much space for any of her family's grand portraits or statuary or massive Turkish rugs.

As the others talked, Thomas could not help but look distractedly about the room. He noticed a soldier wearing the familiar red military coat, only his dripped with decorations. And then Thomas witnessed a most peculiar thing. The soldier looked long and hard at Colonel Gordon, then crossed to the opposite side of the room as if to keep his distance from the former officer.

His actions seemed very odd. At first Thomas thought possibly the man had been in trouble with the colonel at one time, but then Thomas remembered all the military decorations the man sported. A man who

was not in his officers' graces was hardly likely to
have earned so many medals.

No, Thomas thought, it must be something else.

"We missed you at last night's assembly," Carlotta
said to Felicity.

"I had the bad head, but as you can see, I am now
fine," Felicity replied.

"I must say you look especially lovely in blue," the
colonel said.

Yes, doesn't she, Thomas thought. It was his favorite
dress. She looked like some heavenly body he longed
to hold in his arms. She would be even lovelier without the blue gown. He imagined himself helping her
disrobe, his lips nibbling at the satin-smooth skin on
her bare shoulders. *Good Lord,* life sprang to his groin
at the very thought. Only Felicity could affect him so
profoundly.

Though he stayed slightly attuned to the conversation around him, Thomas kept his eyes on the lone
soldier. The man walked over to the attendant and received his glass of water.

He appeared to be looking about the room for a
familiar face—avoiding a glance in the colonel's direction. He obviously found none and left the Pump
Room.

If Thomas hadn't had his sister with him, he would
have followed the soldier.

"Will you come, Mr. Moreland?" Carlotta asked.

He snapped to attention. "Come where?"

"To the dinner I'm hosting at my house tonight."

"Do say you'll come," Glee implored. "Felicity and
I are to be there, and we'd be ever so happy to have
you and Miss Moreland among the company."

He glanced at Felicity, then at Carlotta. "It would
be my pleasure."

George kept looking at the door. Before long, he wondered aloud. "I don't suppose Blanks is coming today." He shook his head. "Has a terrible aversion to rising before afternoon."

"Not too long ago, you were exactly like him," Felicity said, "and I'm ever so glad you have matured." She shot Thomas a determined glance.

"Yes, Lord Sedgewick, I would say you're now a reformed rake," Carlotta said with affection.

Felicity's eyes narrowed as she looked at Carlotta. "I beg that you do not refer to my brother as a rake, even if you preface it with *reformed*."

Carlotta cast a scathing look at Felicity, then smiled at George. "Allow me to offer my apologies, Lord Sedgewick."

Now George gave all the signs of being embarrassed. He could not even look Dianna in the eye.

But to Thomas's pleasure, Dianna smoothed everything over in her own gracious way. "Lord Sedgewick is as fine a gentleman as I've ever encountered. In fact," she added with a snippet of laughter, "I should be honored if he would stroll about the room with me."

It was quite a forward action for Dianna, who would never force herself on any man, as Carlotta did. On the other hand, Dianna had always been keenly aware of those who were in difficult circumstances. Thomas had lost count of all the orphaned girls she had dragged home from school for the holidays. And he hated to think how many cats and dogs she had offered a home. Or all the pet funerals he had attended with her in back of their cottage in Brampton.

He frowned as he watched George and Dianna, arm in arm, stroll about the room, her happy face smiling up at Sedgewick's. He had never before seen two people appear so much in love or look so good together. The fair-haired George with his golden skin and the pale Dianna with strikingly black hair. They were compatible opposites. Like Felicity and him. A pity Sedgewick was unworthy of Dianna.

To Thomas's annoyance, no one seemed interested in leaving the Pump Room today even though the morning was now gone. He wanted to locate the soldier and talk to him about Colonel Gordon.

To his relief, Dianna asked if she could spend the afternoon with Glee and her sister, and he readily consented. Then he took his leave.

Where in the city of Bath would a soldier go? Thomas could instantly dismiss the shops. They would be the last place to attract men.

He pulled his watch from his pocket and noted it was past noon. And he smiled. The public houses were now open, and he could think of no likelier place to find a soldier.

He went first to the pub nearest the Pump Room, but he saw no soldiers there.

He walked down toward Broad Quay, an area by the river that Thomas deemed of appeal to soldiers. There he found a pub called Bird in Bath, and he walked in. The room was dark and smelled of ale and fish. And standing at the bar was the soldier.

Thomas walked to the bar and stood next to the soldier.

"Can I help you, sir?" the bartender asked Thomas.

"A bumper of ale for me." Pointing to the man beside him, Thomas added, "And when this brave soldier is finished, I would be honored if he would allow me to purchase his next drink."

"Very kind of ye, sir," the soldier said, smiling at Thomas. The man's voice was that of the lower classes. He was a typical foot soldier who had served the Crown well. Had likely done so for most of his life, for the man was not young.

The soldier emptied his glass, and the bartender poured him another.

When the bartender moved down the bar to tend to another customer, Thomas initiated conversation. "I saw you back at the Pump Room."

"A loftier gatherin' than I'm used to," the soldier said. "I know me place. I know, too, you're the nabob from India. I heard of you from a soldier who served with me. Are you not the Englishman who established an orphanage in Bombay before you returned to England?"

Thomas shrugged. " 'Twas the least I could do for a country that had been so good to me." He was quick to talk of other matters. "I'd say from all your medals, your place is definitely in the army."

"Thank ye."

"In the Pump Room I saw that you looked at Colonel Gordon with what I perceived to be recognition."

"I know 'im." The man's ruddy face was inscrutable.

"I also perceived that you did not like the colonel."

The soldier took a long drink, then wiped his lips on his sleeve. "You ain't come to throw me in the brig, are ye?"

Thomas laughed. "Of course not, my good man." Then he lowered his voice. "It so happens I am not overly fond of Colonel Gordon."

Now a smile broke across the soldier's face. "I'm not only not overly fond of the man, I downright dislike 'im."

Thomas nodded, a smile curving his lip as he went to take another sip. "May I ask why?"

The man set his bumper down with a great noise. "I'll tell you why, and I wish I 'ad told the authorities in Portugal, but I was too busy keeping meself alive to go worrying after a coward officer."

"A coward?"

The soldier nodded. "Worst I ever saw. I've seen 'em cry, I've even seen 'em call out for their mamas, but I ain't never but once saw one shoot himself in order to get out of fightin'. And that once was Colonel Gordon."

"Who wanted to come home," Thomas added quietly.

The soldier paid no heed but kept on talking. "Yep. Sure as I'm sittin' here, the yellow-bellied colonel shot himself in the leg. Course, he didn't know I was watchin'."

"A more peculiar thing I've not heard," Thomas said, frowning. "Tell me, did you know Captain Harrison?"

The soldier's voice became reverent. "I was proud to be one of his men."

Another person who clearly worshiped Michael Harrison. Though he was long dead, the man who had been Felicity's husband had earned still another admirer. Respect had followed him to the grave, Thomas thought. "Where was the captain when the colonel shot himself? Do you know?"

"Oh, yessir. I had found his body just minutes before I 'appened on the colonel a-shootin' 'imself."

"Did you find anything unusual in this?" Thomas asked. "In Captain Harrison's death?"

The soldier pondered a moment. "Now that I thinks about it . . . I remember at the time I was wonderin' who'd killed him because the enemy was behind us."

Thomas nodded thoughtfully. The soldier had indeed repaid him for his trouble. "Drink up, my good man," Thomas said, patting his back and setting two guineas on the bar. "It's been a pleasure."

The man pocketed one coin. "The pleasure's mine, sir!"

Thomas did not know where he was going when he left the public house. Like the day before, this day was fair and sunny, and he felt like walking. With the low hills as his guide, he kept walking to the north of the city, to the same place they had walked yesterday. When Felicity had grown jealous and fled.

He saw Mrs. Simmons's millinery shop and the lad out front. Jamie was swinging his useless legs under him as he perched on a pair of crutches.

Thomas crossed the street to him. "Good afternoon, Jamie," he said.

The boy looked up and smiled at him. Thomas noted his front teeth had come in.

"Have you taken the baths today?" Thomas asked.

"Yes, sir."

"And were you able to move your legs in the warm water?"

"I was!"

"Good. Did you eat your oranges?"

Jaime nodded. "And they are ever so good. Better'n any comfits. Mum says oranges don't grow in England unless they're in a big glass house."

"Your mum's right." Thomas squatted to the boy's height. "I agree with you about oranges being better than comfits. Give me oranges over them any day." He put a gentle hand to the boy's back. "Tell me, Jamie, have you ridden your pony today?"

"I rode the pony, but I don't believe it's mine."

"Of course he is. I bought him just for you. But since you've got no place to keep him, I take care of

him for you. Unless your mum would allow him to
sleep with you?"

The boy broke into gales of laughter.

"So you must give a name to your pony. What shall
you call him?"

His face still delighted, the lad thought on it for a
moment. "I shall call him Snowy 'cause he's white."

Thomas ruffled the boy's hair, then stood up. "A
very good choice, I should say."

Thomas said his farewells and continued on to the
Royal Crescent. Seeing the lad in such good spirits
lightened his own mood.

He kept thinking of what the soldier had told him.
The colonel had shot himself. Though the infantryman
had thought the colonel's actions a result of cowardice,
Thomas knew he had maimed himself in order to return to England with the newly widowed Felicity Harrison.

Had the colonel also murdered Captain Harrison?
The truth might never be learned.

The damned colonel would get off scot-free. With
no witnesses, it would be impossible to convict him
of Harrison's murder, and Thomas doubted there was
a law prohibiting a man from shooting himself in the
leg.

One thing was certain. Thomas did not trust him.
Instinctively, he feared the man would harm Felicity.

And Thomas could not allow that.

Twenty-one

As Felicity took her seat at the bottom of Carlotta's table, she cast a bitter glance at her hostess. Carlotta had seen to it that Thomas sat next to her at the head of the table. Unfortunately, Felicity's seat offered a perfect spot from which to witness Carlotta's outrageous flirting with Thomas. Which left Felicity with little appetite.

To do her justice, Carlotta had seated Dianna and George opposite each other, which facilitated their cheery conversation. Thank goodness Balmoral etiquette was not observed here. Felicity hated to think the royal table was so wide from side to side that speaking across the table was simply not done. That would make for a most stiff assemblage indeed.

Felicity could not say she missed the colonel's presence tonight. He had begged off because he was dining with an old military chum. It had pained him, she could tell, not to join them. The man hated to allow Felicity in the same room with Thomas without his being there to prevent any camaraderie between Felicity and Thomas.

Felicity positively steamed when Carlotta said, "I had my cook prepare lobster for you, Mr. Moreland, for I know how dearly you like it."

It was as if Carlotta had the funds to hire men to

spy on Thomas, though Felicity was well aware that Carlotta's funds were quite limited. She even wondered how Carlotta had managed to set so grand a table.

"You are too good," Thomas answered, not looking up from his forkful of shellfish.

"Tell me, Mrs. Ennis," Glee said, a wickedness shining in her eyes, "how old is your little boy now?"

Thomas put down his fork and looked at Carlotta with a puzzled expression.

Carlotta's face went even whiter than its usual milky shade. She swallowed hard and avoided looking at the man to her left. "He is five."

"Why have I not met him?" Thomas inquired.

Carlotta slapped a false smile on her face. "Oh, he doesn't live here in Bath. Whatever would a lad find to do here?" Not allowing anyone to answer, she continued. "He lives in the country where there is so much more to occupy a lad. I find he is far better off with my grandmother, who raised five sons of her own, than ever he would be with me."

Thomas lowered his brows as Carlotta spoke. "Would not your grandmother be somewhat old to be raising a rambunctious lad?"

"She *is* getting on in years, but the boy's nurse is quite young and lively. He adores her."

Felicity's heart went out to the little boy who had lost his mother as well as his father. And inexorably, she was even more jealous of Carlotta than ever. For Felicity had longed for a son. At first she had wanted a son in Michael's image so Michael would never be completely gone. Now that she had managed to close the page on Michael's chapter in her life, she still longed for a child of her own. It had occurred to her more than once that though Jamie's mother was poor in material wealth, she was rich for having so precious a son.

"How often do you see him?" Thomas asked.

"Oh, I make it a point to see him every year on his birthday. I've only missed once. He looks forward ever so much to my visits—and the toys I bring for him. My grandmother is rather stern about lavishing toys on children."

"Does he have his own pony?" Thomas asked.

"Oh, no, Grandmama's money doesn't run to that."

Felicity wondered what Thomas would think of all this. She suspected he would not approve of a mother who chose to send her child away. In fact, she was almost certain he would disdain a mother who could do so. For when it came to matters of right and wrong and good and evil, it seemed she and Thomas exactly agreed. Though his circumstances of birth were quite different than hers, Felicity had never known a man whose opinions so mirrored her own.

She thought of the pony rides Thomas had arranged for little Jamie, and a smile lifted the corners of her mouth.

After dinner the ladies retired to the saloon, and Thomas and George followed soon after, having drunk their port rather quickly.

Carlotta was bent on singing for Thomas. She was in possession of a rather distinctive alto. It was throaty and altogether sensuous.

To Felicity's surprise, Thomas came to sit on the settee beside her as Carlotta began to sing. Her surprise was even greater at the adversarial remark she addressed to him. "I am disappointed you do not find my brother worthy of your sister."

He turned to her, his dark brows plunging, his eyes fiery. "How do you know that?"

Her stomach sank. He had all but admitted her claim. "It's a feeling formed after observing you."

"Let me say that at this stage of his life, your brother has not yet demonstrated the maturity I would like in Dianna's husband."

"I'll admit," Felicity countered, "that when you came to Bath he *was* immature, but he has shown a marked improvement."

"I cannot deny he has changed—for the better—but I've yet to see evidence that gaming no longer appeals to him."

Carlotta continued singing, but she was clearly disturbed that Thomas could talk during her performance.

"Ssh," Felicity warned, shooting her attention on Carlotta while scorning Thomas. How dare he find fault with her brother!

He had shot himself in the foot, Thomas mused angrily. Felicity was actually speaking with him, and he had ruined everything.

A moment later he thought about warning Felicity against Colonel Gordon, but it seemed a petty thing to do. Instead, he vowed to protect her from the colonel. She need never know that the endless suffering she had endured was because of the fiendish man.

Thomas suppressed an overwhelming urge to take her hand in his. This was actually the first time she had spoken to him privately all week. Even if it was a confrontation. Being near her had almost been worth it.

He attempted to look interested in Carlotta's singing when in reality all he could think of was his proximity to Felicity.

When she finished the first song, Carlotta began another. He gazed with pride at his sister who accompanied Carlotta on the pianoforte. He knew the best tutors and masters in all the world could not have made Dianna the great lady she had become. She had been born with grace and compassion and intelligence and a facility for adapting to new ways. He couldn't have been prouder.

George would always be good to her. He was no fortune hunter. Yet Thomas could not bless a marriage between them—at this time.

At least Sedgewick wasn't like the scheming Carlotta—who didn't even want her own child!

Something deep within him stirred when he smelled Felicity's light floral scent. He cautioned himself that he really had to pay more attention to the singer. He did not fancy being boxed in the ears by Carlotta.

Carlotta's song came to an end and she stormed across the carpet, but she turned calm as she faced the two who had not had the decency to remain quiet while she sang. "Come, Felicity, you must sing now."

Felicity walked gracefully to the instrument, told Dianna what song she would sing, and then began.

Though Carlotta, who now sat where Felicity had sat, tried to engage him in conversation any number of times, Thomas refused to rise to the bait. It was as if each melodic note Felicity sang came from a heavenly choir. She looked like an angel. A halo of gold framed her lovely dimpled face. With pleasure, he saw she wore the soft blue silk gown. His favorite.

He could scarcely believe only a week had passed since the day she had surprised him by wearing the pale blue wool dress. It seemed so long ago.

She sang just one song, followed by Dianna, who sang just one while Glee accompanied her.

"I have made my musical contribution for the night," Glee insisted when she was asked to sing next.

After the singing, Thomas insisted on a game of whist, despite the hostess's protestations.

"But I don't play whist," Carlotta said, her lower lip working into a pout.

"I'm sure we'll have enough," Thomas said. "Mrs. Harrison and my sister play, and Lord Sedgewick will make an able fourth."

Carlotta quickly suppressed her anger. "Whatever pleases you, Mr. Moreland."

It was the males versus females, and all four of them took their play seriously. Though Dianna was not competitive, she was conscientious, and was no doubt trying to impress Sedgewick. Few words were said. Thomas was somewhat inhibited by Carlotta, who stood at his shoulder. "So I can learn from a master," she had said.

Yet Carlotta showed no signs of really desiring to learn. She had not asked a single question. He suspected she merely wanted to prevent him from engaging in conversation with Felicity. The cat! He could imagine her with arched back and could almost hear her hiss.

The men won one game, and the women the other before it was time for them to leave. "We must finish this soon," Thomas said as he scooted from the table.

Felicity and her siblings bundled up for the two-block walk back to Charles Street.

"Why do you not allow my brother to take you home?" Dianna suggested to them.

"I believe Mrs. Ennis needs my opinion on a legal matter," Thomas said with disappointment. "But, please, feel free to take my coach. It can come back for me."

Felicity glared at Carlotta. "Thank you, Mr. Moreland, but we prefer to walk."

Thomas cursed himself for agreeing earlier to Carlotta's request. He should have seen it was a ploy to keep him from talking to Felicity. From telling her he loved her.

Colonel Gordon was not meeting with an old army chum, as he had told the others. He was with Lady Catherine. He had called for her at the hotel, and the two of them had ridden in private around the city in his red carriage. Like a good military man, he had wanted to drill her for her meeting with Thomas the following day.

"I am afraid if you act too amiable, the Usurper will grow suspicious. After all, you have not hidden your dislike of him."

"I can think of no situation that would render me agreeable to Thomas Moreland," she said.

The colonel's eyes sparkled. "The other matter is to convince him you have truly injured your ankle. Do your best to elicit his concern—if he's capable of showing concern for anyone, that is."

"Don't worry, Colonel, you can depend on me. He will be thoroughly convinced of my injury."

"And . . ." the colonel continued, "you must make certain your cloak cannot easily be found."

When he was assured she would be able to carry it off, Gordon ordered his coach to take her back to the St. George. As the coach slowed down in front of the hotel, he presented her with a hundred pounds, "as a token of my trust that you will complete our scheme as planned."

She moved to step down from the carriage.

"There's much more money to come upon the successful fruition of your, er, mission," he told her.

She turned back, stuffed the money into the bodice of her dress, and disembarked.

Twenty-two

Thomas rode his phaeton to the St. George Hotel. The weather had turned noticeably colder, and a thick mist hung in the air. On the way into Bath, he had noticed ice forming at the banks of the River Avon.

Lady Catherine's sudden communication after weeks of snubbing him puzzled Thomas. Not that she had been overly friendly yesterday in the Pump Room. It was as if she only barely managed to tolerate him. Like an uneasy truce between sworn enemies.

All of which was quite all right with him for he didn't particularly like her, either. She was snobbish, rude and icy of demeanor. Altogether, Lady Catherine was a most unpleasant lady.

He arrived at the hotel at exactly noon. In the warm lobby he found Lady Catherine waiting for him.

She stood and greeted him stiffly, her manner contradicting her words. "It was so very good of you to come, Mr. Moreland. Do let's sit down."

To his consternation, she sat next to him on the plump velvet settee. Her lush green skirts brushed against his thigh. At least the woman still dressed finely, he thought.

"I am told it grows colder today," she began.

"Yes, my lady, 'tis miserable out there. If you can

avoid being outdoors, I would advise you to do so. Ice is lapping at the banks of the River Avon."

She frowned. "I was so in hopes of the winter being behind us. I am only too ready to welcome the spring."

Did she ask me here to talk about the weather? he wondered.

"You and your sister are comfortable in Winston Hall, I trust?"

If one could be comfortable in a mausoleum. "Yes, quite. The estate is no doubt one of the finest in England."

A small smile played at her lips. "I believe it to be so. I can boast about it now that it is no longer mine."

"You must miss it very much."

A martyred look on her face, she said, "It *was* the only home I'd ever known. 'Tis rather difficult becoming used to such compact quarters now, but I should not complain. At least I don't have the problems that come with commanding so large a staff."

"I have grown to rely on my housekeeper and steward to deal with many of those problems," he said.

She shrugged. "The neglect of my father's steward is no doubt responsible for my reduced circumstances."

She *would* blame her loss of fortune on someone other than her drunkard father. "I am very sorry, my lady. If there is any way I can smooth things, you have only to command me."

"You really are too kind," she said.

This time he was detecting a fraction less chill in her voice. Could she be warming to him?

She scooted closer to him and dropped her voice. "But since you are offering, I must tell you there hangs at Winston Hall a portrait of my grandmother that I have a keen desire to be reunited with. One just doesn't realize at such a stressed time as a move, what one will want as time passes. Seeing her portrait again—possessing it—would afford me great pleasure.

How insensitive he had been to her. Although he had encouraged her to take her parents' portraits, he had obviously not realized there were a great many other things she would miss. "My dear Lady Catherine, you can have every portrait at Winston Hall for all I care. They will, quite naturally, mean far more to you than ever they will mean to me."

"You cannot know what you are saying, Mr. Moreland. Some of those portraits were painted by Gainsborough, and I daresay all of them are quite valuable."

"But I'm already a rich man," he explained. "How much money do you think one man can spend?"

She laughed at this. It was the first time he had ever seen her smile. And he thought now she really wasn't so homely after all.

"You must know I have little room to hang them here at the St. George."

"Perhaps you will marry and have a home of your own one day. Then I should be most happy to present you with a gallery of your ancestors."

"I regret that the men whose birth matches my own have little desire for a wife who is plain as well as penniless." A look of complete sadness came over her.

Knowing the wisdom of her words, he felt even sorrier for the displaced noblewoman. "Perhaps you would like to reclaim some of the art that has no sentimental value to you. The money you could get from them should allow you to buy a comfortable home of your own."

"You don't have to offer me the art, you know," she

said. "Winston Hall was yours for settling the many debts my family and I had amassed over a long period of years. We no longer have any legal claim to its possessions."

"The world does not always move according to English law, you know. Your former possessions happen now to belong to me, and it is my hope that you would help yourself to any of them you would like."

Her eyes rounded in wonderment. "You really mean that, don't you?"

"Of course. I have all I could ever want." *All except Felicity.*

Tears welled in her gray-green eyes. "I have done you a great disservice, Mr. Moreland. I thought of you as a usurper, and I held you in the greatest dislike."

" 'Twas only natural, given the fact I swept you out of the only house you had ever lived in."

Her head inclined and her voice was soft, almost remorseful, when she replied. "You are really much too kind."

As soon as the words were out of her mouth, Lady Catherine began sobbing. He moved closer to her, put an arm around her shaking shoulder and he spoke in a soothing voice. "I hope I have not offended you?"

"I am s-s-s-so utterly ashamed of myself for what I had planned to do today."

He gave her a puzzled look.

"You see," she stopped to sniff, "I was party to a wicked scheme to entrap you here at the St. George. I had planned to accuse you of attempting to . . . to force yourself upon my person."

"Here in the lobby?"

"No. I was going to feign a twisted ankle and then ask you to fetch my cloak from my room. Then I was to sneak upstairs and surprise you in my chambers at the same time I broke out screaming."

So wicked a scheme could only have been hatched by one man. A man determined to get Thomas out of the way. "Surely you did not devise so devious a plot on your own?"

She shook her head. "No, I was merely a puppet of the man who would wish to see you dead."

Thomas nodded. "Colonel Gordon."

"Yes," she managed between sobs.

Thomas offered her a handkerchief. The colonel must be stopped, he thought grimly. There was no telling how many lives Gordon would take in his pursuit of Felicity.

After he left the hotel, Thomas sent a message to the Bow Street runner who had previously discovered so much information about Felicity and her family. The man was extremely capable. Knowing the matter would be in Mr. Brown's hands, Thomas already felt more at ease.

Lady Catherine refused to get into the colonel's tasteless carriage. She did not trust the former military man. In broad daylight on the street in front of her hotel, she handed him a parcel containing the hundred pounds. "I could not do it," she told him.

His face turned red, his eyes steely. "You what?" he demanded in a loud voice.

"I could not discredit Mr. Moreland. He is a very kind man. Altogether a gentleman, though I know he was not born to such manners. Also," she mumbled, "I could not discredit myself. I have stooped as low as I am going to."

He grabbed her, digging his fingers into the soft flesh beneath her upper arm.

"You're hurting me," she shouted.

"You won't know what hurt is until I get finished with you," he said in a guttural voice.

She spit in his face. "You won't lay a finger on me, or I'll report you to the authorities." She pulled herself free. "How would you like for me to scream *Rape!* right now?" Her eyes flashed with anger.

He raised his hand as if to strike her, then he realized there were too many people about.

"How fitting it would be were you to be the victim of your own evil scheme," she sneered.

"Why, I could . . ."

She lifted her chin defiantly. "You will not lift a finger against me. My solicitor has locked away a document pointing to you if any unexpected tragedy should befall me."

He shoved her against the brick wall of her hotel, then released her and turned his back, muttering an oath as he climbed into his waiting carriage.

It took several minutes before his roiling anger subsided. Then he told himself he was just as glad his plan had not worked out. He should have known better than to have welcomed another into his illicit schemes. Especially a woman. The woman who could keep a secret had never been born. And one more person knowing of his plan to discredit Thomas Moreland was one person too many.

Gordon was confident the reason he had never been suspected in Captain Harrison's death was that either no one else had known he had been murdered or had witnessed it.

And no one else would ever know.

He consoled himself that he was far better off without Lady Catherine.

But now to think of another plan that would assure him a clear path to Felicity.

Of course it *would* be best to eliminate Moreland, but since everyone knew of his dislike for the man, he would quite naturally be the first suspect if Mr. Moreland met with an unexpected end.

What was needed was a situation that demanded that Felicity Harrison become his wife. Mrs. Gordon. Ah, he liked the sound of it.

Surely he could think of a way to make his dreams a reality.

Later that day, Thomas decided to pay a call on Felicity. She seemed clearly surprised as she moved gracefully down the stairs, her sister right behind her.

"Won't you take tea with us?" Glee asked him.

That Felicity shot her sister an angry glance did not escape his notice. She, no doubt, was angry over what he had said about Sedgewick.

The invitation was more than he had hoped for. "Hot tea would be the very thing on so cold a day," he said.

Felicity and Glee shared the settee in the small drawing room, and Thomas found the sturdiest chair— one that looked English more than French—and sat down.

"It's so good to see you, Mr. Moreland," Glee said. *Why couldn't Felicity have said it?* "It has been rather a long while since I have been given entry to your home, you must know," he said.

He could have sworn the color rose in Felicity's fair cheeks.

"I have come to tell you your mounts need exercising. No one has ridden them this past month."

"Oh, the poor beasts," Glee exclaimed. "I must tell you I have missed our riding terribly."

To his pleasant surprise, Felicity agreed. "I, too, have longed to renew my riding lessons."

"Tomorrow?" he asked.

Glee turned to her sister, a questioning look on her expectant face.

"If the weather gets no worse," Felicity answered.

A smile tipping his mouth, Thomas pressed his suit further. "Will the weather prevent you from going to the Assembly Rooms tonight?" he asked Felicity.

"I'd rather not—since the weather is so horrid."

"My carriage will protect you from the elements. May I call on you?"

"That would be most generous of you," Glee said. When Stanton brought the tea service and laid the cloth on the tea table, Felicity presided over the serving. She did not have to ask Thomas how he prepared his tea but added just the exact amount of sugar he preferred and then stirred in cream until the tea was the color of sand. *She had remembered.* It was such a small thing, but it touched him deeply.

They discussed the dance that night, then Felicity surprised him by saying, "Will Mrs. Ennis not mind your collecting us tonight?"

"What Mrs. Ennis minds is of no concern to me." He watched Glee's bemused expression slide to her sister, who showed no emotion at all.

"It's very kind—all that you have done for little Jamie," Glee began.

Felicity's gaze whirled to Thomas.

"How did you know?" he demanded, his brows lowering. As soon as he said the words, he realized he should have played ignorant and asked who Jamie was. But it was too late now.

"It wasn't difficult to piece together the information about his benefactor and realize it was you. Felicity also deduced that you were the man helping the boy. After all, how many people in Bath have an orangery? I believe, with your help, the lad will be walking in no time."

"Though the doctor will give no assures, it's my belief he will. But of course he'll always be lame."

"And if you hadn't come to Bath," Glee said dramatically, "I shudder to think what a dreary life the boy would have been forced to endure."

"What good is money if one cannot help others with it? There is a limit to my own needs, you must know."

A door creaked open, and Stanton announced that Misters Pope and Smythe desired to pay a morning call.

Thomas sized up the young men as they shyly entered the drawing room, deciding the bone-thin youths who were barely out of the schoolroom must be interested in Lady Glee. Indeed, one of them presented her with a nosegay of lilacs.

Handing his empty cup back to Felicity, Thomas rose and said his farewells. His step was light, as was his heart. He could not wait until evening. Somehow, he would find a way to tell Felicity how dearly he loved her.

Twenty-three

After their gentlemen callers left, Glee faced her sister. "I am so happy you received Mr. Moreland today. He is the very man for you, you know."

Yes, I know, Felicity thought. "I cannot believe Mr. Moreland feels anything more than gratitude toward me." *And malice toward my dear brother.*

"Then you are a very poor judge," Glee exclaimed. "From the first time we met him, I was keenly aware that he treated you rather special."

Felicity's pulse accelerated, and she was so breathless she could barely manage to speak. That had been a great many weeks ago. She must not allow herself to get her hopes up. No doubt Carlotta held Thomas's affections now, Felicity tried to persuade herself. "Would you not have special feelings for a person who saved you from dying?" She began to gather up the cups and saucers and put them on the tray for Stanton.

"It's more than that, Felicity! The way he looks at you, the way you two are when you're together . . . Oh, I cannot put it into words. I just know. I believe he has always been in love with you."

Felicity's heart fluttered at the thought. She still cared for Thomas, despite his aversion to George. *Drat!* She could not allow herself to give such amorous thoughts to Thomas Moreland. "I daresay Carlotta feels the same. He treats her with great regard as of late. No doubt, he was happy when I freed him from my company."

"How can you believe anything so foolish?" Glee asked with exasperation. "Did you not hear Mr. Moreland say he cared not what Mrs. Ennis thought?"

Dare she hope? Felicity wanted to believe Thomas's attentions to Carlotta were merely because she had made herself unavailable. "We will see," Felicity said, sweeping biscuit crumbs from the white tea cloth. "I cannot give a great deal of credit to *your* judgment, pet. After all, you fancied yourself in love with Mr. Salvado."

A deep flush crept up Glee's fair face. "I am ever so humiliated that I could have thought myself in love with him. The very minute I was alone in the carriage with him, I realized how grave a mistake I had made. Even then, when I looked at him, he seemed dark and menacing, and I grew quite frightened. And when he tried to sit beside me and kiss me, I was forced to box his ears."

Felicity burst out laughing. "I cannot think what you ever saw in the man."

"Nor can I." Glee twisted an auburn curl around her finger. "I believe I was in love with love, and he was the only man I was exposed to."

"Then I am happy you are now in society. Have you not found any other young man you fancy? I take it neither Mr. Pope nor Mr. Smythe has engaged your affections."

Glee wrinkled her nose. "Not at all, though I am excessively enjoying having half a dozen eligible men dance attendance upon me. It's just that I cannot imagine myself spending the rest of my life with any of them."

"Now you're showing maturity. But don't distress. There's time. You are but seventeen."

Glee got to her feet and started for the door. "Perhaps a new man will come to the Assembly Rooms tonight and sweep me off my feet."

Felicity followed her sister as she climbed up the stairs. "I hope not, pet. You're still much too young. Enjoy being adored by half the young men in Bath. Soon enough you will settle down."

That night Thomas and his sister called for Felicity and Glee. For the first time in a week, Felicity was able to sit next to Thomas in his carriage. She heartily hoped he could not see the way her knees trembled. For his very proximity had quite an odd effect on her. She felt like a miss directly from the schoolroom, all joyous jitters over her first romance.

She was keenly aware of the length of his legs and the solid muscles beneath his breeches. She smelled his scent of sandalwood and in the silence heard his breathing. It had been a very long time since she was so drawn to a man.

It had been like this with Michael. She had been achingly aware of his masculinity, too. And she had reveled in the intimacy she had shared with the man she loved. Could she and Thomas ever blend in such a manner? Such thoughts had a profound physical effect on her.

She could not remember ever wanting anything so desperately as she wanted Thomas Moreland. The pity of it was she still felt this way after he had maligned George.

Carlotta was already at the Assembly Rooms when Thomas's group entered. With a somber face, Felicity met Carlotta's malicious stare.

Ignoring Felicity, Carlotta spoke jauntily to Thomas. "Oh here you are, Mr. Moreland. I did not know if I would see you tonight since we did not meet today."

Felicity's gaze swept over Carlotta from her luscious black hair to her breasts that were barely confined in the purple silk that hugged the soft curves of her figure. A Greek goddess could have been no lovelier, Felicity thought with disappointment.

"I am here, Mrs. Ennis," Thomas said. "You must honor me by standing up with me." He offered Carlotta his hand, and they turned their backs on Felicity.

Felicity fumed as she watched them walk to the dance floor. So that was that. He had turned his back on her in order to dance with Carlotta.

Felicity met her sister's pitying glace. "Do you see how mistaken you are about Mr. Moreland's feeling, my pet?" Felicity whispered.

"The night is still young. You will see," Glee responded with assurance.

"Ah, there you are!" George said to Dianna. He had crossed the room to speak with her. "I beg that you will stand up with me for this set."

Dianna's brown eyes danced as she gracefully gave her hand to him.

Which left George's friend Blanks alone with Felicity and Glee. He looked at Glee. "Miss Pembroke?" He merely held out his hand, and Glee took it.

Felicity sat down where she was and watched Glee and Blanks. It was generally agreed—before Thomas had come to Bath—that Mr. Blankenship was the most eligible man in the watering city. He was quite rich and extremely handsome. The problem was that he was but twenty-three and very immature still. He showed no interest in settling down with one woman, as George appeared to be content to do with Dianna. Blanks had a habit of gaming heavily, drinking heartily, and bedding women of questionable morals.

A pity because he was the very man for Glee, thought Felicity. She thought, too, that Glee might secretly harbor deep affection for Mr. Blankenship but knew how futile such affection would be.

"Good evening, Mrs. Harrison," the colonel said, strolling up behind her from the direction of the gaming rooms. "I hope you don't object to me sitting with you for a while."

"Not at all," she said, patting the seat next to her. He came to sit beside her.

After the set, all four couples joined in a circle and talked. "May I get ratafia for you, Mrs. Harrison?" the colonel asked.

Before she could consent, the other three gentlemen delivered similar invitations to their previous dancing partners. All the women were in agreement that a refreshing drink would be in order.

" 'Tis so terribly hot in here tonight," Carlotta remarked to the other females after the men had departed. She unfurled a fan with plump feathers of deep purple and commenced to fanning herself.

"It has been my observation," Felicity said, "that those who become the hottest are those who carry more soft flesh around their bones. Would that I could fill the bodice of my dress as you do, Carlotta."

Carlotta's lilac eyes glowed. "Then it's happy I am to be hot!"

The other ladies laughed and were still laughing when the men returned with their refreshments.

Felicity took hers from the colonel and drank as her

eyes watched the way Carlotta's fingers brushed against Thomas's when he handed her the ratafia. *Why can't it be me?* Felicity wondered.

Soon the orchestra began playing again. This time it was a waltz. Knowing Thomas usually waltzed with her, Felicity was afraid to look at him. Her heart pounding, she saw his feet step in her direction.

"Mrs. Harrison," Thomas said, "would you do me the goodness of standing up with me?"

Hallelujah! she wanted to say. But she could really say nothing for she could not trust her voice not to tremble. She placed her hand in his and followed him to the dance floor, certain she had completely lost her breath. The feathery touch of his hand did positively provocative things to her. Things no respectable woman dare admit.

When he set one hand on her waist and pulled her closer, she felt a molten heat surge through her. Which did nothing to still the trembling in her hands. Surely he was aware of his effect on her. She was afraid to meet his gaze for fear he would see the naked hunger in her eyes, yet she could not avoid lifting her lashes to see his dark face bent to hers. There was intensity on his solemn face, an intensity that drew them inexorably together. Was it her hopeful imagination that made her see hunger in his black eyes, too?

Her trembling would not calm. *He was aware of it.* For he pressed his fingers more tightly into her palm. Then she realized *he* was trembling, too.

Though the music called for sweeping steps, Thomas's steps slowed, and he pulled her even closer. Indecently close. Though Felicity had no desire for her maiden sister to witness their intimate dancing, she was powerless to pull away from him.

She enjoyed the way his body felt against hers.

'Twas so much like lying with her Michael, bare flesh to bare flesh. What would it feel like to have Thomas's hands gliding along the rounded slopes of her body? To feel her own hands gently stroking his solid muscles? To feel her fingers splay into the mat of dark hair on his magnificent chest? To feel him inside her?

Suddenly she felt the swelling below his waist as it pressed into her. Down low. And she responded with a noticeable melting. Down low.

Blue eyes locked with black. Though unspoken, there was a magical blending.

Finally he spoke. "You are trembling."

"Yes," she answered, unable to remove her hungry gaze from his.

The colonel watched the pair of them, despite the murderous effect it had on him. He had not seen such naked hunger since he had witnessed Felicity dancing with her husband so many years ago. The night he had vowed to get rid of Michael so he could claim Felicity and the pleasures bedding her promised.

Had they not been in a public place tonight, the colonel would have run a sword through the handsome Usurper. Why did women—why did Felicity—not understand that a man such as himself could do so much more for her than a well-built man of thirty summers? Why must women be blinded by the good looks of well-built men? It had been the same with Captain Harrison. He had been rather taller than average, though not as tall as the Usurper. And like the Usurper, Captain Harrison had been considered an exceptionally handsome man.

It was while Felicity and the Usurper were gazing hungrily at each other, the colonel looked away. *Before the Usurper gets the opportunity to bed her, she will be mine,* Colonel Gordon vowed.

When the waltz was over, Thomas chided himself for not telling Felicity then and there on the dance floor that he loved her. That he had since that night six years ago.

The moment was lost, but he decided he would not lose her. Not now. For he knew that at long last he had won her affection. Soon, he would declare himself to her. *Soon.*

Despite his acute desire, he would not allow himself to dance with her again that night. It was far too painful. Soon, he promised himself. *Soon* it would be right for him to unburden his heart to her.

If he could only wait until the proper time. Perhaps tomorrow when they went riding.

Twenty-four

Lettie had waited up for Felicity to help remove her evening gown.

"You should have gone to bed," Felicity told her as she glided into the room.

"Allow an old woman the pleasure of seeing her charge sail happily into her chamber." With hands withered from age, Lettie began to unfasten Felicity's dress. "I can tell by the lightness in yer step things are going much better for ye and Mr. Moreland."

Felicity spun to face her abigail. "What do you mean by that, pray tell?"

"I've known ye and loved ye too long not to know yer heart, lass. Ye can't hide your affection for Mr. Moreland from old Lettie."

Felicity smiled and once more presented her back to the abigail. "Is it that obvious?"

"To me."

Once her dress was off and Lettie was rehanging it, Felicity stripped off her ivory gloves. "I'm afraid I've been much too much the open book to Mr. Moreland. I've feared that his interest in me is because he feels indebted to me for having saved his life. I've worried that after realizing my affection for him, he would court me only to repay a debt, not out of any true feelings toward me as a woman."

"Then ye must be blind as a bat. First of all, ye are the loveliest woman in all of Bath. And second, the man is unable to hide his adoration of you. Both Lady Glee and Lord George have remarked to me of the way he hungers after ye with those dark eyes of his."

Such a thought sent Felicity's heart fluttering. She sat on the edge of her bed while Lettie removed her satin slippers. She remembered the feel of Thomas pressed against her for the waltz, and something stirred within her deep and low. "I must confide in you that Mr. Moreland surprised me tonight with his marked attentions. I had begun to fear that Carlotta had captured his affection."

"Pooh! From what I've heard of the man, he could never be attracted to Mrs. Ennis, unless he thinks she's as free with her favors as she appears to be." The old woman harrumphed as she bent to pick up Felicity's slippers. "It's scandalous the way her dresses almost don't cover her breasts. Even in broad daylight. And always wearing purple! Why, she looks like a tart, that's what. It's my belief Mr. Moreland is looking for a real lady, like ye—and I'm not referring to your family's peerage, either."

"I hope you're right," Felicity said. "He's invited me—and Glee, of course—to ride with him tomorrow."

A frown dropped on Lettie's face. "It's gonna rain."

Felicity lifted her arms as Lettie slipped on her night shift. "Pray that it doesn't."

Lettie waited for Felicity to slip beneath the covers; then she doused the candle and left. "I will pray that it doesn't rain, lass."

Felicity was so exhilarated with anticipation of the morrow that sleep eluded her. When at last she dropped off into slumber, she dreamed of Thomas . . .

It was a magnificent day. The skies were exceptionally blue and cloudless. The sun shone brightly without being too hot. Daffodils spread their yellow glory over the fields. And she was with Thomas. They were riding. She did not know where Glee and Dianna were, but it was as if they did not exist. No one else existed. In fact, it seemed as if she and Thomas were the only two people on Earth.

They rode for a long time until they came into a clearing, a meadow actually. It didn't look like the terrain around Bath, more like a lovely meadow in Sussex or Kent. They dismounted, and Thomas tethered their mounts to a huge shade tree.

Then he removed his coat and spread it on the grass near the tree but still in the warm sun. He beckoned for Felicity to come lie with him.

She gave him her hand, and he walked with her over to the coat. Then his face bent to hers. She raised her lips to meet his. As their soft lips merged, she had a heady feeling she and Thomas blended together into one being.

She did not remember how they became undressed, but by the time they lay beside each other on the coat, their naked flesh also blended together. Again, she could not tell where she ended and Thomas began, for they seemed like one.

Low in her body she felt a molten heat, and soon her beloved Thomas began to plunge into her pool of liquid.

Felicity bolted up in her bed, her breath coming only with great difficulty. She looked around for Thomas and with a deep, wrenching disappointment realized she had been dreaming. Her void was as distressing as losing a limb.

She also became aware of something else. A steady

rain drummed on her window. Now she was doubly bereft. She would have no opportunity to be alone with Thomas this day.

When Thomas awoke the next morning, the sky was unusually gray. Worse than that, rain beat against his window. All the hopes and expectations that had sent him off to contented sleep the night before withered as he morosely watched the rain spatter on the pane. He would not be able to go riding with Felicity today. Another day he would be unable to tell her how deeply and for how long he had been in love with her.

Lethargically, he swung his legs over the side of the bed and then heard a knock at his chamber door. "Yes?" he shouted, getting to his feet.

His butler eased open the door just a crack. "You have a caller, Mr. Moreland."

"In this blasted rain?"

"Yes sir, a Lord Sedgewick. I have taken his dripping coat and sat him in front of the fire in your library."

"See to it he gets some hot tea, will you, Bryce?"

"I have already taken the liberty, sir," Bryce said as he closed the door behind him.

What could be so important that George would walk three miles in this miserable weather? Thomas's stomach plummeted. *Something had happened to Felicity.* She needed him. With help from his valet, a trembling Thomas was shaved, dressed, and downstairs in ten minutes.

He threw open the door to the library, and a smiling but thoroughly wet George stood up to greet him. George's cheery countenance eased Thomas's worry.

Felicity must be all right. Thomas closed the door and crossed the room to welcome Felicity's brother.

"Whatever brings you out on such a wretched day?" Thomas wanted to point out that George did not even possess a horse, which could have shortened his time getting drenched, but he thought better of mentioning it. A man of George's class without a horse was somewhat emasculated.

George returned to his chair, but he appeared nervous. "I've come to speak to you, sir, about an important personal matter."

Felicity? Did George want him to see less of his sister? Did he find Thomas's birth not satisfactory for the daughter and sister of a viscount? Or had something happened to Felicity? But, of course, Thomas assured himself, if that were the case George would not have been smiling when Thomas entered the library.

Perhaps Sedgewick had been back to the gaming hells and needed Thomas to pay off his markers. "Yes?" Thomas said warily.

George cleared his throat. "You may have noticed that I have a marked preference for Miss Moreland."

The boy wanted Dianna's hand! Relief washed over Thomas. He nodded, barely able to prevent a smile from lifting the corners of his mouth.

George looked him straight in the eye. "I must tell you your sister affects me as no other woman ever has."

As your sister affects me. Thomas merely nodded.

"Miss Moreland is the most beautiful, graceful, sensitive—wonderful—girl I've ever had the pleasure of knowing." George stopped and nervously cleared his throat. "To cut right to the chase, I must tell you, Moreland, I'm desperately in love with your sister."

"And does my sister know your feelings?"

George shook his head. "I dared not press my suit without your approval. I believe Miss Moreland has a partiality toward me, but I did not want to encourage it if you were going to deny me—which you have every right to do—given my past indiscretions.

"But I want you to know that my deep feelings for Miss Moreland have made a new man of me. I have no desire to continue with my former ways of debauchery."

Thomas leaned back in his chair. "I wish I could be convinced you will not regress. Tell me, what is it you want from life now?"

George thought on it a moment. "Gambling and womanizing no longer hold any appeal for me. I find more than anything I want to be married." His voice seemed far away, as if he were dreaming aloud, when he continued. "I would like to have children with Miss Moreland. And one day I hope to get my lands back and see to it they are restored to a profitable state." He peered intensely at Thomas. "But the only woman I could ever desire to marry is your sister. As far as I'm concerned, there *is* no other woman. I vow I will always be true and constant to her."

Thomas understood completely. It was as if Sedgewick were describing his own feelings for Felicity. "I admit your behavior has improved—"

"Since I met Miss Moreland."

"Yes, quite. I wish I could have assurances you would not return to your former ways."

George hung his head. "I pray that you allow me to prove myself."

"How do I know you're not a fortune hunter?" Thomas hated asking the boy that, but he wanted to see George's mettle.

George's hand clenched on the arm of his chair. "Because I don't want your money. I know that sounds foolish, given that my settlement from you is the principal thing that keeps me from the poor house. But *if* you were to favor my suit and *if* Miss Moreland were to favor my suit, I would propose to accept only one marriage settlement from you: the redemption of Hornsby Manor, which you'll remember, is the Sedgewick estate. Has been for centuries. I would propose to spend every waking minute seeing to the success of the estate. Already I've been reading about new labor-saving farming techniques as well as some hybrids that would produce larger crops. You see, I've been spending a good bit of time learning about farming. This next phase of my life is going to be serious."

"I am indeed impressed." Thomas believed George was earnest. He already had little doubt that George was in love with Dianna. The fellow could no more hide his feelings than he could change his fair coloring. But Sedgewick still had a great deal of growing up to do.

George was silent, his green eyes locked with Thomas's.

"I believe you are sincere, and I believe you are in love with my sister—not her brother's money." Thomas paused. "Are you certain now—and in the years to come—you will not come to regret the marriage because of Dianna's lack of noble birth?"

"It wouldn't matter to me if she worked in a book-shop," George protested. "I would love her still and want to make her the viscountess Sedgewick. I also believe I've never known a lady born who is as much the lady as Miss Moreland."

Thomas smiled. "I believe you, and I give you permission to speak to Dianna, but I cannot sanction a marriage until you demonstrate that gaming no longer holds an attraction for you."

"How long?"

The poor fellow was terribly in love. "A few months should suffice. If my sister is agreeable to your suit, I would rather the engagement not be made public until your behavior has satisfied me."

"I can tell you now my behavior will be exemplary," George said with a smile.

"Since you are here today," Thomas said, his chest tight, "I am given to believe you have no objection to uniting our houses. If the tables were turned, say, would you object to me marrying one of your sisters?"

George's brows plunged. "Felicity?"

Thomas nodded, his heart hammering. "I came to Bath because I was in love with her."

"Does she know?"

Thomas shook his head. "I haven't had the opportunity to tell her. I had hoped to when we went riding today, but that is impossible now because of the rain."

A smile broke across George's face. "I honestly cannot imagine Felicity with anyone else. You two are perfect for each other."

Thomas shrugged. "I don't know about that, but I do know no one could ever cherish her more than I."

" 'Tis exactly how I feel about your sister. Fancy that!"

Thomas stood and offered George his hand. "Don't let me keep you. I suggest you go and speak with my sister now."

"Thank you, Moreland." He started toward the door, and Thomas called to him.

"You're to take the carriage back to Bath. I can't have my future brother taking lung fever."

A smile spread across George's face as he turned to leave.

Twenty-five

After waking from her wrenching dream, Felicity was not able to go back to sleep. She lay on her tester bed, listening morosely to the rain's beat, beat, beat against the windowpane. It seemed as if each time the rain tapped against the window, it carried Thomas farther away from her.

She lay there within the blackness—then later, grayness—of her chamber, somber and blue-deviled.

Eventually Lettie entered with a breakfast tray. "It looks like our prayers for fair skies today weren't heeded by the Almighty."

Felicity sat up in bed and shrugged. "I have the most terrible feeling Mr. Moreland slips farther from my reach with each drop of rain."

"Pooh!" Lettie said, pouring Felicity's tea. " 'Tis only a minor setback. I believe ye will see yer Mr. Moreland today. Mark my words, he will brave the day's wretched weather to call on ye." She handed Felicity her tea. "So ye will assuredly want to look yer best today. What dress shall ye wear?"

"The blue," Felicity said solemnly. " 'Tis his favorite on me, though I lack your optimism that Mr. Moreland will come today."

Lettie busied herself getting Felicity's blue dress from the linen press. "Ye will never believe what yer brother has gone and done. He not only has taken to rising early, but this morning the daft lad refused his breakfast, donned a big greatcoat, and took off walking through the wet streets of Bath."

"Whatever could be so important he should want to brave such inclement weather?" Felicity wondered aloud.

Lettie removed stockings from the drawer. "I wasn't privy to his destination."

Felicity finished her tea and got out of bed, and Lettie assisted her in getting dressed for the day.

With great disappointment Dianna awoke to the dismal sound of a healthy rain drumming against her windows. *I shall not see Lord Sedgewick today,* she thought morosely.

She sat up so her maid could place the breakfast tray in front of her. It was Dianna's custom to take a leisurely breakfast in bed while she perused the day's post. Her brother kept such erratic hours, the two of them never seemed able to meet for breakfast.

Today Dianna had no desire to leave her bed. The house would be damp and chilly, and she would have to cover herself in shawls and don wool stockings. Even then she would still be chilled. She thought back to the thatched cottage where she had lived with her parents during her childhood, and she longed for its coziness—but not as much as she longed to see blue skies and Lord Sedgewick today.

She had almost decided not to get out of bed at all when Bryce rapped at her chamber door.

Collette answered it.

Dianna's heart soared as she listened to his words.

"Lord Sedgewick desires to see Miss Moreland. He awaits her in the drawing room."

He had come on so horrid a day to see her! Since he had neither horse nor carriage, she wondered if he had come on foot through the sodden mire, the wind and rain slamming against him. Such thoughts troubled her but not enough to dampen her uplifted spirits.

She could scarcely believe her good fortune. Flying from her bed, she began to bark orders at Collette. "Pray, fetch the ivory promenade dress! I should like the ivory boots, too, I think. Oh, do please hurry. You must dress my hair. I want it to look ravishingly beautiful. Do you think you can manage that?"

A smile on her youthful face, Collette answered, *"Oui, mademoiselle."*

A half-hour later, Dianna glided into the drawing room, puzzled over the serious expression on Lord Sedgewick's golden skinned face as he stood and met her gaze. His warm eyes flashed with intensity.

Her heart beat wildly. She was frightened. Was he going to tell her something dreadful? Had he become betrothed to another? Nothing could possibly be worse. She swept gracefully across the carpeted room to give him her hand. "How surprised I am to see you in this wretched weather, my lord." She winced at how wet his boots were. The man needed to soak his cold feet in a tub of warm water. He must be utterly miserable. She could not bear it.

"I fear I'm a most impatient man," he said. "I had determined to speak to your brother today, and nothing—not even this dismal weather—could dissuade me."

Whatever was so important that it couldn't wait until the skies cleared? she wondered. "Come, my lord, you must sit before the warm fire. I fear this room is far too big and far too cold unless one sits directly in front of the fire." She moved to scoot a chair closer to the hearth.

"Allow me," he said. George moved two French chairs near the fireplace; then the two of them sat down.

She was aware of the mere foot that separated them and was reminded of the night he had taken her hand at the musicale. Oddly, she wished he would clasp her hand here and now. Then, suddenly she realized Collette had not come downstairs to chaperon her. And she was enormously glad to be alone with Lord Sedgewick. Perhaps he *would* take her hand again. Her eyes darted to his wet hair. Wet, it looked more brown than blond. "You must be chilled to the bone, my lord."

"Actually, I haven't given it a thought. I've had more important things on my mind."

Her heart pounded. She was seized with fear. His uncommon behavior was most definitely alarming. Of course, she tried to persuade herself, gray skies always had the effect of lowering her spirits. Perhaps that was all it was. "I hope everything goes well for you and your family, my lord."

Then he smiled. A heart-stopping, spirit-lifting, wonderful smile. "Yes, everything is quite splendid. I'm in fairly high spirits now that I've spoken with your brother."

She gave him a puzzled look. "Pray, what could my brother have said to make you so happy?"

George leaned closer to her. She could smell his musk scent, and she could see the fine stubble from where he had shaved that morning. "Can you not guess?" he asked her in a low voice.

Now she looked even more puzzled. "What could

my broth——" Before the words were out of her mouth, she had a jubilant thought. Had he? Oh, my. Dare she hope? What if she merely embarrassed herself? In a flash, she thought of all the warm gestures Lord Sedgewick had made to her and of how he never danced with anyone but her.

And all at once she knew. "You offered for me," she whispered.

He nodded.

She saw the doubt, the fear of rejection in his countenance, and she could not bear for him to think there was any possibility she would reject him. She smiled and teasingly asked, "And what did my brother say to you?"

"He said I was free to declare myself to you, but he would withhold permission to wed until I demonstrate I have reformed."

She could not remove her eyes from his. "Reformed from what?"

"I regret to say I gamed heavily before I met you."

"Oh, dear." Then seeing the troubled look on his face, she added, "It is my desire to accept you, my lord."

George sprang from his chair, and she rose to meet him. He gathered her into his arms and held her for a moment.

Here in George's arms is where she wanted to spend the rest of her life. She lifted her face to his, and he lowered his lips to hers for a chaste kiss.

"You have made me the happiest man on earth, my love."

She reached out her hand to tenderly stroke the side of his golden face. She could not wait until they truly belonged to each other. "I feel the very same, my lord."

He pulled both her hands to his lips for a nibbling kiss. "You are to call me George now."

"Yes, George." She happily basked in whatever it was he was doing to her hands.

"Any number of men would beg for your beautiful hand. I am completely honored that you have chosen me, though I realize I'm not worthy of you."

"I've never noticed any other man since the night I met you. I knew when you walked through our door that you were the only man for me."

He squeezed her hand. " 'Twas the same with me."

There was a knock on the door. "Come in," Dianna said.

Thomas walked into the drawing room, his gaze resting on his sister and George holding each other's hand. "I take it my sister is favorable to your suit."

George turned his smiling face on Thomas. "Indeed, she has made me the happiest of men."

"And where is your maid, my dear?" Thomas asked Dianna with a wink.

Her eyes widened.

"You silly girl, I told her not to follow you," Thomas said. "Really, you cannot expect a man to deliver a proposal of marriage when his intended's maid is present."

Dressed in Thomas's favorite blue dress, Felicity sat by the window in the upstairs sitting room reading her slim volume of Shakespeare's sonnets. She had reread "Shall I Compare Thee to a Summer's Day" so many times, she had learned all the words by heart. And with every new reading, she pictured Thomas the way he had looked that night as he lay in George's bed, a bandage wrapped around his broad chest. He had known all the words to the sonnet and as he had mouthed them, she allowed herself to imagine he meant the words for her. Something in his demeanor that night had convincingly suggested he associated the sonnet with her.

A knock sounded at her door. "Yes?"

The butler stepped into the room. "You have a caller, Mrs. Harrison."

Her heart leaped. *Thomas had come!* A smile on her face, she stood up.

" 'Tis Colonel Gordon," he said.

Her shoulders sagged, as did her voice when she replied. "I'm coming right down."

The colonel stood when she entered the drawing room.

"My dear Colonel, whatever possessed you to come out on a day like this?"

A thin smile lit his face. "You must remember, my dear, men are not nearly as adverse to a little rain as women are. We don't have to worry about our skirts or our hair becoming limp."

She strolled into the room, stiffly offered him her hand and sat on the settee next to his chair. "I do suppose you are right, which could possibly explain my brother's peculiar behavior. I have been thinking him quite mad. George actually left the house this morning on foot in this wretched weather and hasn't been seen since. I cannot imagine what could have beckoned him."

A smile slid across the colonel's face. "I would wager it's a woman, and I don't think I'd be far from the mark if I guessed it was Miss Moreland. Such a union—bringing in her hefty portion—would restore your family's finances. George is being sensible."

"George would never marry without love!" Felicity

protested. "It is my belief he is sincerely attracted to Miss Moreland."

"I must admit the woman is not at all coarse like her brother."

Felicity stiffened and shot the colonel a cold glance. "Pray, in what way do you find Mr. Moreland coarse, for I declare I cannot understand what you are speaking of? I find him to be a gentleman in every way."

His eyes narrowed. "The way the man flaunts his wealth is so *bourgeois.*"

"I am in no way aware that Mr. Moreland flaunts his wealth," she said, trying to keep the hostility from edging into her voice.

"Did he not *purchase* the most opulent estate in this part of England?"

The butler entered the drawing room and met Felicity's gaze. "Mr. Moreland has called for you, Mrs. Harrison. Is it all right to send him in?"

"Yes," Felicity said, her heart beginning to dance. The day's gray skies seemed suddenly brighter.

Seconds later, Thomas stood at the room's doorway, his glance skirting the chamber. When he saw Colonel Gordon, a frown lowered the corners of his mouth.

He crossed the room and bowed in front of Felicity. "Your servant, Mrs. Harrison."

She extended her hand.

He took her hand in his, slowly brought it to his mouth, and pressed his lips into her palm.

It was an unbelievably intimate gesture, Felicity thought. "I beg that you sit down, Mr. Moreland." She was surprised she had found her voice—and even more surprised that it did not tremble.

Thomas then sat on the settee beside her.

She almost broke into laughter at the anger that

transformed the colonel's face. Really, the man was an open book.

Like her.

"I regret that we cannot ride today," Thomas began, still without having acknowledged the colonel's presence.

"Yes," she lamented. "Glee and I were so looking forward to it."

"We shall go when the weather clears, though I can't tomorrow for I have business matters that will require my attention."

When, then? she wondered morosely.

"If you are so keen to ride," the colonel said, "it would be my pleasure to furnish you with a mount tomorrow—if the weather turns fair."

Suddenly the door to the room swung open, and George came bouncing in, his smile nearly stretching from ear to ear.

Felicity was relieved she would be spared from having to answer Colonel Gordon. Her glance trailed from her brother's wet mop of hair to his sodden boots. "Wherever did you go in this wretched rain?" Felicity asked George.

"I had a deep desire to see Miss Moreland."

"Miss Moreland must count herself fortunate to merit such marked attentions from a viscount," Colonel Gordon said.

George's eyes narrowed. "I hope, Colonel, you are not suggesting Miss Moreland suffers my company only for my title."

"Not at all, my boy. You have many fine qualities that I'm sure someone as lowly born as Miss Moreland must sincerely appreciate."

Thomas leaped to his feet, and George's hand fisted. The two men shouted at the colonel at once.

"You will apologize for calling my sister lowly born," Thomas demanded.

George spit out his words. "How dare you malign the woman I hope to make my wife!"

Felicity jumped to her feet and placed herself between Thomas and the colonel, facing Thomas. "Please, Mr. Moreland, do sit down and cool off."

He met her gaze, then nodded softly and sat down.

The colonel looked apologetically at George. "Terribly sorry, my boy, if I offended you—or your future wife. I am sure you and Miss Moreland will suit admirably. After all, there is nothing of the shop about her, and I must say she is quite lovely and comports herself in a genteel manner."

George's hand unfisted, but he continued to glare at Colonel Gordon while imperceptibly nodding his forgiveness.

"So is it official? Is Miss Moreland to become your wife?" Colonel Gordon asked.

George's glance shot to Thomas. "Mr. Moreland withholds his permission until I demonstrate sufficient maturity."

The four of them continued to sit in the drawing room for the next hour. Then Glee entered the room and sat beside George on the settee that faced Felicity's. "Why did you take off this morning in the rain?" Glee asked George. "All morning the staff was abuzz with the news that Lord Sedgewick had lost his marbles and was walking about in a rainstorm."

"I wished to see Miss Moreland," he answered.

"Why couldn't it wait until the rain stopped?" Glee asked.

George shrugged. "I have been having a difficult time sleeping for thinking of Miss Moreland and hoping . . . I wished to declare myself to her brother."

Glee shrieked in excitement. "That's wonderful! Miss Moreland is to be my sister."

A look of disappointment disturbed George's face. "Well . . . not yet, anyway. Her brother thinks I'm too immature."

"How dare he!" Glee said with outrage.

The five of them continued sitting there. And none of them would budge. Felicity wished the colonel would leave so she could speak more freely with Mr. Moreland, but she knew he would likely die before he would allow her to be alone with Thomas. It was obvious each man wanted to outlast the other. How long, pray tell, would they sit here?

When one hour stretched to two, Felicity stood up and addressed them. "You gentlemen are free to stay, but I really must leave. I have things that demand my attention now."

The colonel grasped his cane and pulled himself to a standing position. "I beg that you forgive me, madam, for keeping you from your duties." He tossed an irritated glance at Thomas.

Thomas stood up. "I, too, beg your pardon, Mrs. Harrison."

Felicity nodded at them and swept from the room, angry that she could not speak to Thomas.

Twenty-six

The next morning's sunny skies had offered Felicity fleeting hope she would be able to ride with Thomas; then she remembered him telling her the previous day that he had business matters that required his attention.

Carlotta paid a morning call, which caused Felicity to wonder if her friend's reason for coming was motivated by goodwill or by the expectancy that Thomas would call. A smug smile crept across Felicity's face because Thomas was not coming. She felt as if she were scoring one against Carlotta.

When Felicity entered the morning room, Carlotta was busy examining one of her lavender slippers. "I am so very vexed!" Carlotta said, stomping her shoeless foot. "I believe the wet pavement has positively ruined my shoes."

Felicity sat across from her. "Why did you not wear boots instead of slippers? Were you unaware of the huge amount of rain that fell yesterday?"

A pout tugging at her face, Carlotta put her slipper back on. "Of course I was aware of the wretched weather! I thought I would go mad yesterday. I have never been so bored in all my life."

"Then you should have realized the pavement would still be wet—and possibly muddy today."

Carlotta shrugged. "I was fooled by the sun."

"The sun is rather welcome today, after yesterday. Is the air chilled?"

"No, it's quite pleasant with no more than a pelisse."

"Then I propose we go for a walk," Felicity said.

Carlotta rolled her eyes. "I've never known one such as you who would rather walk than ride."

"But neither of us has a means of riding," Felicity pointed out.

"Well, not today, of course, but other times—when you do have a choice—you still promulgate walking."

"It has been my observation that those who seldom walk have a tendency toward corpulence," Felicity said.

Realizing Carlotta would not budge until she was assured Thomas wasn't coming, Felicity added, "A pity Mr. Moreland must conduct estate business today."

"He told you?"

Felicity nodded. "Yesterday."

Carlotta could barely conceal her jealousy. "He called here yesterday?"

"Yes. By the way, I must tell you our family's delightful news."

Carlotta's face went white.

Felicity could not resist dragging out her information awhile longer. Uncharitably, she rather enjoyed watching her rival squirm. "There's to be a wedding."

Carlotta swallowed; then she spoke in a shaking voice. "Really?"

"Oh, yes. Can you imagine my house uniting with that of a bookseller's offspring?"

Carlotta was unable to answer.

"George desires to marry Miss Moreland, and she looks favorably on his suit," Felicity said.

A smile broke across Carlotta's face. "Then he's offered for her?"

"He spoke to Mr. Moreland, who desires that George wait until he is a bit more mature."

"What a wicked thing for Mr. Moreland to do! Does he not realize Lord Sedgewick is a very good catch for his sister?"

Felicity shrugged. "I must admit I'm most vexed with him."

"You do not object at all to Dianna Moreland's misfortune of birth?"

Carlotta certainly didn't. "I know of no one noble born who is more a lady than Miss Moreland."

"If they should marry, your papa would likely roll in his grave," Carlotta said bitterly.

Felicity could not bear for anyone to malign Thomas's family. Neither he nor Dianna warranted it. "You know the lame little boy in front of the milliner's?"

Carlotta nodded. "He's much the age of my own lad."

"Mr. Moreland—anonymously, you must understand—has been helping the boy. He hopes the boy will one day be able to walk. Please don't tell Mr. Moreland I told you. He doesn't like for people to know of his many charities. He has paid for the lad to see the best doctor in Bath. He's determined the lad's misshapen legs come from having little sunshine and no citrus. Therefore, he sees to it the lad gets fresh oranges and sunshine every day. Mr. Moreland even instructs his groom to take the boy pony riding each day."

Carlotta's eyes narrowed. "How do you know all this?"

"I deduced it on my own, if you must know. The

lad's mama doesn't even know her son's benefactor's name. From her description, I surmised it was Mr. Moreland. Then Glee tricked him into admitting it."

Carlotta shrugged with feigned disinterest. "It's not as if he doesn't have hoards of money."

Yet Felicity knew the first chance Carlotta faced Thomas alone, she would gush rapturously over his benevolency. Even if Felicity had told her not to mention it.

Felicity got to her feet. "Come, let's walk to Crescent Fields." Then with a sheepish smile, Felicity added, "You mustn't allow yourself to become corpulent." She smiled wickedly at the picture of a fat Carlotta.

On those words, Carlotta sprang into her sodden slippers. The two women donned their pelisses, then left the town house.

"I do hope the weather stays this fine," Felicity said, once they were on the pavement.

"I believe it will. You can see the sky is cloudless."

They strolled toward Gay Street.

"I have the most wonderful idea!" Carlotta said. "We could get a party of us to have a picnic at the old ruins over in Hammersmith tomorrow."

A smile crossed Felicity's face. "That would be pleasant, would it not? Who would come?" From the corner of her eye, she saw they were nearing the milliner's where little Jamie played with his tin soldiers on the pavement.

Carlotta did not spare him a glance. "Your family, of course. You, Glee, and Lord Sedgewick. Me. Mr. and Miss Moreland. Colonel Gordon and Mr. Blankenship."

"It would be fun. Why do you not tell Mr. Moreland of your proposal. Perhaps he will offer his cook to prepare the baskets. I daresay he can afford it far more than you or I," Felicity said.

"I thought perhaps your family had come into money lately. How else could you have afforded a new wardrobe for Glee as well as the new dresses you have?"

"It's much easier to hang on to one's money when one's brother is not deep in play."

"I didn't know he had changed."

Felicity nodded. He hasn't gamed at all in the past week and had cut down considerably before that. You knew he sold his horse, did you not?" Felicity commended herself on her ability to skirt the truth about their source of income while not actually lying.

"So the proceeds from his horse bought your new dresses?" Carlotta said thoughtfully.

Let her think that. "Since there's no entertainment tonight, how will you inform everyone of the picnic?"

Carlotta thought on this a moment. "I believe I'll send around notes."

They came upon the Royal Crescent and then turned into the nearby park and strolled beneath the still-barren tree branches. As they were walking about the park, Thomas pulled up in his phaeton, got down, and tethered his horses. Then he joined them.

"I thought you had business matters to tend to today," Felicity said by way of a greeting.

"I just finished." He bowed to her first, then to Carlotta.

Carlotta's lavender eyes sparkled. "How fortuitous for us you were driving this way."

"Fortuitous for me," he said.

"I must tell you of my exciting scheme." Carlotta linked her arm through Thomas's. "Tomorrow we shall all go for a picnic at the Roman ruins in Hammersmith. Have you been there, Mr. Moreland?"

"No. How far away are they?"

She shrugged and glanced at Felicity. "How far would you say, Felicity?"

"An hour. No more."

He looked up at the skies. "I believe the rain has left us, and I think your scheme excellent. Should you like my cook to prepare the baskets?"

Felicity and Carlotta exchanged amused glances. "How very kind of you to offer," Carlotta purred.

"How many shall there be?" he asked.

"Eight," Felicity answered instantly. "Three from my family, two from yours, Mrs. Ennis, Mr. Blankenship, and Colonel Gordon."

At the last name Thomas frowned. "Must we invite all of them?"

"Yes," Felicity said with authority. Really, the two men were going to have to learn to get along with each other. After all, they traveled in the same circles and enjoyed the same group of friends.

"Let's see," he said, "you, Mrs. Ennis, know of it. And Mrs. Harrison can inform her brother and sister, and I can inform my sister. Who does that leave to inform?"

"Mr. Blankenship and the colonel," Felicity said.

"I'll send them notes," Carlotta offered.

"Could you not misplace the colonel's?" Thomas asked teasingly.

"You know how distressed he would be were Felicity to picnic without him. 'Twould surely break his heart. The man is totally besotted with her."

"Yes, I know," Thomas said grimly. "I had the dubious pleasure of spending the afternoon with him at Mrs. Harrison's house yesterday."

Carlotta pouted. "I shall be most jealous, Mr. Moreland, that you came to Mrs. Harrison's house yesterday and not to mine."

"By the time I left Mrs. Harrison's, it was far too late to call on you, my dear Mrs. Ennis."

"Whatever were you doing there for so long?" Carlotta asked.

Thomas shrugged. "Wearing out our welcome, I daresay."

They all laughed at that. Then Thomas offered Felicity his other arm.

She slipped her arm into his and became blazingly aware of his masculinity.

"You will be most proud of me, Mr. Moreland," Felicity said.

"Why is that?" he asked.

"Because I have memorized the words to your favorite Shakespearean sonnet."

A softness covered his tanned face. "Ah, Shall I Compare Thee to a Summer's Day?"

"I should ever so much love to hear you say the words, Mr. Moreland," Carlotta said.

He turned to Felicity. " 'Shall I compare thee to a summer's day? Thou art more lovely and more temperate. Rough winds do shake the darling buds of May, and summer's lease hath too short a date.' "

It *was* as if he said the words to her. About her. Oh, my. Felicity's heart beat faster with each word.

He recited the words to only half the sonnet, then turned to Carlotta. "I daresay I'm boring you to tears, Mrs. Ennis."

"You could never bore me," Carlotta protested. "And how true those words 'summer's lease hath too short a date.' "

They walked in silence for a moment before Carlotta said, "I declare, I never can remember sonnets, but I recall they were so rigidly constructed I positively marveled at those who could write them. Sixteen lines, are they not?"

"Fourteen," Thomas answered.

"Do you write poetry, Mr. Moreland?" Carlotta asked.

"I do not possess that talent."

"Mr. Moreland's talent is in memorization. He can recite poetry by heart and he has mastered several languages," Felicity said.

"I declare, Mr. Moreland, you are truly a marvel," Carlotta said with admiration.

Felicity began once again to long for that big handkerchief. Even more than that, she wished Carlotta to the devil and Thomas to herself.

"Not at all," Thomas protested. He turned to Felicity. "So you like my sonnet?"

" 'Tis lovely, but I wouldn't call it yours."

He laughed. "Are there others you admire?"

"Many. 'Herein lies wisdom, beauty, and increase; without this, folly, age and cold decay.' "

His eyes alive, he nodded knowingly. "A bit maudlin but very well written. Tell me, do you know *'Those Lips That Love's Hand Did Make'*?" he asked.

She smiled. "That followed it as gentle day doth follow night."

"Could you find Shakespeare's works in India?" Carlotta interrupted.

He shook his head. "I took my own."

"But surely you had no servants to carry trunks for you. I'd have thought you would merely have taken a single bag when you went to India."

"I did."

"How odd that you would choose to fill your limited space with books," Carlotta said incredulously. " 'Tis exactly the same with Felicity. I declare the entire time we were in Portugal she had her nose in a book."

Thomas turned to Felicity and smiled warmly.

On the way to Charles Street, Carlotta saw to it there was no more opportunity for Thomas to ignore her.

Twenty-seven

The next day dawned glorious and sunny for the picnic to Hammersmith, Thomas thought. The night before he had arranged that Mr. Blankenship call for the colonel, Carlotta, and Glee in his coach-and-four. Thomas would bring Dianna, George, and Felicity. He took perverse satisfaction in thinking of the colonel's wrath over the transportation arrangements.

If the colonel had wished Thomas dead before, he would surely want to run his sword through him now—especially if Thomas had his way this day.

Today I will make Felicity mine. Such thoughts enabled Thomas to greet his valet cheerily and assist the man in selecting an especially taking suit of clothing in shades of brown ranging from chocolate to milked coffee.

"I've never known you to be so particular in your choice of clothes before," the valet said. "Have you something special planned for today, sir?"

Thomas held out his arms for the valet to fasten his cuffs. "I do. If my plans go as I hope, perhaps I will become betrothed."

The valet's eyes widened. "I was not aware you had a special lady."

Thomas smiled. "She is indeed special."

Once he was dressed, he left the room. "Wish me luck, Hopkins."

Next, Thomas went downstairs to the kitchen to check his cook's progress in preparing their baskets. Already, she had lined up three baskets, each so full that plump loaves of bread poked over their tops.

"I see you don't need me to facilitate the eating plans," Thomas said with satisfaction to the cook.

The portly woman, an apron tied around her waist, looked up at him and smiled. "You did say to have enough food for eight, did you not, sir?"

"I did, indeed, and it looks as though none of us shall go hungry today. You have done a fine job, Meg."

"It wasn't just me," she said. "Jeremy fetched the oranges from the orangery for me. Eight of them. One for each of you."

"Excellent. By the way, did you find enough bottles of Bordeaux in the wine cellar?"

"Bryce did, sir. I've already packed 'em."

"Good."

Next, Thomas sent a maid to check on his sister's progress in dressing for the day, but it was Dianna herself who came back downstairs to assure him she was ready to leave.

He was only too happy to get into the coach. Soon he would see Felicity. She would actually sit beside him during the hour ride to Hammersmith.

He walked with his sister to the carriage, then sat across from her.

"Have you brought the baskets?" she asked.

"They're coming in a separate cart."

She nodded. "I can tell you're rather excited about the picnic. I am, too."

"I daresay you'd be excited over anything that would bring you together with Sedgewick for several hours."

She smiled shyly. "I daresay that's true, and I think you're being an ogre not to give us permission to marry."

"I hope my decision will only be temporary."

The coach turned onto Charles Street and came to a stop in front of Felicity's town house.

"Stay here, Dianna. We shouldn't be more than a moment." He hopped down and strode to Felicity's door.

Before he had the opportunity to knock, George swung the door open. "Ah, good day, Moreland," he said with a smile. "Isn't this picnic a deuced good idea?"

Thomas nodded. "You must thank Mrs. Ennis, for it was her scheme."

"I bloody well will," George said as he climbed into the coach with Dianna.

Felicity, wearing her blue dress again and crowned with a straw bonnet topped with hollyhocks and blue ribbons, glided down the stairs to him and gave him her hand. "Good day to you, Mr. Moreland."

He took her hand and turned it palm-side up, and gently kissed the warm cup of her hand. "Good day to you, Felicity. It's beautiful outside. Just like you."

Color crept up her cheeks as she moved with him toward the door. "I cannot believe Carlotta had so excellent a plan," she said, clearly intending to change the subject.

" 'Twas a very good idea." He helped Felicity into the carriage just as Mr. Blankenship's carriage drew up. He watched as Glee flew out the door and up to the open door of Blanks's coach, negating any need for Blanks to remove himself from his carriage to fetch her.

Thomas settled back in his seat next to Felicity. He saw that his sister and Sedgewick sat close to each other and were holding hands, which gave him an even more overwhelming urge to draw Felicity's hand within his. Instead, he turned to look at the perfection of her dimpled face. "You really do look quite lovely. I see you have taken my advice about wearing the blue. 'Tis the very color of your eyes."

He watched as the corners of her full mouth lifted into a smile, deepening her dimples. "I'm happy it pleases you," she murmured.

He seemed unable to remove his eyes from her sweet mouth. How he wanted to feel her lips upon his! His earlier taste of them had left him longing for more. His Felicity might look like an ice maiden with her silvery blond hair and steely blue eyes, but he knew better. Beneath her gracious exterior lay a woman of warmth and sensuous responses. He nearly trembled with his need for her.

He would not be able to wait much longer. *Soon.*

George really wasn't all that objectionable, Thomas thought, his resolve beginning to waver. If Sedgewick could avoid the gaming parlors, he would win Dianna's hand. Thomas watched the two of them.

"I respect him for doing what he thinks is best for his sister," George said. "Now I plan to live up to Miss Moreland's expectations."

It was almost unfathomable that anyone could love with the intensity he felt for Felicity, but if anyone could, it was Sedgewick.

On the way to Hammersmith, twists and turns jostled Felicity into him a number of times. Each time she would carefully scoot back to her side of the carriage. After half a dozen of these sharp turns and the successive reclaiming of her seat, she stayed close to him. Their thighs ran side by side, hers soft and slight, his hard and long.

Despite that it was daylight, he was to the point of boldly taking her hand into his, but then the coach came to a stop. They had arrived at the ruins. Behind their carriage, Blanks's carriage drew up, and they all streamed out of their conveyances like ants scattering from footsteps.

Thomas pulled his watch from his pocket. One o'clock. Everyone was sure to want to eat before exploring the ruins. He looked to see if the cart carrying the blankets and baskets was close and saw that it was only a two-minute drive away.

Even though Thomas had made arrangements for the food and transportation, Carlotta behaved as if the gathering were hers. She walked forward to a clearing unprotected from shade. "I think we'll set up here," she said decidedly.

Within a few minutes Thomas's footmen arrived and spread blankets on the spot selected by Carlotta. They returned to the cart and brought back the baskets, then one of them proceeded to lay out the food while the other uncorked each wine bottle and began to pour the wine into eight glasses.

In the meantime each of the eight claimed a spot on the blankets. Thomas waited until Felicity sat down, then he was able to beat the limping colonel and sit beside her. He completely expected the colonel to be shaking his cane at him, but he would not look.

Felicity tucked her feet under her skirts. Thomas's boots planted on the blanket, one knee level with his chest. While the footmen set food before each of them,

Thomas watched George and Dianna, who shared a blanket.

"Should you like cold mutton, my lord?" she asked George.

His finger brushed the tip of her nose. "You are to call me by my Christian name. And, yes, I would like the mutton."

Dianna smiled shyly and gave him a large portion from the plate the footman was passing around.

Thomas's glance flicked to Carlotta, who sat between Blanks and the colonel. His gaze then trailed to Glee, who sat with her sister on one side of her and Blanks on the other. The winsome look that had been on her excited countenance when she had flown to Blanks's carriage an hour earlier had been replaced with one of gloom. Thomas wondered if she was being snubbed by Blanks, who gave every indication of being smitten with Carlotta. It had occurred to Thomas on more than one occasion that Glee might be hiding tender feelings for her brother's best friend.

"Mrs. Ennis," Blanks said, leaning to peer into Carlotta's eyes, "I have never before noticed your eyes are lavender. In fact, I don't believe I've ever seen anyone with lavender eyes before."

It seemed to Thomas the reason Blankenship had never before noticed her unusual eyes was that he was too preoccupied with her generous bosom.

"They quite match your dress," Blanks added. "I say, do you always wear clothing that is purple or lavender or some such similar shade?"

A soothing smile passed over her exotic face. "I'm flattered that you noticed, Mr. Blankenship."

From his peripheral vision Thomas saw that the colonel, who had stretched his legs before him on the blanket, was already pouring himself a second glass of wine. Was he trying to cool his raging temper?

Thomas took two oranges, peeled one and handed it to Felicity. How he wished he could take the same proprietary role with her that George was taking with Dianna. *Soon,* he told himself.

Felicity's lashes lifted and she met Thomas's gaze before taking the orange from his outstretched hand, her fingers brushing against his. "Thank you, Mr. Moreland. 'Tis most kind of you."

"Kindness had nothing to do with it," the colonel barked angrily.

Everyone froze at his antagonistic remark. Only Glee seemed able to find her voice. "I beg to differ, Colonel. Mr. Moreland is a very kind man. Though he doesn't wish for people to know of his many acts of charity, I can testify to them."

His lips folded into a grim line, the colonel grabbed another wine bottle and poured his third glass.

"I declare," Carlotta said, "this is a most perfect day for a picnic in the country."

"That it is," Blanks agreed. "I understand this outing was your idea, Mrs. Ennis. I must say it was a very good one."

"Yes, I'm so very happy you planned this," Felicity said to Carlotta.

By now Felicity had finished her glass. "More wine?" Thomas asked her.

She looked up at him and nodded. Must everything she did have to be so damned seductive? 'Twas a trial indeed to be so close to her. So close he could see the rise and fall of her breasts and smell the intoxicating scent of her soft floral perfume.

Carlotta wistfully watched Dianna and George, then

sighed. "There's nothing as exciting as that first love. I'm terribly jealous of you, Miss Moreland."

"How do you know Sedgewick's her first?" the colonel asked, sneering.

George angrily went to get up, but Dianna stopped him with a hand across his chest, just as Felicity did with Thomas.

"I think you and I should take a stroll to the ruins," George said to Dianna, getting up and offering Dianna his hand. "I have a strong desire to be where the air is less offensive." He shot an angry glance at the colonel.

"Oh, dear," Carlotta said, "Lord Sedgewick did not even finish his food."

Thomas's glance flicked to the unfinished food on his sister's and George's plates, then to the colonel, whose eyelids appeared to be growing heavy.

Thomas took up a pair of hard cooked eggs, peeled one and handed it to Felicity.

Nothing could have given him greater pleasure than the smile that brightened her face when she took the egg from his hand. "You are much too kind, Mr. Moreland. I could become quite spoiled."

I would love to spoil you for the rest of my life. Though he wanted to say the words to her, he could not in front of the others. Not now. *Soon.*

Copying Thomas, Blanks took up an orange, peeled it and offered it to Carlotta, who gave him a most seductive look when she slowly withdrew it from his hands.

Thomas watched Glee for a reaction. Her tiny chest heaved, her eyes misted and she jerked her glance away from Blanks. Thomas saw, too, that her hands trembled. The poor girl.

I pity Blanks if he thinks Carlotta superior to Glee, Thomas thought.

Colonel Gordon leaned back on the blanket, propping himself on his elbows. His lids began to droop, and he jerked himself back to an upright position, only to repeat the pattern a moment later. Before long he stretched out on the blanket and went immediately to sleep.

Too much wine, Thomas thought. *Now I shall have Felicity to myself.* His heart began to pump erratically and his stomach coiled. He had never been so nervous in his life. Always before in all his endeavors he had moved to a swift conquest with the ease of a Goliath, but now he felt like a green country boy. As he had been the night he met Felicity.

He turned to her and watched as she finished the egg. "Would you like to explore the ruins now?" he asked.

"I should love to," she said.

He stood first, then helped her up.

Soon, he told himself.

Twenty-eight

When Felicity smoothed her skirts and then tucked her arm into his, Thomas actually felt like a Goliath. A Goliath bursting his buttons with pride. Never mind that winter's icy hand had stripped the color from the landscape. All that mattered was that he was with Felicity here and now. And the sun smiled down at them as they began to climb the hill to where the old Roman ruins had crumbled centuries ago.

"I never thought I'd be thanking the colonel for anything," Thomas said. "Whatever exorbitant price I paid for the Bordeaux, it was worth every shilling."

"You've been most uncharitable to Colonel Gordon, but today I, too, am vexed over his bitterness. His dislike of you makes him say wicked things to your sweet sister, and that I cannot abide."

"Then you think it permissible for him to malign me?" Thomas teased.

"No, but you can give tit for tat, which is quite alien to Miss Moreland's sweet nature."

Her face lifted to him and her eyes shone. It was the look one would give a lover. *Soon.* He grew nervous just pondering what he would say to her, how he would tell her that he was in love with her. Had she been cold to him he would not have had the courage to declare himself to someone so far above his touch, but he had reason to believe she was not without feeling toward him.

"Will you tell the colonel of your change of feelings toward him?" Thomas asked.

Felicity nodded. "It will be difficult, given his extreme kindnesses to me, but I think I shall."

They were within feet of the ruins now and winded from the uphill walk. Dianna and George were already leaving, going downhill toward the lake west of the ruins.

"It seems so strange to think people like you and me lived within those crumbling walls so many years ago," Felicity mused aloud, her gaze taking in the ruins that stretched before them. "People who worked and worshiped and loved . . ."

"And now they've lain in graves for more years than there's been an England."

Her hand pressed into the flesh of his arm. "Please don't be maudlin. Not today."

Thomas stopped and looked down at her. "I assure you that's the last thing I want to be today."

In silence, they walked closer to the main building. All that remained was a stone frame from which all wood had rotted or been stripped long ago. Many of the walls had fallen into heaps of rock, which had been overgrown with dirt and weeds and wildflowers that were yet to bloom. He took her hand so she could step into the main building over a wall that was no more than a foot high now.

Then Thomas, too, stepped over the smooth rocks and captured her hand once more. Hand in hand, they walked through abandoned rooms, now inhabited only by a nest of birds, the blue sky their ceiling.

"It makes our lives seem so insignificant when you

realize how many people have gone before us, people who have long been forgotten," she said.

"Now, who's being maudlin?" he said cheerfully. "Though there is nothing insignificant about you, Felicity."

She gave a little laugh and walked into the next room. "What do you suppose this room was used for, Thomas?"

His pulse accelerated. She had called him Thomas. With that one word she had lowered the barrier between them. There were still other barriers he wished to remove. *Soon,* he told himself. "If you'll look," he said, "you can see there was once a wide chimney here. It would not surprise me if this was formerly a kitchen."

Her blue eyes met his. "You have a very fine mind," she said in a low voice filled with admiration. "I wish people like the colonel understood that you are not only as good as them, but better than most."

She stood in the corner of the room that had been a kitchen. Shade from the sturdy walls put her in shadow, though the silvery shimmer of her hair would not be dulled. Wordlessly, he walked toward her and lifted her hand to press his lips against it. She allowed him to continue kissing her hand as though it were something to be worshiped, and when he raised his face he saw the hunger burning in her eyes. That she had not stopped him must mean she did not find it objectionable. Which was good. Very good.

He seemed unable to remove his gaze from hers. "You must know how deeply I care for you," he said throatily.

A solemn nod was her only response.

That was enough. He moved closer to her, backing her farther into the corner, and bent to taste her lips.

Lips that readily parted for him. Waves of sensual pleasure washed over him as he drew in her floral scent and felt the moistening that filmed on her satin skin. He settled his arms around her, buffering her back from colliding against the cold stone wall. The kiss continued, and he realized she whimpered with each new breath.

He grew so wretchedly hot. And breathless. He had never wanted anything as he wanted her. Here and now. Vibrant life sprang to his groin, and he moved even closer to her. Like the last time they danced together, 'twas as if she were a continuation of himself, this time joined at the mouth. She sucked at his lower lip; then he began to drop soft kisses on her eyes, her mouth, her nose, her graceful neck, and lower still.

He began to unbutton her pelisse, and she made no move to stop him. Which was good. He continued, button by agonizing button; then he lowered the bodice of her dress, allowing one breast to spill out. He bent to kiss it. Reverently. He closed his mouth around her nipple and she cried out with pleasure.

Her lower torso cleaved to his. His Felicity was no maiden. She had lain with a man before. She knew what she was doing to him with her incessant grinding motion. She wanted to make love with him.

But he could not take her here. His Felicity should lie with him on a bed fit for a queen, should lie with him as the wife he would cherish eternally.

Then Felicity did something that swiftly and completely destroyed his resolve. She fitted her hand to his arousal. *She wants me.* A chorus of angels should be singing in the skies around them.

As she slid her hand along the length of him, he knew he could stand it no longer. Over her skirts he began to knead the juncture of her thighs. She whimpered deeper now.

He began to nudge up her skirt slowly until his hand slipped beneath the hem. As he stroked the silken skin of her inner thighs, she parted her legs.

It was as if his whole life had been in darkness until this minute when the sun seemed blazingly hot and a molten heat surged within him. He looked down at her face. His Felicity's. Her lids were lowered, her lips sucking the linen that covered his shoulders, her breath unsteady, labored.

Soon his fingers slipped into her. *There.* She was warm and slick. And welcoming.

He adjusted his breeches, then replaced his hand, planting himself within her. She frantically moved her hips to meet him. He came fast and hard, his breath vibrating within the walls of his chest.

It must be the wine, Felicity told herself as she languidly allowed Thomas to feast on her hand. With each soft kiss, she had grown more sexually aware of him. She longed to feel herself against him as close as skin to his muscled body, to feel her fingers sliding through the black hair on his bare chest. To feel his pulse deep within her.

Then when he had kissed her, it had been she who boldly parted her lips. But she still had not succumbed completely to her physical yearning. Then her thoughts trailed to the days when she thought she had lost him to Carlotta, had thought to never again feel his lips against hers. She had begged to have another chance, and now she basked in the sensuousness of Thomas Moreland. Her second chance had come.

This moment of passionate pleasure compensated for

the years she had been cloaked in grief. *Thomas cares!* She kept telling herself. *Thomas cares for me!* Nothing else mattered. No one else existed, save her dark lover.

Yet she found even the long desired kiss was not enough. She wanted more. She wanted to feel him within her more than she had ever wanted anything. Only that would complete their union. Hers and Thomas's. They had to be one.

Yes, it was surely the wine that made her forget she was a lady, forget that they were not in a private place. All that mattered at the moment was that Thomas take possession of her. It most certainly must be the wine that was urging her to act so recklessly.

She was powerless to resist when his fingers moved to unfasten her pelisse. And when he closed his lips over her breast, she thought she would ignite from the swirling heat that consumed her.

Now that she felt Thomas's lifeblood pumping into her, she could no more stop it than she could pluck the stars from the night skies. Even if she *had* wanted it to stop. Which she didn't.

Soon she felt Thomas's essence begin to slip down her thighs, and still she could not bring herself to part from him. This—being within Thomas's arms, joined at the bottom of their torsos—was where she had dreamed of being. She could not bear to stop it even when their rhythm slowed and their breathing returned to normal.

Then Thomas suddenly pulled away, hurriedly readjusting his breeches and smoothing down her skirt. "Someone's coming!" he warned, urgency in his voice.

She stood still and listened, then heard Carlotta's laughter. Thank God, Thomas had heard. How shocking it would have looked for her to be seen with her skirts up, Thomas taking his pleasure from her.

Then out of the blue, the wantonness of her own actions hit her like a bucket of ice water.

Her mouth opened and she gazed at Thomas with watery eyes. "What you must think of me," she murmured, her eyes lowered in shame.

He moved to her and lifted her chin possessively. "I love you. You're the most wonderful woman I've ever known."

She slapped his hand away as tears sprang to her eyes. "Please leave me alone," she hissed, pulling up the hem of her skirt and taking off at a run.

The colonel dreamed of Felicity. She greedily lifted her lips, but it wasn't him who tasted them. Something deep and depressing gnawed at him. Then he realized what it was. Felicity would not kiss him. The Upstart had stolen her kisses and her heart.

He jerked awake and sat up, only to discover he had been dreaming. He saw that all the blankets were empty. Everyone had gone to see the ruins. No doubt Felicity was enjoying them this very minute with the Upstart. Damn.

His gaze drifted to the hill to where the ruins stood, and he saw a blond woman in blue running down the hill toward him. Felicity.

As she drew closer, he saw that her pelisse gaped open where it had been buttoned.

And he knew.

He would have to act fast.

Twenty-nine

It was the wine, Felicity told herself as she sat on the blanket and solemnly watched Thomas start down the hill. How else could she explain her reckless behavior? What terrible things must Thomas think of her! Certainly, he had told her he loved her, but what man wouldn't say those words to a woman who had just given him total access to her body?

Michael had told her about the sexual drives of men. Nay, he had done more than tell her, he had showed her. Making love was something men never tired of. They were not like women. Michael had said that most men did not even have to be in love with the woman to lie with her.

Thomas Moreland was most certainly a man. More of one than anyone she had ever known. Even Michael. Thomas must have lain with many women of easy virtue. Women like her, she thought morosely. Surely she had lost him with her foolish lack of control. What gentleman would wish to align himself with a harlot like her?

"I wish to ride home in Mr. Blankenship's carriage," Felicity told the colonel.

"Then I shall look forward to the journey," Gordon answered.

Perhaps it was the alcohol that dulled his response,

for the colonel's voice lacked the usual jubilation that inflected his words when she was favoring him with her company. *Could he know? About Thomas and me?*

When Thomas came back to the blanket area, he sat beside Felicity again and poured himself a glass of wine. "More wine, Mrs. Harrison? Colonel?"

"I think the colonel and I both have had far more than we should have."

"Yes," the colonel said, "I suppose that is what made my eyelids so devilishly heavy."

Thomas's face was grim. "It certainly can do that."

If only the wine had affected her as it had affected the colonel, she lamented. But, oh no, it had turned her into a trollop!

Soon Blanks returned with Carlotta and Glee. Carlotta was laughing and animated; Glee, quiet and solemn.

"I believe I would like to ride back in your coach," Felicity told Blanks.

"Then I will swap places with you," Glee snapped.

Her brows sinking, Felicity gazed at her sister. Whatever could have made her so solemn? She had been in the best of spirits this morning.

Then so had Felicity. Now she could gladly hide her face so she wouldn't have to see Thomas. After she had . . . Oh, how could she have been so devoid of propriety?

It was not just the wine. Thomas's touch had the power to make her lose all sense of right and wrong. After all, the line separating good from bad was so insignificant, especially when she was with Thomas. She had only herself to blame for her wanton behavior.

Another five minutes passed before George and Dianna returned. With misty eyes, Felicity noticed that Dianna's pelisse also had been unbuttoned. Then Felicity suddenly realized she had not taken time to re-fasten hers. A quick glance at her chest confirmed the disappointing reality. It was too late to fasten it now. There was only one thing to do. She must pretend to be terribly hot.

"I daresay walking up those hills will make one quite hot. Is that not correct, Dianna?"

Dianna's glance flickered to her open pelisse. "Yes, I became terribly hot myself."

"Well, I thought it was most pleasant," Carlotta countered.

It was obvious Carlotta had not broken a sweat.

Blanks turned to Glee. "Did you find it hot, Miss Pembroke?"

"I was quite comfortable, thank you."

Whatever had made Glee so very curt and glum? Surely she hadn't seen Felicity and Thomas.

"I see that my footmen have cleaned up the leavings of our picnic," Thomas remarked.

"Well, we've eaten and we've hiked to the ruins," Blanks said. "Anyone ready to return to Bath?"

"I should think all of us are," the colonel said. His voice lacked the bitterness that had been in it earlier in the afternoon.

As Felicity sat there still moistened from Thomas's essence, she prayed it would not bleed through her skirts. She prayed, too, that she would not have to sit beside him much longer. She needed to be away from him. Away from his debilitating presence and the wantonness he evoked in her.

Thomas was the first to get up. He offered Glee his hand, then George and Dianna followed. Felicity stood and, with tightened chest and misty eyes, watched them walk to Thomas's carriage.

With lead in her steps, she walked beside the colonel, who followed Blanks to his coach.

On the return to Bath, Felicity spoke little and gave no encouragement to the colonel, who tried to engage her in conversation. She ignored Blanks's flirting with Carlotta, her own thoughts on the strange union that had occurred between Thomas and herself.

Her cheeks flamed as she remembered the way her hand had curled around him, below his waist. He must think her very fast indeed. With her galling behavior, she surely had lost his affections.

When Blanks's carriage drew up at her town house, she flew into her house, ran upstairs to her chamber, and bolted the door behind her. She wanted no intrusion. In fact, all she wanted at this moment was to never have to face Thomas again. She would have to leave Bath. But how could she? She *did* have the settlement from Thomas. Of course, she could no longer accept it. Not now. Now that she had truly earned the settlement as surely as a mistress earned her keep. Heat spread up her cheeks.

No, she could never face Thomas again. Wanton creature that she was.

An hour later, Stanton informed her that Thomas was downstairs, begging to speak to her.

"Tell him I am not in," Felicity instructed.

Her answer was the same the following day when Thomas called. She dared not leave her home for fear of having to face him. Would she never breathe fresh air again?

It had been three days since Felicity had so freely given herself to him. Three days of hell. How could an act that was so wondrous bring him such agony?

Did Felicity—his Felicity—not understand how deeply he loved her? Worshiped the ground she trod?

Did she not realize that since she had given herself to him so completely, he loved her even more than he had thought possible? With every breath he drew, he thought of her. Longed for her.

Yet she had refused to see him. He'd come to her door every morning and every afternoon, and each time the butler conveyed the same lie. *Mrs. Harrison is not in.*

Finally he had broken down and written her a long letter in which he tried to capture the depth of his feelings toward her. It had taken him all of one long, tortured night to write it. It had to emphasize how dear she was to him—even more now that she had allowed him to love her so thoroughly.

When a day passed and he had no answer and was still being barred from seeing her, he realized she must have thrown his unopened letter upon her fire. She would not bend to his will. Ever again.

He grew desperate to see her. There was nothing to do but to throw himself on George's mercy. With that thought, Thomas went to his big desk and withdrew a sheet of vellum and began to spill his heart onto the pages of a letter to his beloved's brother. Then he read the letter and decided to tear it up. Far better to speak to Sedgewick himself.

Though it was nine o'clock at night, he called for his horse and donned his greatcoat. Ten minutes later, he was rapping at the door of the Charles Street house.

"Mrs. Harrison is not in," the butler told him.

"It's not Mrs. Harrison I wish to see," Thomas answered. "I have come to speak to her brother."

A look of mistrust on his aging face, Stanton eased

open the door. "Please take a seat in the library. I will tell Lord Sedgewick you are here."

Thomas was pleased Sedgewick wasn't out with Blankenship tonight. A moment later, George entered the chamber, glanced at Thomas and grew alarmed. "Is everything all right?"

Thomas smiled. "Everything is all right with my sister. I wish I could say the same for me."

George's brows drew together in concern. "What's the problem? Anything I can help with?"

Thomas gave a bitter laugh. "My problem is your stubborn sister."

George shrugged, then sat down near Thomas. "Don't know why she's refusing to see you again, old chap. Then, I'd be enormously rich if I possessed knowledge of the female mind. Any number of men would beg to purchase such."

"I would, though I believe I know why your sister refuses to see me."

"Do you, now?" Clearly, George expected forthcoming elaboration.

All Thomas did was nod. "I have come here tonight to throw myself upon your mercy."

"My mercy?" George asked quizzically.

"I need for you to convey a message to Felicity from me."

"I will be happy to."

"I want you to tell her I love her. I've never loved anyone but her. I've loved her since the night I met her." He stopped for a moment, then cleared his throat. "Tell her since the day at the ruins I love her more than I ever thought it possible to love another being. Tell her I want to marry her and to be hers to command for all eternity."

"Don't see how my sister could turn a cold shoulder

to that eloquence." George stood up. "I better fetch paper and write all this down. Don't want to forget anything vital."

He was back a moment later, quill and paper in hand. He stood with the paper on the liquor cabinet's surface and began to write. "First point. You love her. Second point. Always have. Third point—"

Thomas interrupted. "Second point is I have always loved her since the first night I met her."

George nodded. "Quite so. Let me add that." He wrote for a moment, then said, "Third point, since what happened at the ruins, you love her more than ever." George sent Thomas a shimmering, admiring gaze. "Is that correct?"

"It is."

"The fourth point is you want to marry her. Fifth point, you want to live forever with her. Does that cover everything?"

"Everything except when I can expect you to impart the information to her. You must realize I'm on tenterhooks."

"Quite so, I expect. I can only say I'm grateful your sister is not given to the flights my sisters are. In answer to your question, expect her to receive your message no later than tomorrow morning. I'll try to speak with her tonight, but you know how unpredictable women are."

Thomas smiled. "Will you tell Felicity to send me a reply? If it's in the affirmative, I shall fly here to propose on bended knee."

George folded the paper. "I'll tell her all of that."

Even though it had been three days, Felicity's door was still barred. Only Lettie had been allowed in to bring Felicity modest meals, even though Felicity protested that she wanted to die. Such thoughts, however, did not actually extend to refusing *all* food.

George knocked at her chamber door.

"Who is it?" she demanded in an agitated voice.

"It's George. I have to talk to you."

She crossed the room and opened the door to him. He strolled into her room and plopped on her bed.

She faced him, sincerely hoping nothing had happened to cause a rift between himself and Miss Moreland. "What did you want to talk to me about?"

"Moreland has just left." He pulled his paper from his pocket and unfolded it.

"I will not listen to anything he has to say," she protested.

"This ain't a letter for you, I'll have you know."

Her brows arched.

"I'll make this quick, and you must listen carefully." His glance flickered to the paper for the briefest of seconds, then he looked back to her. "Moreland's in love with you. Has been since the first night he met you. He says he loves you even more since what happened at the ruins, and he wants to marry you and have you—no, make that, have each other—for all eternity."

He looked up and saw the watery pools shimmering around her eyes. "What's wrong, pet?"

"Can't you see? He feels compelled to offer for me because he feels he has compromised my good name."

"Oh, dear," George said, unable to meet his sister's stare. "I never thought of it that way." He sat quietly for a moment. "But I'll swear that's not it, pet. He told me the day I asked for Dianna's hand that he was in love with you."

"He did?"

"He did indeed. Can you not believe him?"

Tears began to trickle down her fair cheeks, but she made no move to wipe them. "I don't know what to believe. Think of it from my point of view. I cannot accept a man whose offer comes only from gallantry."

" 'Tis not gallantry, Sis. The man truly loves you and has since he met you. If you must know, he looks wretched. I'll wager he's not slept these past three nights. He begs you send him a response. If he's anything like I was the day I begged for Dianna's hand, he would likely walk through a snowstorm to get it."

Felicity moved to hug her brother. "Thank you for coming. You've made my heart far less heavy." She stepped back and looked at him and realized she had experienced no shame when she all but told her brother she and Thomas had made love. "I will give him my response tomorrow."

Thirty

After George left, Felicity pondered over the fact she had been without embarrassment when she had told her brother she had lain with Thomas. Could that mean something? Was what had happened between Thomas and her really not so terrible after all, given that they loved each other? For she knew without doubt she loved him, and she was beginning to understand that he must love her in the same way.

As she lay down to sleep, hope bubbled in her bruised heart. Tomorrow she would tell her Thomas the truth. That she loved him as she had never loved Michael. As she never knew she could love a man. Tomorrow, her Thomas would ask her to become his wife.

And she would accept.

With such happy thoughts, she drifted off to sleep for the first time in four days.

When she woke to clear skies the following morning, she allowed Lettie to dress her in the blue silk. 'Twas beginning to look as much her uniform as Lord Nelson's red coat. Then Stanton rapped at her chamber door.

Her chest felt lighter than air. She could soar to the heavens. Thomas was here. "Yes?" she answered in a melodious voice. Thomas had come.

"You have a caller, madam. Colonel Gordon."

Her chest fell as if whacked by falling timber. It wasn't Thomas. Only Colonel Gordon. She would tell the colonel today she did not wish to see him anymore. After all, she would soon wed his fiercest rival.

Even if she never spoke to her beloved Thomas again, she knew she could no longer maintain a friendship with a man as bitter and mean-spirited as Colonel Gordon.

"I'll be right down," she said, her voice heavy.

It was more imperative than ever that she dispatch Colonel Gordon as soon as possible. Thomas would likely be calling before afternoon.

When she entered the drawing room, his cane stabbed the rug, and Colonel Gordon pulled himself up to greet her.

"Sit back, Colonel," she said, not deigning to allow him to kiss her hand today. She sat on the nearby settee and looked at him, noticing distress on his face. "Are you all right?" she asked.

"I am fine, my dear, but I have somewhat stressful news to impart."

She lifted her brows.

"You'll remember Sergeant Fordyce and his wife from Portugal?"

"I do. Beth Fordyce was a particularly good friend of mine. They don't live far from Bath, do they?"

"Only a two-hour drive."

Her brows lowered. "Pray, what distressing news have you brought?"

"I've had a letter from Mrs. Fordyce. It's very sad, my dear. She informs me her husband is gravely ill and not expected to live."

A shadow passed over Felicity's face. "But he was no older than Michael . . ."

"I know," the colonel said. "Such a pity, really. It would seem from her letter that he has been calling for you. Claims he has to tell you Captain Harrison's dying words before he can go to his own reward."

"But Sergeant Fordyce wasn't with Michael when he died!" Felicity challenged.

"Actually, he was." The colonel's delivery was as solemn as a death knell. "Sergeant Fordyce thought if you heard your husband's dying words, it would push you over the edge. Your grief, you'll remember, was quite great."

What could Michael have been wanting to tell her? Why hadn't the sergeant come forward before now? "It's been four years, I believe I can handle his message now." Especially now that she had Thomas.

His hand gripped the silver handle of the cane beside him. "Exactly as I wrote to Mrs. Fordyce."

"What *exactly* did you write to Beth?" Felicity asked, her eyes narrowing suspiciously.

"I wrote to tell her I would bring you to them today. It's not yet ten. If we leave now, we can be back this afternoon."

She sighed. What a horrid decision she was being forced to make! This was the very day she was to give her answer to Thomas. The day she would get to see him again. However . . . she *could* send him her response and ask him to call in the afternoon. "Very well," she said. "Allow me to fetch my pelisse and tell my family where I'm going. The Fordyces live in Blye, do they not?"

"They do."

Felicity scurried upstairs and sat at the desk in her

chamber, where she penned a note to Thomas. Her message was brief:

> Dearest Thomas,
> My answer is yes. Please call at Charles Street this afternoon.
> All my love,
> F.

She folded it up, then got her pelisse and bonnet, the same she had worn to the ruins that day Thomas and she had . . . She swallowed, remembering his smooth touch and the bliss that overcame her whenever he touched her.

She heard George stirring in his room, and she knocked at his door. "George," she called.

He opened the door and stood before her, shirtless and wearing only his breeches. "Yes?"

"I must go to Blye with the colonel to see my old friends from Portugal, Sergeant and Beth Fordyce. Sarge is gravely ill and asking for me, Colonel Gordon said. We'll be back this afternoon." She handed him the letter for Thomas. "Please have this delivered to Thomas this morning."

Frowning, he took the letter. "I don't like you going off with the colonel. In fact, I don't like you associating with him at all. He's not right in the head, if you ask me. He's nothing but a bitter old man."

"I'll not argue with you," she countered. "In fact, I plan to terminate my friendship with him today."

"Good," he said, "tell him now so you won't have to go with him."

"But I do. It's not for him I go but for the Fordyces. We were the best of friends in Portugal."

"I cannot talk you out of it?"

"You cannot."

He solemnly watched her as she turned to go downstairs. He should have told her to wait until he dressed so he could go with her.

Anger welled within the colonel as he watched Felicity sitting across the carriage from him, stiff as a poker. Certainly different than she sat when she was with the Upstart. Then he smiled a bitter smile. *Soon she'll be mine.* It did not matter to him that she carried to their union her love for another man. All that mattered to him was the union. The union he had longed for for five years. The union that had caused him to kill—and to maim himself.

Felicity would be worth all of it, he told himself. He imagined removing her clothing, piece by exciting piece. He had dreamed of it for so long, and now he was so close. This first time, the potions he would slip into her drink would assure her drugged compliance. After that, she would be forced to admit she belonged to him. He would see to it that no one else would ever claim his Felicity.

She had sat gazing from the coach window for two hours now, with hardly a word for him. At noon, she began to grow suspicious. "Haven't we come to Blye yet? Surely it's been more than two hours."

"Soon," he said.

Then his bright red coach pulled alongside the Bull Pit Inn.

Felicity glared at him. "Why are we stopping here?"

"We mustn't barge in on Mrs. Fordyce with hungry bellies. The woman has enough on her mind as it is. We'll have a bit of a repast here, then we'll move along toward Blye. It shouldn't be far now."

He was keenly aware of Felicity's lack of response and the anger that flashed across her face. Yes, it was a very good thing he was abducting her today. Today, before he completely lost her to that brute of a man who smelled of the shop.

His man bespoke a private parlor for them. Felicity slapped herself down on a wooden bench in front of a matching wooden table and glared at him across the table in the darkened room.

"Just a quick bite," he reminded her. "I think a bowl of hot soup would be just what we need to tide us over for the visit, which surely promises to be wrenching."

" 'Twould be potato soup today," the innkeeper's wife told them as she brought each of them a bumper of ale.

Felicity removed her bonnet and set it on the left side of the trestle table, close enough to the edge of the table that his cane could drag it to the very edge. And over.

She blew on the steaming soup, then began to swallow it, unaware that the colonel's cane scooted her bonnet over a hair at a time until it plunged off the side of the table.

"Oh, dear me," the colonel said. "My cane has gone and knocked your hat off the table, my dear."

She glanced up quickly at him, saw the cane, then said, "I'll get it."

As she bent for the hat, he removed the lid from a small bottle and sprinkled his potion into her soup, using her own spoon to stir it.

She set her bonnet back on the table, then took another spoonful of soup. Then another. She yawned once. Then again.

He smiled.

He would soon carry her to the upstairs room his coachman had procured for them. Then later, after he had his way with her, the preacher would come and say the words that would make her his.

When she awoke he would tell her she had drunk too much ale, so much, in fact, that she had consented to become his wife. And it just so happened he had in his pocket a special license.

After reading Felicity's note, Thomas was donning his best black frock coat. He had read and reread her letter a dozen times, his heart leaping with unbound joy. *She's going to be mine!* Of course, he would be unable to wait until afternoon to see her. He would go there straightaway this morning.

It came as a surprise when Bryce told him he had a caller. Felicity had not said she would call on him. This was even better than he had hoped! All these thoughts flitted through his mind before Bryce added, "A Mr. Brown to see you, sir."

The Bow Street runner! Thomas's spirits fell. What could have happened to make the runner come here when he was supposed to be following Colonel Gordon?

Thomas hastened downstairs and met the man in his library. "Have a seat," Thomas said.

"I canna, sir." The man sounded winded. As if he had been running. "The colonel left the Charles Street house with Mrs. Harrison more 'n half an hour ago, and like you told me, I followed. To my surprise, his bright red coach just kept on going. We left Bath, then Chippenham. Then I knew I'd best get back here and tell you."

Thomas jerked his watch from his pocket. "What time did they leave her town house?"

The man looked at his own watch. " 'Twas half past nine."

It was half past ten now. Thomas cursed and began to storm from the room. "Which road did they take? Is Chippenham not on the way to the North Road?"

"It is."

Thomas froze. *Gretna Green.* But Felicity had told him just yesterday she would sever her relationship with the colonel. Then why had she gotten into the carriage with him? His heart hammered so loudly he could hardly think. He yelled for his butler and told Bryce, when he entered the library, to have his horse brought around immediately.

He looked once again at the runner. "Did Mrs. Harrison go willingly?"

"She did, but she did not look to be in especially good spirits."

Good Lord, what had the man said to her? Did he plan to . . . Thomas could not think on it. He had to take action to prevent it from happening.

"You take the London road, I'll take the North. Whatever you do, you must get her away from that beast," Thomas barked.

"I give you my word," the man said.

Thomas took a pistol from his wall and asked Bryce to bring his shot.

When his pistol was loaded, he and Brown left the house, leaped on their horses, and were off.

Thomas thanked God he had a fast mount. And thanked him even more that he was as good a rider as there was. Even so, 'twould be most difficult to gain on a coach that had an hour on him. He dug in his heels, and Thunder blazed ahead.

Thomas tried to put his mind into the devious colonel's. Then with a jolt to his insides, he remembered Colonel Gordon was a madman. He had likely killed once for Felicity. A sickening fear settled into Thomas like strong whiskey. What if the monster planned to do Felicity harm? Why hadn't he warned her about Gordon?

He cracked his whip, and Thunder went even faster. He had to get Felicity before . . . it was too late. Pain seared through him.

Thirty-one

Now suitably dressed for the day, George scrambled down the stairs. He would walk the three miles to Winston Hall and see his beloved today.

A knock sounded at the front door, and Stanton answered it.

A woman's voice spoke. "Beth Fordyce and Sergeant Fordyce to see Mrs. Harrison."

George froze halfway down the stairs. *What the bloody hell?* Then gathering his senses about him, he stopped Stanton from sending the couple away. "Wait! Please tell them to come in." He took the rest of the stairs two at a time.

He didn't give Stanton a chance to seat them in the morning room but stopped them in the entry hall. He eyed the tall man, who must be Sergeant Fordyce. "You are Sergeant Fordyce?"

The man not only looked perfectly healthy, but he sounded so as well when he answered. "I am."

"But my sister—Mrs. Harrison—was told you are gravely ill. She has gone off to Blye with Colonel Gordon."

The sergeant's eyes narrowed. "Who could have told your sister such a lie?"

"I believe Colonel Gordon received a letter from your wife," George said.

Mrs. Fordyce's mouth dropped open.

"That's ridiculous! My wife would never write to the man. I don't like him, and well she knows it."

"Truly, I didn't," Mrs. Fordyce said. "I didn't even know he was in Bath."

George muttered an oath. "I shouldn't have let her go off with that man. I knew he was mentally unbalanced."

"Do you think he's abducted Mrs. Harrison?" the sergeant asked, his brows lowered in concern.

The recent picnic flashed through George's mind. Even before Felicity had told him she had given herself to Moreland, he had known. And if he knew, the colonel—who had lived and breathed for Felicity all these years—would also have known. "Of course! He's abducted her." The thought was like a kick in his gut.

The sergeant started for the door. "Come on, man, my carriage is outside. We must go after the fiend."

"Wait," George said, "while I fetch my father's pistol."

Felicity's mouth gaped open in a huge yawn. "I don't know why I'm so sleepy. I had a good night's sleep last night."

The colonel watched the firelight from the private parlor's hearth play on her lovely face. "I daresay the fresh air outside will wake you. Come, my dear, finish your soup."

Even though the soup was no longer hot, she blew into the full bowl of her spoon, then swallowed another spoonful.

His eyes danced as he watched her grow sleepier and sleepier. *Soon.*

The innkeeper's wife returned to their table. "Anything else I can fetch for you?"

"Yes, two more bumpers," he said.

"I don't know," Felicity interrupted. "The ale must be what's making me so sleepy."

"Nonsense, my dear. All you need is fresh air," he said.

The innkeeper's wife raised her brows. "How many ales will it be, sir?"

"Two," he said emphatically.

He watched greedily as Felicity finished the last of her soup. *Soon.*

The aproned woman returned with their ale, then left them alone in the room.

Felicity's arm moved slowly to bring the bumper to her lips. She tried to take a swallow but was unable to do so. Her lids began to droop. "I don't know what's wrong with—"

She was unable to finish her sentence. The ale spilled over her dress, and she collapsed onto the bench, stretching out as if it were a bed.

The colonel jumped up and, using the table as a crutch, moved to her. Speed was essential. The innkeeper's wife must not see Felicity like this. He bent over her, fastening one arm under her and pulling her up, then he stood with her flopping at his side like a limp cloth doll.

Because of his bad leg, he would not be able to make it upstairs with her. He couldn't hold her and a cane, too. It wouldn't do at all to fall down. It would be bloody hell to get back up.

Where in the hell was his coachman? He'd told the fellow to come back in half an hour. There was nothing to do but to try to struggle along with her. He could lean into the wall. If he could just round the corner, he could make it to the stairway with her. Then he could hold on to the banister as he pulled them up, stair by stair, to the chamber reserved for Colonel and Mrs. Gordon. The problem would be holding on to the rail with one hand and her with the other. Even though she was slight of build, she was far from being featherlight. A pity he didn't have three hands.

His greatcoat flapping behind him like a sailing kite, Thomas spurred his mount forward. He prayed the colonel had not switched coaches. That bright red coach would serve as a beacon signaling his presence. Which would save Thomas the effort of having to stop and make inquiries at every posting inn along the way. He would keep going until he saw the madman's red coach. He prayed he wouldn't be too late.

Though he traveled at a breakneck pace, Thomas's progress was impeded by the frequency of villages along the road. He had to ride through each one, look-ing for the colonel's distinctive coach. There were few coaches to be seen, and all of them were black. He even rode by the livery stables and glanced inside to see if the colonel had hidden his coach within.

The villages began to run together in Thomas's mind. One after another, all with inns and stables. And no sign of the colonel's vehicle.

On leaving each village, Thomas would ride like the wind to make up for lost time. Then there would be another village. And more lost time.

And no sign of his precious Felicity.

The farther he went, the stronger his conviction the colonel had indeed abducted Felicity. What heinous scheme did the colonel plan? White-hot fear flooded Thomas. He told himself he could accept anything that had been done to her. Anything but death. And he sorely feared the colonel would kill her before he would let another man have her.

Had the colonel guessed that she had made love to Thomas at the ruins? In a blissful stupor of recollection, Thomas remembered that her pelisse had been unfastened. Her skirts, too, were likely wrinkled, where he had hiked them up. In front. Still, that memory had the power to weaken him. He remembered, too, how embarrassed she had been when she had run away—back to the blankets. Where the wakened colonel had witnessed everything. With violently wrenching resignation, Thomas realized the colonel *knew*.

Thomas blazed along a road lined with an alley of trees; then he came to still another village, the name of which he did not know. When he slowed down at signs of habitation, he looked far and wide for the colonel's carriage, but it was not in this village. He rode past the livery stable and cast a glance inside. It held but a dozen horses. He continued on through the village, saw nothing, then turned and raced back down the main street and back to the North Road.

He hadn't gone more than a mile when Thunder came up lame.

To get a full panoramic view, George sat up on the box with the sergeant's coachman. That way he would be assured of spotting the colonel's gaudy red coach. With each clop of the hooves, George cursed himself. *Why did I let her go? How could I have been so bloody stupid?* He knew what the colonel was, yet he'd allowed his sister to run off with the monster. If he couldn't prevent her from going, he should at least have insisted on going with her. *If anything happens to her, I'll* . . . Not since his father had died suddenly had George been swamped with such feelings of raw hurt. But this time, he had only himself to blame for the grief. *If only* . . .

He recalled the colonel's intense bitterness the day they went to the ruins. And realized the colonel knew Felicity loved Moreland—had probably guessed that she and Moreland had made love in the ruins. And the vicious man had now stolen Felicity away. The question was, Did the colonel plan to force himself on Felicity, or kill her?

For George knew without a doubt that the madman was capable of both. He only prayed Gordon's love for Felicity would spare her life.

Fortunately, the sergeant's coachman could skillfully handle the cattle at so grueling a speed. They swung through each of the succession of villages that dotted the North Road. And in none of them was the colonel's coach visible.

George prayed he wouldn't be too late. *Too late for what?* What *did* the colonel have planned for Felicity? George sombered, thinking of his sweet sister, who always put him and Glee before herself. She had never in her life done anything that would warrant so cruel a fate. She'd had so little happiness in her short life. Harrison's death was cruel enough a blow for one woman to bear. And just as she was at the precipice of finding true happiness with Moreland, who would cherish her as George cherished his Dianna, the colonel planned . . . What?

If only I can get to her in time.

Then, remembering that Colonel Gordon had an hour on them, George issued an oath.

* * *

Colonel Gordon had never before realized his Felicity was so very heavy. He had thought he knew her as one knows his own face. He knew the very size of her ripe breasts. And her tiny waist. In his chamber on the darkest night, he could picture her blond hair with each of its silvery, shimmery strands. Yet he had not known she would be so difficult to carry.

His arm ached from holding the dead weight of her body. Where was his damned man? He had to get out of the parlor before that cursed woman came back. He backed himself into the wall and used it to brace himself, to keep him from falling.

Ah, now he had a free hand. He could hold her with both hands now. In no time, he had scooted to the corner of the room and, blessedly, to the door that led to the stairwell. He kicked open the door and looked around him to make sure the noise had not brought the innkeeper's wife.

The hallway was still dark and empty. He pushed Felicity through the door first, then swung himself after her. He kicked the door closed and smiled. Now he stood in the stairwell at the base of the steep wooden staircase and looked up. How his leg ached whenever he climbed stairs. At his own house, he had converted the morning room to his sleeping chamber to eliminate his need for hiking up the daunting staircase.

Damn! Where was that blasted coachman?

He took consolation in the fact that, since it was daylight, there would be no comings and goings to the upstairs rooms. Rooms in the inn were generally occupied only at night. And since it was afternoon, the maid would have tidied the rooms by now. He should have the staircase to himself. He could take his time.

Rest after each step. And hope that his man would arrive and take Felicity off his hands—literally.

Thomas cursed the horse. Cursed himself. Most of all, he cursed the colonel. Under normal circumstances, he would have dismounted and gently walked his horse back to a stable. After all, this was no nag. This was one of the finest horses in England. Thunder had cost nearly four hundred guineas. But today, saving the horse was the least of Thomas's worries.

So he turned around, dug in, and forced the beast back to the village they had just left. Just five minutes before, he had been pleased Thunder had covered so much ground after leaving the village. Now he regretted every furlong they had traveled. It would only mean taking longer to return.

Finally, Thomas dismounted and tied Thunder to a tree. Then Thomas took off on foot. He had long legs and could run well. That would be much faster than limping into the village on Thunder's back.

In ten minutes a winded Thomas began to slow down as the livery stable came into view. A minute later, he was within. "Hurry!" he barked. "I must hire a horse. Immediately."

A young man quit brushing a gelding and came forward. "I can help."

Thomas reached into his pocket and offered the man a handful of coins. "Hurry. Saddle your fastest horse as quickly as you can."

As the man slung the saddle over a bay's back, Thomas asked, "Have you, by any chance, seen a red coach go through here today?"

"Actually, I did, sir," the man said. "I was sittin' out front 'bout half an hour ago. I thought I was seein' things when I saw a red coach going down the North Road."

Thomas's heart thumped. *Maybe it isn't too late.* Apparently, he had already gained a half hour on the colonel. "Would you say the coach was traveling fast?"

The man thought on it for a moment. "Not particularly. I'd say they was travelin' at a regular rate of speed."

Thank God.

In less than two minutes, Thomas was atop the beast and fairly flying from the village, encouraged that a single horse could go a great deal faster than a coach.

He had to catch up with Felicity.

Thirty-two

The colonel's coachman finally came when Colonel Gordon was halfway up the staircase. "It's bloody well time you got here," the colonel growled. "Here, carry my wife-to-be, will you?"

The man threw a long glance at Felicity. "Are you sure she's all right?"

"Quite sure," the colonel said. "Can you not smell the ale on her? She's merely had too much to drink. After she sleeps it off, she'll be fit as a fiddle."

"Whatever you say, sir," the burly coachman said, bending to pick up Felicity. He threw her over his shoulder as if she were a rolled-up rug.

"What is the number of the room you procured?" the colonel asked.

"Room Number Five."

Without his cane, the colonel held tightly onto the banister as he painfully mounted the rest of the stairs. Then he leaned into the wall and scooted himself a few feet at a time, using the strength in his good leg. The first room he came to was Number One. He cursed. The colonel scooted along the dimly lit hall until he came to Number Five. Its door stood open and the coachman was putting Felicity on the bed.

The colonel entered the room and gazed at Felicity. Pure excitement filled him like water spraying from a fountain. "Go back to the private parlor and get my cane," Gordon snapped.

"Yes, sir." The coachman left the room, closing the door behind him.

As hard as it was not to plunge into Felicity, the colonel decided to wait until the coachman returned. He had waited a very long time for this and had no wish for it to be interrupted.

A moment later the coachman tapped on the door to Room Five, then tried the knob and entered the room. "Here it is, sir. Will you be needing me further?"

The man would have to fetch the cleric. "Yes. You are to watch my window. When you see a white cloth waving there, you are to go to the vicarage and bring the vicar to this room. You're to tell him my sweetheart is on her deathbed, and I wish to marry her before she dies. Do you understand?"

"I thought you said she was all right."

"She is, you idiot. Don't think. Just do as I say."

"How will I know which room it is?"

"You bloody idiot, count. There's only one more room on this side of the hall. That would make this the next to last one. Is that so bloody difficult a concept for you?" Anger flashed in his eyes.

"No, sir. I'll do as you say. Be sure to wave the white cloth for a good long while. You can't count on me seeing it first thing, you know."

"How bloody well I do know, you idiot!"

Now that he had his cane, the colonel hobbled to the door and locked it behind the oaf. Then he turned to gaze at Felicity. After five years of worshiping her, now, at last, he would taste her pleasures. And he was assured of a compliant body. No bloody fighting.

He limped to the bed and, smiling, looked down at

her beautiful face. "Now I will see your face on the pillow beside mine for the rest of our days, my beloved."

He wanted to see more of her. All of her. But his bulging need was too great. He must take his own pleasure first. He sat on a chair to pull off his boots. Then, trembling with his mounting need, he removed his breeches and stood facing her.

Just as he heard the handle of his door turn. Whoever it was could not open the door. The colonel climbed onto the bed beside the lifeless Felicity, his weight on his knees.

Then he heard a loud crash and looked back. The door splintered, and a hole gaped in its center. A man's hand reached through the gap and unbolted the door.

The next thing the colonel knew, Thomas Moreland, a pistol in his hand and fury on his face, rushed into the room. His glance swept over the scene before him. "I'll kill you, Gordon!" Then Moreland lunged at him. The colonel fell back into bed. His hand could just reach the pants he had removed. Moreland flew over the foot of the bed. As Moreland's fist slammed into his face, Gordon pulled his knife from his breeches.

He enjoyed the look of fear on Thomas's face as he saw the glint of the long blade. The colonel slashed at Thomas, as Thomas tumbled away from him. The knife scored Thomas's forearm, forcing him to drop his pistol in the folds of the blanket.

Now the bed lay between the two enemies: Thomas standing on one side, unarmed; the colonel at the other, poised to hurl the knife. Then, cursing, Thomas leaped on the bed, his long arms lurching toward the knife.

Gordon lunged forward and stabbed Thomas's hands, but even then Thomas kept trying to disarm his assailant. Blood gushing down his arm, Thomas heaved himself forward and grabbed the colonel's forearm. Still, Gordon managed to turn the knife toward Thomas's face. "I'll kill you, Moreland," he growled. "I've killed once for her, and I'll gladly kill again."

With one hand securing the colonel's arm, Thomas used his other hand to twist the knife toward Gordon's chest. But he was stronger than Thomas had expected.

There was a flash of movement at the room's open doorway. Then a sound as loud as an exploding cannon filled the room, shook it. Thomas saw blood begin to ooze from the colonel's chest, and he turned to the open doorway.

There stood George, smoking gun in his trembling hand. "I was afraid he'd kill you, old chap. And I can't say that I particularly wanted the bloke to live, anyway."

Thomas looked at the dying man with disgust. Now he could see the hole where the bullet had torn through his chest. He saw, too, that blood had spilled down his shirt—and lower, to where the colonel's prominent manhood was wrapped in scarlet.

All Thomas could say was, "Thank God."

Behind George stood Sergeant Fordyce. "What the hell was the bloody fiend trying to do?"

By now Thomas had his wits about him and was feeling for Felicity's pulse. "She's all right." Thomas lifted her and cradled her in his arms. "Thank God." Then he faced her brother. "I think he gave her a sleeping draught."

"So he could have his way with the blessed angel," the sergeant said.

George's eyes rounded. "Thomas . . . he didn't . . . Could you see?"

"Her skirts haven't been disturbed," Thomas said, his voice filled with relief. "Had we been a moment later . . ." Tears filled his eyes.

Now the innkeeper and his wife rushed into the room. "What happened?" the innkeeper yelled, his glance taking in the grim scene. "Is the lady . . . dead?"

"No, but the man is," Thomas said.

"Why isn't she moving?" the man's wife asked.

Thomas spat out the words. "This fiend gave my wife-to-be a sleeping draught so he could ravish her."

"Oh, how awful—and what an awful mess," the woman cried.

"I'll take the beast out of here and clean up, too," the sergeant offered. "Never could tolerate the man, and it appears now with good reason."

"How—" Thomas began.

"How—" George began at the same time.

"You first," Thomas said.

"How did you know Gordon had abducted Felicity?"

"I've been suspicious of him for some time, so I hired a Bow Street runner to follow him. The runner stormed into my house this morning, telling me the colonel had picked up Felicity and appeared to be going some distance with her. Since she had told me that she was going to terminate her relationship with him, I was understandably wary. Now tell me how you knew." Thomas stroked Felicity's golden hair.

"Sis told me this morning the colonel had received a letter from their friends from Portugal, the Fordyces." He indicated the sergeant, who stooped over the colonel, muttering oaths with every breath. "This is Sergeant Fordyce, by the way. Felicity said the colonel told her the sergeant was dying and had to speak with her before he died. Damn, but I should have prevented her from coming."

"How were you to know the man is a murderer?" Thomas asked.

"You mean an almost-murderer," George said.

Thomas's glance was steady when he looked at George. "No, I mean a murderer. He killed Captain Harrison so he could have Felicity. He also shot himself in the leg in order to come home from Portugal with her."

George winced when he heard Thomas say the colonel had killed Harrison. "How do you know he killed Michael?"

"He told me just before you came on the scene."

George closed his eyes as if he were in great pain. "Poor Michael."

"He was as fine an officer as there ever was," Sergeant Fordyce said. "I'd heard the rumors about Colonel Gordon shooting himself. I thought he was just a coward. Little did I know the man was a bloody fiend."

"I actually met the soldier who saw Gordon shoot himself," Thomas said. "He was here in Bath, and I talked with him after noticing how he avoided the colonel."

"I suppose we'd better get the colonel's breeches back on before I lug him downstairs." The sergeant picked up the breeches, which were torn where the knife had sliced them, and dressed the colonel. "A bloody blight this man is to our army."

At her home on Charles Street, Thomas sat with Felicity throughout the night, burning a candle so she would not be frightened if she were to awaken.

Saying he could not leave his unconscious sister, George had sat with Thomas until past midnight, when Thomas urged him to get some sleep. Putting a hand to George's shoulder, Thomas said, "You showed great maturity today, Sedgewick."

"Does that mean . . . ?"

Thomas nodded. "Perhaps we can have a double wedding ceremony."

For the rest of the long night, Thomas watched Felicity, drinking in her loveliness. 'Twas a face he would never tire of. In her sound slumber, her dimples were barely visible. He longed to see a smile pierce them. He longed for so much more but happily realized their tomorrows stretched endlessly before them.

Once her chamber was bathed in the late-morning sunlight, Felicity began to stir. Thomas watched as she rolled to her other side. He waited anxiously to see her lids flutter open. When they did, she looked straight ahead—out of sight from Thomas, who sat on her other side. Disoriented, she spun her head around to his side.

Her brows lowered. "Where . . . what . . . I feel so terribly confused."

He moved to the side of her bed and smoothed his hand over her face. "Everything's all right now, my love."

"Why are you here?" She sat up. "How did I get here? The last thing I remember . . ."

"The innkeepers tell me you had soup at midday yesterday. I believe the colonel somehow put a sleeping draught in your soup."

Her hand flew to her mouth, her eyes widening in fear. "That explains . . . But—"

Thomas gathered her hand in both of his. "Don't worry, love. Colonel Gordon's dead."

"How? Where was I?" She gripped his hands.

"He brought you to an upstairs room at the inn. I believe he intended to compromise you there. His coachman said the colonel planned to wave a white cloth in front of the window. That would have signaled the coachman to fetch a cleric to perform a marriage ceremony." He paused and continued to hold her gaze within his. "We found a special license in Colonel Gordon's pocket."

"Dear God . . ."

A painful expression on his face, Thomas nodded. "I believe he planned to tell you that you had drunk too much ale, and while in such a state, you agreed to marry him."

"Never!"

"I know, my love."

"But I couldn't have had that much to drink. I don't even like ale." She stopped, putting nose to chest. "Yet I smell of it."

"He probably poured it on you while you were unconscious."

"Good Lord, what else did he do?"

"Fortunately, your brother and I showed up in time to prevent any real harm from occurring."

"How did you two know to come?"

"I had known for some time Gordon was a devious man. In my concern for you, I had hired a Bow Street runner to always keep the colonel within his sight. The runner notified me yesterday morning that the colonel had left town with you. Knowing what I knew of him, I grew suspicious and gave chase."

"And George was with you?"

"No, your brother became suspicious when a very healthy Sergeant Fordyce and his wife showed up at your door at the very same time you were supposedly fleeing to the dying man. George, quite correctly, smelled a rat."

"So he began the journey to Blye."

Thomas nodded. "Which is probably most fortunate for me. Your brother bounded up the stairs at the same time Colonel Gordon drew a very long knife on me."

She saw the cuts and bandages on Thomas, and she bolted up, her face angry. "You could have been killed! Colonel Gordon has been trained to kill. Oh, I would never forgive myself if anything happened to you because of me."

A smile played at his lips. "Is that so?"

"Oh, Thomas, I'm so very hurt and angry and . . . embarrassed. To think of all the people who have been hurt because of me."

"Not because of you, Felicity, because of a madman." He sat back and faced her, a sorrowful look on his handsome face. "There's more."

It seemed as if she could hardly breathe, yet her heart pounded in her chest. "What?"

"Colonel Gordon killed your husband."

Tears sprang to her eyes. "Oh, no," she moaned. "Because of me?"

Thomas nodded. "Don't blame yourself. The colonel was wicked through and through."

"Poor Michael, his life was cut short because—"

"Hush, my darling." He gathered her in his arms and held her as she wept. "None of this is your fault. You never asked for the man's attention."

She wept for a moment, then looked up at Thomas. "And to think, if it hadn't been for George, you would have been killed."

He offered her his handkerchief.

She wiped her tears and handed it back to him. "I'm glad he's dead."

"There's still more."

"Oh, I cannot bear any more." Her voice was a moan.

"I do hope you can bear this. I was coming to your home yesterday to beg your hand. Now, I will do so."

She gazed at him. At the sincerity she saw in his earnest face. God, but she could never tire of his face. Nor of him. It was so different than it had been with Michael. There were times she had turned away from Michael in their bed. Something she could never do to Thomas. His very touch debilitated her. It had never—not even at first—been like that with poor, dear Michael. Who was dead because of her. "I cannot accept a gesture offered out of either indebtedness or gallantry because you think you have compromised me."

He trailed his fingertips along the smooth planes of her face. "I offer for neither reason. I offer because I love you. I always have."

"But how can I believe that when I know how very much a gentleman you are? After what happened between us at the ruins, you would feel obliged to offer for me."

"But I loved you long before that precious day at the ruins. I've loved you for more than six years." He stood up, and from his pocket he withdrew the piece of white linen. "I don't suppose you remember this?"

Her brows lowered. "What is it?"

" 'Tis the piece of your petticoat. You bandaged me with it that night on the road more than six years ago."

Her mouth opened, but no words would come.

"I knew you were to wed a fine gentleman, an officer. I knew I had no chance, but still I carried this with me. I compared every woman I ever saw to you, and they all came up wanting. I used you as my inspiration to earn a fortune so that I could be a fine gentleman like Captain Harrison. So I could one day win a woman like you. But I didn't want a woman *like* you. I wanted you. The news that Captain Harrison had been killed gave me hope. You—and only you—are the reason I came to Bath. All I've ever wanted was to love you. Only you, Felicity."

Tears pooled in her eyes. "Oh, Thomas, I do love you so. I'm ashamed that I never loved Michael as I love you."

His eyes moistened, too. He moved toward her, and she moved toward him, and they merged in one blindingly happy kiss.

When it was finished, he settled his arms about her. "I propose to make you the most cherished nabob's wife on Earth. There is just one request I have of you."

Felicity trailed a lazy finger down his nose. "Yes, my love?"

"I beg that your wedding dress be blue."

We hope you enjoyed the first
Brides of Bath book.
Turn the page for a sneak peek at
the next title in the series,

WITH THIS RING

available wherever books are sold in April 2002.

One

The prick of her needle sent Glee into hysterics. She carelessly flung aside her imperfect embroidery, stomped her kid slippers, and commenced wailing. "I simply was not made for a life buried here at Hornsby Manor. Why can I not live in Bath by myself? Other spinsters do."

Her elegant sister-in-law calmly set aside her own flawless needlework and directed a sympathetic gaze at Glee. "You're not a spinster. You're a nineteen-year-old maiden, and it's not acceptable for you to live alone."

"I prefer to think of myself as a spinster," Glee protested, her lower lip working into a lovely pout. "After all, I've two Seasons behind me."

"And seven proposals of marriage," Dianna smugly pointed out.

"Seven and a half—if you count Percy Wittingham, whom I persuaded not to address my brother."

The impeccable Dianna gave a bemused smile. "I know how very dull it must be here for you, with my recent confinement and with Felicity on the Grand Tour."

Glee emphatically shook her head. "Nothing—not even a presentation to the queen—could have kept me away from baby Georgette's birth." Her face softened and her voice grew sweet. "My niece is without a doubt the most precious baby ever to draw breath."

Dianna lowered her impossibly long lashes, a glow of contentment suffusing her. "George and I think so."

Glee sighed. "You and George . . . and Felicity and Thomas . . . I'm surrounded by happily besotted married couples, and all I can ever aspire to is being an aunt." Despite the unrivaled success of her two Seasons, the one man she had adored since earliest childhood, the only man she could ever truly love, remained as elusive as seraph's wings. Gregory "Blanks" Blankenship was so completely removed from her touch, she had never even given voice to her adulation of him. And if she could not have Blanks, she vowed to die a spinster.

Dianna's doelike eyes softened. "Have patience, Glee. I'm two years older than you, Felicity's seven. If you had truly been desperate, you would have accepted one of those *seven-and-a-half* proposals. And there will most likely be seven more. You're a very lovely young lady." A smug, mischievous smile settled over Dianna's normally placid face. "I know why you could not fall in love with any of those young men." The graceful young mother casually took up her sewing again.

"Pray, enlighten me," Glee said impatiently. Watching Dianna pick up her sewing, Glee was embarrassed to have her own meager snatches of embroidery in the same room with her sister-in-law's meticulous creations. How fortunate she was that Dianna was already married, for Glee compared most poorly to her beautiful raven-haired sister-in-law's perfection.

"Whether you realize it, you have long been in love

with a man who has not yet realized how eligible you are," Dianna continued.

Glee's brow arched. "Indeed?"

Dianna nodded. "A young man you've known almost all of your life, or at least since he and George attended Eton together."

"Blanks." The name tumbled from Glee's lips almost reverently. How had Dianna guessed? She met Dianna's gaze squarely. "You realize in Mr. Gregory Blankenship's eyes I will always be twelve years old."

Dianna nodded. "It is for you to force him to notice otherwise."

Glee pulled her shawl more closely about her and rose from the silk damask chair to stride to the fireplace and its crackling warmth. With her back to Dianna, she said, "Then, too, there's the fact that Mr. Blankenship has never been attracted to decent young ladies. Does he not keep a mistress?"

"You are not supposed to know of such things!" Dianna chided.

"Perhaps if I acted like a doxy, Blanks would find me appealing."

"Then you *do* care for him!"

Glee sighed, bit her lip, then met her sister-in-law's probing gaze with an embarrassed nod.

Had Dianna known that Glee compared every man to Blanks, and they all came up wanting? It was not just that he was taller and better looking than all the others. Or that he was enormously wealthy and displayed incomparable taste. Or that he was a noted whip. Though he was all those things, he was so much more.

He was uncommonly personable and solicitous of all he met. It had been Blanks—not her own brother—who extracted her first tooth. And Blanks had been the one to console her when her favorite dog had died. And with a peculiar racing in her heart, she remembered a twelve-year-old Blanks stoically carrying her back to the manor house after she had tumbled from a tree and hurt her foot.

She remembered, too, that his ready smile could fill the gloomiest day with warm sunshine. She shuddered even now as she pictured his devastating grin.

Dianna smiled like the cat who caught the canary. "When Blanks is ready to settle down, he will want a good girl, not a doxy."

Glee turned around to face Dianna. "Despite that I'm five years younger than he, this red hair of mine could turn quite gray by the time Mr. Gregory Blankenship decides to settle down."

"You know as well as I that George had no intentions of settling down when he met me, but love has a way of changing things—even a bachelor's toughest resolve."

How remarkably love had changed her brother, Glee thought. Not a day went by Glee did not marvel over George's metamorphosis from a heavy drinking, wildly gaming rake to a besotted husband and devoted father. Of course, it had helped that he removed himself from his hedonistic friends in Bath and settled at Hornsby Manor.

"It's as likely that Blanks will suddenly fall in love with me as it is that faro and the races at Newmarket will cease to hold his interest. Not like George with you. I could almost see Cupid's arrow snare George's heart the minute he set eyes on you. And I assure you, my brother had no intention of marrying before he was thirty."

Glee's gaze dropped to the hearth where the flames leaped in a blaze of yellow and orange and blue. "Of course, I'm not adverse to offering Cupid a little encouragement, where Blanks is concerned." She looked mischievously at Dianna. "Tell me, does George have a book that tells one . . ." She turned her back to Dianna once again. "Tells one about sex. You know, how to go about it and all that."

She turned to face Dianna, who had suddenly colored, and watched Dianna intently for a moment.

Finally, Dianna answered in an embarrassed voice. "I'm sure I've never heard of such a book."

"Then how do you know what to do?"

Dianna avoided meeting Glee's gaze. Taking up her sewing again, she cleared her throat. "I suppose it's somewhat like breathing. It seems to come automatically, provided one is in love with one's partner."

The large door creaked open, and George came striding into the room. He was blond and burly and young and exuberant. And completely in love with his wife. His dancing eyes settled on Dianna. "What comes automatically?"

The two young women exchanged amused glances.

George planted a kiss on Dianna's cheek.

She looked up at him with adoring eyes. "Falling in love, my dear."

He glanced at Glee. "Is Glee in love?"

"How could I possibly even meet an eligible gentleman buried here in Warwickshire?"

He nodded sympathetically.

Glee strode to the door. "I shall leave you two lovebirds alone and take a walk. The only thing better here than in Bath is that here I can walk without a maid."

Company was thin in Bath this winter, Gregory "Blanks" Blankenship lamented as he flipped a woolen scarf about his neck with one hand while maneuvering the reins to his tilbury with the other. How he missed good old George. There was nothing they could not persuade the pleasure-loving fellow to do, especially when he was in his cups. Gregory chuckled to himself as he recalled the time Appleton dared George to drink a tankard of hog's urine, which George promptly did, earning a fat five pounds from Gregory.

Remembering his solemn mission today, Gregory's smile vanished. He pulled his gig in front of his solicitor's place of business, eyeing a waiting young boy.

Coatless with a single toe poking through a hole of his well-worn shoes, the lad fairly bounced in front of Gregory, a wide smile revealing missing front teeth. He must be around six years old, Gregory decided.

"Morning, Gov'nah," the boy said.

Gregory leaped to the pavement and addressed the lad. "I'll wager you're a young man who has a way with horses. Keep an eye on mine, and there's a crown in it for you." Gregory knew a crown was an exorbitant amount to pay for so menial a task, but the boy looked as if he could certainly use it.

The lad's eyes rounded. "Right, Gov'nah! I ain't never seen a crown before." The little fellow took the reins and began gently to stroke the gray, speaking soothing words as Gregory mounted the steps.

Mr. Willowby's young clerk greeted Gregory. "Good morning, Mr. Blankenship. 'Twas sorry I was to learn of your father's death."

Gregory, who had had six weeks to become accustomed to the idea of his father's demise, acknowledged the man's condolences with a grim nod before withdrawing a guinea from his pocket and slapping it on the man's desk. "Be a good man, won't you, and see to it the little urchin who hangs about in front of your building gets a warm coat and new shoes."

The clerk took the coin, pushed back his chair and got up to walk to the window and peer out at the child. A light snow was beginning to fall. "His mum cleans for us, and I don't believe he has a father. Poor lad."

The door to Willowby's office opened, and a slender man with a pointed chin spoke to Gregory. "Won't you step into my office, Mr. Blankenship?"

Gregory followed him into the chamber and settled in a chair facing Willowby across an immaculate desk.

"I asked you to come today because I wanted to talk to you privately before we meet with the entire family," Willowby said.

Gregory cocked a brow.

Willowby cleared his throat and met Gregory's quizzing gaze with openness. "I wanted to prepare you."

Gregory's brows lowered. "Prepare me for what?"

Willowby expelled a deep sigh. "Your late father's will is a bit unusual."

Gregory shifted in his chair. His heart began to pound. Somehow, he knew this was not going to be pleasant. Not removing his eyes from Willowby, he said, "Go on."

"The last time I saw your father, he was somewhat out of charity with you. He kept mumbling that you were entirely too ah, unsettled."

Gregory nodded.

"You'll have the opportunity to read his exact words, but they were something to the effect that he did not want you to squander away his money on your frivolous pursuits."

"So, he's cut me out of the will."

Mr. Willowby hesitated a moment. "Not exactly. According to your father's latest will, if you are not married by your twenty-fifth birthday, all properties will go to the next eldest, your half-brother Jonathan."

"The good one!" Gregory interjected, his ever-present smile spreading across his face. Not that he was happy. The smile was to conceal his pain, a mask cultivated from years of practice with his stepmother who resented that he—not her own son—would inherit her husband's wealth. So, Gregory thought with sorrow, Jonathan would get the Blankenship fortune. Their sedate father had always preferred Jonathan and probably with justification. Jonathan was just like their father. Serious. Frugal. And incapable of having fun. In short, totally opposite of Gregory.

Gregory scooted back his chair. "I'm grateful that you let me in on my father's scheme," he said, rising and striding toward the door.

Mr. Willowby cleared his throat. "How old are you now, Mr. Blankenship?"

Gregory stopped and turned to watch Willowby's amused gaze. "I'll be twenty-five in June."

"It's not too late for you to comply with the terms of your father's will."

"To get married?" Gregory's eyes narrowed suspiciously.

Willowby nodded.

"But I've got less than five months and no prospective bride." Nor did he desire a bride. Ever.

"I should think any number of women would be more than happy to accommodate you, especially with such a great deal of money at stake."

"My brother would see through such a scheme readily and challenge such an action."

"It is possible to actually fall in love in a very short period of time. Take Mrs. Willowby and me. I offered for her a week after we met."

Gregory, who had never met Mrs. Willowby, suddenly pictured the sharp-chinned solicitor with an equally sharp-chinned bride leading a trail of little pointy-chinned youngsters. A sure reason to avoid matrimony. "Would that I could be so fortunate," Gregory murmured.

He stepped toward the solicitor and placed a firm hand on his shoulder. "Thank you, Willowby."

Willowby's clerk was gone when Gregory passed through the chamber again, drawing on his gloves before braving the day's chill. He hoped the clerk was off procuring a coat and shoes for the wretched lad now tending his horse.

The boy stood faithfully beside Gregory's mount, despite the snowflakes that settled on his blond hair. Gregory patted the lad's head. "I see you're as good as your word." He tossed the boy a crown. "It's much too cold for you to be outdoors without a coat. Be a good lad and go warm yourself in Mr. Willowby's second-floor office." Gregory shot a glance toward the building.

He watched the boy, clutching his coin, enter the building, then Gregory took a seat on the box and directed his conveyance down Bath's Milsom Street. Despite the bitter cold, he had no desire to return to his town house. He did not feel like making polite conversation or flashing smiles he did not feel. Though he had presented a stoic front to Willowby, Gregory felt lower than an adder's belly.

Once more, his father had played him cruelly in favor of Jonathan. Gregory wanted to hate his half brother as he hated his father, but he could not. Jonathan was younger and smaller and had always evoked a sense of protection in Gregory despite that his brother looked on him as an opponent. They were

only two years apart, but they had never been close.
Jonathan resented it when Gregory was better at his
sums or when Gregory's mount went faster than his.
And Jonathan coveted whatever Gregory had, even
though their tastes were vastly different. Gregory
would weaken and give his brother the toy sword or
the silver spurs or the book of poems Jonathan hun-
gered after, only to watch dust cover them once they
were in Jonathan's possession.

Gregory rode across Pulteney Bridge, noting that
the River Avon was nearly frozen. He was too angry
to take note of the chill in his bones. Never had it
occurred to him that he would not live out his life in
the extravagant style he had lived it these first twenty-
four years.

It was different with Jonathan. Not only was he not
raised with such expectations, he would never know
what to do with such vast sums of money. Jonathan's
life's passion was squeezing as much as he could out
of a shilling. At his own lodgings in London, he denied
himself what other young men of his class considered
necessities. He kept no horse, nor a fire in his chamber, and he substituted inferior tallows for the better
quality wax candles—and used those only sparingly.
Gregory suspected his brother saved a goodly portion
of his three-hundred-a-year. Jonathan frequently put
up at Sutton Manor to spare himself expenses.

Gregory could not understand Jonathan's frugal ob-
session. What good was money if it could not be used
to purchase what made a soul happy? In one bleak
second the full force of how perilously close he was
to losing his fortune walloped Gregory. Good Lord,
would he have to give up his horses? And his tailor?
And his gaming? His heart tripped. Would he have to
dismiss Carlotta?

How was he to get along? He remembered when his best friend George had lost the little bit of fortune that was left him by his viscount father. How had George managed before he married the sister of the fabulously wealthy Mr. Thomas Moreland?

Perhaps George would have some timely advice to offer. Damned if he wouldn't just ride over to Warwickshire and visit his viscount friend.

COMING IN FEBRUARY 2002
FROM ZEBRA BALLAD ROMANCES

__OUTCAST: The Vikings

by Kathryn Hockett   0-8217-7257-0 $5.99US/$7.99CAN

Vengeful clansmen have taken Nordic warrior Torin prisoner. His only hope lies in the beautiful, brazen Erica, who promises to aid his escape provided he take her with him. He cannot anticipate the peril that lies ahead—or the relentless desire that will lead them to a grand empire . . . and glorious love.

__COMING UP ROSES: Meet Me at the Fair

by Alice Duncan   0-8217-7276-7 $5.99US/$7.99CAN

Rose Ellen Gilhooley can see that handsome newsman H.L. May is only interested in one thing. Trouble is, the more he squires her around the grand Columbian Exposition, the more Rose yearns for the same! But when H.L. swears he's not the marrying kind, Rose thinks it's high time she taught *him* a lesson—about listening to his heart . . .

__CASH: The Rock Creek Six

by Linda Devlin   0-8217-7269-4 $5.99US/$7.99CAN

Daniel Cash was a ladies' man with a smile as quick as his draw. Yet the gunslinger harbored painful memories of the girl he'd left behind. Cash believed Nadine Ellington was better off without the man he'd become, but when she rode into town, Cash was tempted to consider another future . . . with her by his side.

__SWEET VIOLET: Daughters of Liberty

by Corinne Everett   0-8217-7146-9 $5.99US/$7.99CAN

Violet Pearson is determined to prove she can manage the Tidewater Nurseries. And now, with the opening of a lavish new conservatory by Gabriel Isling, the Duke of Belmont, she is sure to make the business bloom! She had not, however, counted on her intense attraction to this charming gentleman whose seductive gaze reveals nothing of the dangerous secret that has led him to America.

Call toll free **1-888-345-BOOK** to order by phone or use this coupon to order by mail. *ALL BOOKS AVAILABLE FEBRUARY 01, 2002*

Name _____

Address _____

City _____ State _____ Zip _____

Please send me the books that I have checked above.

I am enclosing $_____

Plus postage and handling* $_____

Sales tax (in NY and TN) $_____

Total amount enclosed $_____

*Add $2.50 for the first book and $.50 for each additional book. Send check or money order (no cash or CODs) to: **Kensington Publishing Corp., Dept. C.O., 850 Third Avenue, New York, NY 10022**

Prices and numbers subject to change without notice. Valid only in the U.S. All orders subject to availability. **NO ADVANCE ORDERS.**

Visit our website at **www.kensingtonbooks.com**.